I0738111

JO BUER

Rest Easy Resort

For MB and our family.

Contents

PROLOGUE

May 11, 1989, site of the new Cooks Hotel Resort, Kulani Island, South Pacific.

Drums beat a hypnotic dirge, drawing the congregation closer to the dirt stage. The female dancers, shimmying their hips in grass skirts and weaving their fingers through the air, tempted the crowd closer with flirtatious smiles.

Pounding their feet upon the soil, the male dancers drew closer to the women. They squatted and kicked, thrusting their fists at the ground, stressing every taut muscle in their bodies.

The few tourists who had gathered pushed themselves to the front of the crowd, beaming in awe at the free performance they had lucked upon. Some tapped their feet in unison or clapped their hands.

Nosey curiosity had also drawn the locals. It was not every day they broke ground for a luxury resort. Not of this size. Not with this much power to pull the island out of a recession. And not on cursed land.

The locals stifled the electric impulses of their bodies from joining in, remembering in time this was a performance for the white men in expensive ironed shirts who hung back, sheltering under a small cluster of palm trees.

Sweat glistened on these men's brows and stained their armpits. They held clipboards and wore large black beepers attached to their belts and looks of boredom on their faces. In contrast to the scooters and bikes belonging to the tourists and locals, they parked their fancy rental four-wheel drives further back under the shade of coconut trees. The locals had noticed them arriving and shook their heads. They knew better than to park anything where large bowling-ball-type objects could fall and smash their vehicles.

The drums built into a bone-shaking crescendo before plummeting into silence. Applause broke out while the business men stood stoic. The dancers dissolved into the crowd, seeking refuge with their friends and families. Only then did they allow their faces to fall into consternation.

The mayor stepped forward, taking centre stage before the humming crowd. With shaky hands, he adjusted his tie and gestured for two of the crisp-shirted men to follow him. His glasses slid halfway down his wide nose as he waited.

The three of them stood before a small mound covered in decorated turmeric tapa cloth, hidden until now by the drama of the dance. Addressing the crowd, the mayor pushed his glasses back up the bridge of his nose and thanked everyone for coming. He wrung his hands and praised the white men for bringing what would be "economic salvation" to their little island. Creating jobs for locals and wealth for the land, the new Cooks Hotel Resort would stand out from all others, a pinnacle for the tourism industry. Words like "prosperity" and "wealth" made the business men stifle smirks and puff out their chests.

When it was the businessmen's chance to talk, they gestured towards an enormous billboard which read "Coming soon… " They boasted of a resort nestled amongst palm trees and tropical gardens with lavish swimming pools, and beach-view villas of a luxury not seen before on the island.

The tourists oohed and aahed and cheered. The locals, thrilled and fearful, whispered and muttered behind their hands.

The sun disappeared behind gathering clouds, and a nervous buzz settled on the group. A little girl in a yellow floral dress wriggled in her mother's arms, squealing and pointing towards the back of the crowd. Heads turned and people moved aside as a curious figure pushed his way to the front. The speakers on stage fell silent. The business men's jaws momentarily dropped, while the mayor used the back of his sleeve to wipe sweat from his brow.

He was an old man, short and solid with a formidable air of authority. Around his shoulders draped a tapa cloak, adorned with red-and-black island designs. Several lengths of sennit wrapped his waist, tying the cloak to his body. A grass kilt hung to his knees, traditional sandals adorned his feet, and a crown of palm leaves and feathers sat upon his head. He leant on a carved tokotoko stick as he made his way to the front. Carved into a line of determination, his mouth held firm, his jaw strong and clenched. His dark eyes pierced the remaining stragglers, who clambered to get out of his way. Those who knew this man, guilty by their presence, diverted their eyes.

Avoiding the old man's stare, the mayor shrunk back, disappearing into the crowd. The two businessmen sought explanation from the faces before them. The crowd's eyes shifted. Confused, the men moved aside to join their associates under the palm trees.

The old man planted himself behind the covered mound. With growing boldness, the crowd murmured. The air tensed.

Using one hand the man reached down and swiped the tapa cloth off the mound, abandoning it to the ground and revealing a shin-high grey stone. Mounted to its face was a bronze plaque. Those at the front of the throng noticed the date and inscription immortalising the breaking of ground for the new resort.

The old man held his staff before him. Shaking it at the crowd, his voice rang out, invoking the gods to hear his words.

Starting in his native tongue, he transitioned to English, so all knew his intent.

"This place—" His voice shook and he paused. "This place," he started again, "it is sacred land. It is not white people's land; it is the land of our ancestors. *My* ancestors!" His gravelly voice chilled the audience despite the warmth of the day.

"Passed on through generations until poisoned by the blood of my sister and her child. Cursed by my mother's tears and then by her tongue. And now—" he grew louder— "stolen from my family and given to the highest bidder."

A nervous twitter drifted amongst the crowd.

"I, Rawiri Tangaroa, again invoke the curse of my ancestors. Until this land is returned to my family and devils put to rest, no enterprise will thrive. No false ambition nor sacred union will flourish. All will rot!"

His voice fell like a weight upon the crowd. The island held its breath. The air grew thicker, and concrete-coloured clouds near eclipsed the sun. The palm fronds of the nearby trees began a gentle dance before whipping themselves into a frenzy. A coconut loosened itself from its stalk, falling to the ground with a percussive thud. Somewhere out of view, a rooster crowed.

The crowd stood motionless, confusion and fear incised their brows. Some shared a sidewards glance with their neighbour.

Rawiri Tangaroa lifted his tokotoko stick to the heavens, waiting for a moment before plunging it down hard upon the memorial stone. A sharp cracking sound reverberated across the building site. It vibrated across the skulls of the onlookers. And, from top to bottom, a thin fissure grew across the rock's surface, missing the plaque by a centimetre.

A child cried out, and the wind died away to nothingness. For a moment, the old man stood stoic, unmoving. Then, almost as if he were shrinking, he folded in upon himself, wearied by his spell.

The trance broke. The clouds shifted, and the sun reappeared once more. One by one, feet shambled, murmurs grew and nervous bodies moved. From the back of the crowd someone started up their scooter's ignition, and the last few people woke from their stupor.

The man in his tapa cloak leant heavily on his tokotoko stick and shuffled back through the crowd. He was a lesser man than when he had arrived. The crowd moved aside for him, but as he passed, the people forgot him, their eyes turning back to their neighbours and families as they floundered in confused conversation.

More engines revved, and one by one people left. Some stole a glance in the memorial stone's direction, others had already forgotten. The mayor wiped sweat from his brow, slinking away unnoticed.

The businessmen, huddled in their own little group,

shrugged their shoulders and dispersed. Their moment had passed. They'd meet up later for a stiff drink and a laugh at the day's events.

The mother and the little girl were two of the last to leave. Holding the toddler against her hip, the mother stood over the memorial stone. Drawing in a breath, she narrowed her eyes, then spat a small pool of saliva onto the stone. With her daughter, she pivoted on her feet and walked away. Rawiri Tangaroa was right, she thought. This site deserves no more.

CHAPTER 1

The plane landed on the tarmac with a shudder and jolt. Hannah's stomach flipped. For a moment, she held still, eyes closed, taking deep breaths, waiting for her insides to settle.

"We're here, Mrs O'Connor." Mike grinned when she peeled open one eye. He bent over, placing a small kiss on her forehead.

Something in her chest fluttered. Mrs O'Connor. Mr and Mrs O'Connor on their honeymoon!

"Ready?" he asked, giving her hand a quick squeeze.

Hannah returned the gesture with a smile. He was handsome, her husband. Playful blue eyes and a child-like grin ever at the ready. How she had won his heart, she'd never know. Her fingers fidgeted with the gold locket hanging around her neck.

The captain's voice came over the loudspeaker, welcoming them to Kulani Island, the Heavenly Island. Temperature, a perfectly humid twenty-seven degrees. Local time, 7:28 p.m.

They stood up, ready to join the queue of people retrieving their carry-on luggage from the overhead bins. A low cursing stole the moment as a balding man in a bright Hawaiian shirt grappled with his bag in the overhead compartment above her.

"Henry! Be careful, Henry!" The urgent high-pitched cries of whom Hannah assumed was his wife, did nothing to calm the old man's mutterings.

"I *am* being careful!" he retorted with another strenuous tug at the bag.

"Here, I can help," Mike offered, leaning over Hannah.

"No need, no need," the man said, sending a smile in Mike's direction. "I've got this. Just one more…"

"Henry!" his wife interrupted. "Let the man help you."

"I've got it!" he said with more determination than before. With a last tug, a large brown duffel bag came ripping out of the compartment, swinging out and hitting Hannah in the head.

"Ouch!" More surprised than in pain, she rubbed the side of her head where the bag had made contact.

"Look what you did, Henry! You near gave the poor thing a concussion!" the woman retorted.

A dull thud and a small exclamation of "Ow" came from behind her. Hannah suspected the woman had given her other half a good whack.

"Are you okay?" Mike rested his hand on her shoulder.

"Oh, I'm so sorry, my dear. I never meant for that to happen. The blasted carriers. I swear they make them smaller and smaller every year. Let me get you some ice when we get off," the old man apologised.

"I should hope so!" the woman behind her muttered. The old man wore a pained expression, his concern genuine.

"There's no need. I'm fine," Hannah replied, still rubbing the side of her head, then self-consciously dropping her hand to her side. It had hurt, but she doubted any actual damage was done.

"No, no, I insist," the old man said. "Once we get off this beast, we'll get you checked out. Worst case, some ice and a good stiff drink are in order."

Hannah grinned. She had never known her grandfathers, but she had imagined this was what grandfathers were like. He was warm and caring. The crown of his head was blotchy with age spots and short, coarse tufts of white hair. He had a ruddy complexion, bulbous nose, and a stomach that strained against the buttons on his shirt.

"No need," Mike chimed in. "Hannah has a hard head. She'll be fine." He gave Hannah's head a quick rub.

Embarrassed, Hannah turned and smiled at the man's wife over the seat.

The passengers behind them had grown impatient. They grunted and huffed their annoyance at the holdup. The man's wife angled her head, giving his arm a tug.

"Alright, alright, we're moving," the man said to the frustrated faces behind him before winking at his wife. "Come on, love. Let's get off this beast before we get thrown off. We can argue some more with this delightful couple when we're on the ground."

Mike chuckled, and Hannah joined in, her queasy tummy practically forgotten. It surprised her to notice she was genuinely happy. Really happy. Everything is going to be alright, she told herself. And mostly, she believed it.

CHAPTER 2

Night had already begun to swallow the day as Hannah took her first steps out of the small passenger plane. A few stars flickered in the sky, and the smell of sea salt scented the air. A wave of warmth and humidity washed over her, making her pull at the front of her shirt, which was already beginning to stick. She readjusted the shoulder strap on her bag and grabbed onto the side rail as she descended the stairs to the tarmac.

She had never been to a tropical island before. In fact, she had barely been *anywhere* before. A teacher's salary allowed little extravagance. But even with the spike of anxiety that came with knowing the sea was so close, the greater thrill was being here on her honeymoon with the man of her dreams. And, come hell or high water, she was going to enjoy it. Phobias be damned.

Mike's hand rested gently on her shoulder as he followed on her heel. The couple from the plane led the way towards the arrival doors of the modest airport building while the rest of the passengers followed suit. Mike picked up his pace, encouraging Hannah to do the same.

From the corner of her eye, she caught Mike tugging at the collar of his shirt. The heat and humidity would be getting to him. He ran hotter than the average person and would crave the AC the airport hopefully granted them.

"Do you have the passports ready?" Mike asked as they drew closer to the small building with open tropical garden walls.

It was a rhetorical question. Of course she did.

The melodic twangs of ukuleles greeted them. Two men in bright Hawaiian shirts, wide grins and smooth voices welcomed them at the entrance. They rocked side to side while strumming and singing a playful song in their native tongue. The music was as colourful as their shirts, and it warmed Hannah in a completely different way.

Her fingers reached up to touch her locket again. "I love it," she whispered with a smile that reached her cheekbones. Mike's eyes shone, as if proud to be sharing this moment with her. He gave her shoulder another gentle squeeze and hmmed in agreement.

The woman from the plane nudged Hannah. "Oh, I just love them." Addressing her husband, she said, "There's no better greeting, don't you think, Henry dear?"

"Uh hmm," Henry said without thought but, on seeing Hannah and Mike, changed tack and leant forward. "We should introduce ourselves, especially as we owe you two a good stiff drink," he said, taking Mike's hand in his own and giving it a sturdy shake. "I'm Henry and this here beautiful maiden is Edith." Teasing, he gestured to the woman.

"Oh, shut up, you big oaf," Edith replied, feigning annoyance.

Hannah held back a snort and took the moment to study Edith. She was petite, her head reaching Henry's shoulder. Short, mousey brown hair framed a delicately lined face. Hannah hoped she would look as good at her age.

"I'm Mike," Mike said in return. "Nice to meet you, Edith."

He gently took the old woman's hand in his own. "This is Hannah. My wife. And you don't owe us a drink or anything."

Hannah offered them both her hand in a quick shake. "I'm fine. Really, I am," she said, embarrassed by all the attention.

"Tell you what." Henry was not so easily put off. "Let's get ourselves through this next part, then we'll discuss just recompense." He gestured at the few airport personnel in their little booths, waiting to greet them.

It took them no time to go through all the necessities.

"Nature of your travel?" a woman with a tightly coiffed bun and navy dress with bright pink and orange flowers asked as Hannah handed over their passports. "Business or pleasure?"

"Well, actually a bit of both," Mike answered.

For a second, Hannah's breath caught in her chest. She wanted to forget the business part of the deal. It had taken Mike a lot to convince her they should spend their honeymoon on Kulani Island. It wasn't just her fear of the sea that put doubts in her mind. Mike had been overseeing the opening of a new luxury resort on behalf of his father's company. It was an enormous investment of both money and time, and eager to please his father, Mike had been travelling back and forth regularly. Now, one week out from the resort's grand opening, they and a few select others – investors, shareholders and the like – would join them for a trial run. And it happened to coincide with their honeymoon. Part of her thought she should be grateful. But, knowing Mike, she wasn't at all sure he'd be able to separate business from pleasure.

The airport attendant wished them a wonderful working holiday, and Hannah and Mike headed towards the small luggage carousel to wait with Edith and Henry for their suitcases to arrive.

"Won't be long now," Henry said as they joined them, "It never takes long. Perk of being on a small island, I suppose."

"You've visited before, then?" Mike asked.

"Oh, yes, we've been coming since the late 1980s." Edith patted Henry's hand. "It's our anniversary."

Edith's eyes sparkled, and a tug pulled deep in Hannah's chest on seeing the look exchanged between the older couple. No mistaking it – it was the expression she remembered her parents sharing. She wanted it so badly for herself and Mike.

"It's our fortieth," Henry said. "Can you believe it? Forty years with this one." He hit Edith with a cheeky grin, and colour flooded her cheeks. She shook her head, a smile playing at the edges of her lips.

Hannah wondered if that was her secret – those in love didn't age. It made sense. She always thought of her parents the same way. Forever a young, baby-faced couple. Then again, she guessed they had been.

"Oh, you tease." Given the way her eyes sparked, Edith thoroughly enjoyed the moment.

Mike was the first to congratulate them. "What a milestone," he said, wiggling his eyebrows at Hannah.

"Congratulations," Hannah interjected, not wanting to be rude.

"We're here on our honeymoon. Any tips for two newly-weds?"

"I knew it," Henry said. "I knew it as soon as I first saw you. The way you look at each other." Henry reached over and gave Mike a slap on the shoulder. Edith smiled in their direction.

"One tip for you, friend," Henry said, staring straight at Mike. "The secret is … yeah, the real secret is…"

Hannah exchanged a smirk of amusement with Edith.

Henry leaned closer to Mike, as if he were about to reveal the meaning of the universe. "Happy wife, happy life!" he said in a stage whisper before dissipating into a wave of raucous laughter. Mike joined in. Edith gave her husband an affectionate whack on the arm and Hannah chuckled.

"I'll keep that in mind," Mike said, winking at Hannah. He absentmindedly swiped a curl of blond hair from his eye, and for a second Hannah felt like her heart would burst.

Henry had been right about the luggage. The carousel started its sluggish cycle, and only a few moments later the first pieces of luggage made their slow migration around the conveyor. One by one, people stepped forward, gathering their bags and suitcases. Hannah's and Mike's arrived not long after Henry and Edith's.

"Where are you staying?" Mike asked Henry and Edith as he loaded his and Hannah's luggage onto a cart and helped Henry and Edith with their own.

"Oh, the Eventide Resort and Spa," Henry replied.

"It's our special place," Edith added.

"In fact, this is our seventh year in a row staying at the Eventide, since we've been coming here annually. It's becoming a bit of a tradition for us, I dare say."

Edith nodded in agreement. "And what about the two of you?" she asked kindly.

Hannah stiffened, somewhat embarrassed. She had heard the opening of Rest Easy Resort was a big thing for the island. The most luxurious of the resorts, if you will.

"Rest Easy Resort," Mike said without missing a beat.

The smiles quickly slipped from Edith and Henry's lips, and they shared a quick look.

"Oh," Henry said, clearing his throat. "I've heard it's real nice. I thought it wasn't to open for another few weeks though?"

Edith stared at the ground, but Mike was oblivious to the change in mood. Excited, he chatted on about his family's investment and development of the property.

Hannah took the moment to excuse herself to use the washroom to freshen up. To her surprise, Edith elected to join her.

As Hannah washed her hands, Edith approached the sink. The small woman appeared smaller as she stood beside her, wringing her aged hands with soap.

"He seems like a lovely man, your husband," she said.

"He is," Hannah said, giving Edith a smile in the mirror, surprised to see the small worry-line between Edith's eyebrows.

"And you love him?" she asked.

Startled, Hannah turned around to face Edith.

Having rinsed the soap from her hands, Edith let the water drip into the sink and partially onto the floor between them.

"Of course," Hannah said. "It's our honeymoon." As if she needed to justify it. An uneasiness crawled across the back of her neck. "Congratulations again on your anniversary," Hannah said, hoping to shake the change in mood. "Forty years is a long time."

"It is," Edith nodded, her face softening. "Henry is a great big pain in the tush most of the time, but I really do love the oaf. I barely think another forty would be enough time with that man." A wistful expression flitted across her face, and Hannah relaxed.

"Luckily, we're soulmates, he and I. We have all of this life and the next together." Edith stared at Hannah as if to gauge her reaction. The prickling crept back along her nape.

"Do you believe in soulmates, Hannah?"

She had done it again. Sent a curve ball Hannah's way. Of course she did. It was all she had ever wanted. Her mother and father had been soulmates. The way they looked at each other. The way they teased each other. The way they balanced each other. Why else would her father have left her, sacrificing his own life to save her mother? Why else would a parent leave their only daughter?

"I do," Hannah said, shaking herself from the memories, which had risen so easily to the surface. She fingered the locket around her neck, stroking its filigree surface, willing her heart to stop thumping in her chest.

"Then, every moment, every second with your soulmate is a thing to treasure. And you don't let go of them, no matter what, understand?"

The air between them hung heavy for a moment. Why hadn't she just said "Mike"? Every second with *Mike* should be a thing to treasure. And why had it felt so much like a warning?

Edith turned her back to her, walked over to where the paper towel dispenser hung on the wall, and dried her hands. As her hand rested on the door to leave, she paused and turned around. "Not even for a resort."

Hannah stood watching her as she walked out of the room.

CHAPTER 3

"And your head's okay, then?" Henry asked again as the four of them waited at the shuttle pickup, ready to say their goodbyes.

"Yes, honestly, it was no big thing. I'm fine." Hannah forced a smile and said a silent prayer no one noticed how rattled she was. She couldn't pinpoint how or why Edith's words had crawled under her skin. Nothing she had said should have done so. But her Spidey-senses, as Mike called them, were tingling.

"Why don't the two of you come join us for a drink at the Eventide later, anyway?" Henry asked.

"Henry! It's their honeymoon." Edith swatted her husband on the arm. "They'll have better things to do."

"Probably not tonight," Mike said, chuckling. "But maybe later in the week. Or you could join us?" he said, almost as an afterthought. "I'd love to show you around the resort."

Henry and Edith eyed each other. "Well, we'll let you get on your way, then," Henry said, ignoring the offer. "But, like I was saying to your hubby" – he raised a brow at Hannah – "if things get too…" Henry paused and Edith looked away.

"If things get too … *much*," he continued, "then I know the owners of the Eventide, and I'm sure they'll be able to accommodate you. We would love to see you again. Isn't that right, Edie?"

Edith turned back, offering a gentle smile. "Absolutely," she said, and Hannah swore she was being genuine.

"And we do owe you both a drink…" Henry grinned broadly.

"Well, we might just take you up on that," Mike replied good-naturedly. "The drink at least – I know we're both going to love the Rest Easy." Mike put his arm around Hannah's shoulders and drew her close to him, pecking her on the forehead. A van pulled up, "Eventide Resort and Spa" emblazoned on its side.

"Henry, dear," Edith said, pointing it out to her husband.

"Oh right, yes. This is us, then. We'll say our goodbyes. But don't be strangers, eh?"

"It was lovely meeting you both," Hannah said as Mike dropped his arm, allowing Henry to draw her into a big bear hug.

"You take care of this one, okay?" he said to Mike, over Hannah's shoulder.

"I'll try to keep her in line," Mike replied with a chuckle before giving Edith a quick hug and Henry a hearty handshake.

Hannah swapped and gave Edith a quick embrace. She felt so frail and small in her arms, but there was warmth too. As she pulled away, Edith gripped her arms for a moment then leaned in, whispering to her while the men loaded the suitcases into the van.

"Soulmates transcend death, but that doesn't mean you should seek it out." The words hung in the air between them on a swath of warm breath. Hannah's first instinct was to recoil, but Edith held her fast, stronger than her slight frame gave her credit for. "Be careful," she said before finally letting go.

As the van pulled away from the curb, another one replaced it – this time with "Rest Easy Resort" scribbled on the side and an image of silhouetted palm trees against an orange sunset.

"Well, this is our ride," Mike said, beaming.

A man rushed around from the driver's side to greet them. He was an older man, maybe in his fifties, Hannah guessed, but she had never been good with ages. He had warm brown skin, smile lines around his eyes, and a grin that reached ear to ear. Island casual, he wore a short-sleeve dress shirt and beige shorts. His trim black hair had veins of silver at the temples, and he stood a head shorter than Mike.

"Ahh, kia orana, Mr O'Connor," he said in greeting, advancing towards them, two white gardenia leis draped over his arm.

"Rua!" Mike replied. "So good to see you." He gave the man a friendly clap with one hand on his back. "I want you to meet my wife, Hannah."

"Mrs O'Connor, so lovely to meet you."

"Hannah," she replied, lips quirking. She shook his outstretched hand.

He smiled wider, showing two straight rows of white teeth. His warmth enveloped her, and the residue of Edith's warnings ebbed away.

"May I?" he asked, offering to place the lei over her head.

Hannah nodded and bowed her head a little, breathing in its sweet fragrance as he placed it around her neck. The flowers prickled, but she didn't mind.

Rua held the second lei up to Mike, who also dipped his head. Rua then bent down, grabbing for the handles of their suitcases.

"Here, let me take that," Michael offered, taking hold of his own to stop any argument. Hannah knew he had done it out of respect for the old man.

Rua shook his head, his lips curving good-naturedly. He opened the back hatch for the suitcases and slid open the side door for Hannah to get in.

"Your first time?" he asked her, indicating the island with a sweep of his arms.

"Yes," she replied. Her shoulders relaxed. The evening's warmth and the scent of her lei wrapped around her.

Climbing into the back of the van, Mike shuffled in beside her and Hannah couldn't stop smiling. Excitement hummed in her belly. Maybe this would be as perfect as she had hoped.

Rua climbed into the front driver's seat and opened a small cooler. He pulled out two bottles of water and passed them back to Mike and Hannah. Hannah gratefully accepted hers and took a sip, allowing the cool water to rehydrate her parched throat.

"Whew, it's warm, isn't it?" Mike said to no one in particular. He wiped his brow with the back of his wrist.

"Oh, it's glorious weather we've been having, Mr O'Connor," Rua replied. "Not too hot, eh? A few rain showers and cooler than normal - the locals love it." He beamed.

Mike gave an exaggerated wide-eyed look at Hannah, and she bit back laughter.

"I think we know each other well enough for you to call me Mike," Mike said with a grin, catching Rua's eye in the rear-view mirror as he pulled away from the curb.

"Okay, Mr O," he said, turning his attention to the road.

Mike shrugged and gave his head a shake. Hannah let a giggle escape.

They were the only two guests with this pickup. Night made it hard to see much of their surroundings. The street seemed narrow, shadowy palm trees gracing both sides of the road. Rua drove at a casual pace until up ahead Hannah saw the tell-tale signs of flashing lights. Slowing down, Rua followed the directions of an officer as he maneuvered around an ambulance and cars that blocked the view of the accident. People in yellow vests walked around. Two loaded a covered stretcher into the back of the ambulance. Hannah turned away, saying a silent prayer for the victim or victims. Rua stole a glance at the two of them in the rear-view mirror.

"Scooter accident," he announced. "Best to be careful," he said, "when riding at night..." He broke off, leaving the sentence hanging in the air between them.

"How's the resort coming along, anyhow?" Mike asked, changing the subject.

"Yeah, yeah, good," Rua replied, flashing another smile their way. "Plants are doing good."

"Rua is the resort's chief gardener and groundskeeper extraordinaire." Mike nudged Hannah. "We're lucky to have him on board with this project."

"No, no," Rua shook his head. "The *plants* are lucky to have me." A throaty chortle pealed through the van. "Left to the spirits, they'd die, eh?"

Hannah shot a confused look at Mike.

"Ah, it's just superstitions," Mike said.

"You haven't told her yet?" Rua raised an eyebrow at them in the rear-view mirror.

"Told me what?" Hannah asked, wondering why Mike had left her out of anything.

"Oh, local superstitions, is all." Mike shrugged it away.

Hannah fidgeted with her necklace.

"Not superstitions, Mr O. I told you, not a good place to bring your new wife either."

"What superstitions?" Hannah asked, not sure she wanted to know. She didn't need to hear ghost stories on her honeymoon.

"Oh, some ridiculous story about the land being cursed. *Stories*, Hannah, like I said." His jaw tightened, even as his thumb rubbed along her knuckles.

"Ah, well, whatever you believe." Rua tipped his head. "I'm here for the plants, is all. As long as they'll have me. Gotta make a living somehow, eh?" He donned a light-hearted air again, lifting his head and winking at them in the rear-view mirror.

Catching his eye, Hannah forced a smile. Her Spidey-senses tingled again. She could swear Rua's smile never reached his eyes.

CHAPTER 4

A large billboard advertising the grand opening of the Rest Easy Resort welcomed them to their destination. Lush jungle lined the circular driveway. Ground lights illuminated palms against a rich navy sky. Rua pulled the van up in front of the reception, a spacious lobby with wall-to-ceiling glass, a thatched roof and a slab of polished mahogany as the front counter.

Rua grabbed their bags with the help of Mike and wheeled them into the foyer. Hannah gawked around her, stunned by how beautiful it all was, even at night. Everything had a laid-back sense of luxury in keeping with the island vibe.

Rua rang the reception bell, and a slim woman with short blonde hair and glasses came out from a room behind the reception desk. She was attractive, Hannah thought, but dark blue circles under her eyes weighed her down.

"Kia orana," the lady said in a melodious voice. "Oh, welcome back, Mike." Her face showed recognition right away. She stepped out from behind the desk and gave him a quick peck on the cheek. "And this must be your wife?" She turned to Hannah, the edges of her mouth quirking upwards.

"It's so good to see you again, Mariana," Mike replied. "I'd like you to meet the new Mrs O'Connor."

"Hannah," Hannah corrected, then blushed. Feeling like Mike's trophy, the way he was introducing her, she held out her hand.

"Mike has told me so much about you," Mariana said, shaking it.

"Hannah," Mike said, turning back to her. "This is Mariana. She manages the resort with her husband, Sam. Although at the moment, Mariana is temporarily running everything."

"Superwoman?" Hannah asked, wondering how one person could oversee an entire resort.

Mariana laughed, her cheeks colouring noticeably. "Not quite," she said. "Plenty of people are helping me out. We have a great team at the Rest Easy. You've already met Rua." She gestured towards him standing beside their suitcases. He nodded back at them.

"How are you, Mariana?" Mike asked.

"Oh, you know me," Mariana replied with an exaggerated sigh. "Keeping this place afloat and all." Her words rolled off her tongue like an old joke between them.

"And Sam?"

"Well, the stomach cancer and all… He's a right grumpy pants, but we get along alright." Her tone was light, under the circumstances.

Hannah had to admire this woman's spunk in the face of such adversity. Maybe her quip about her being superwoman wasn't too far from the truth.

Hoping it not tactless, Hannah changed the subject. "The resort is beautiful," she said, addressing it to Mariana as if it had been of her own conjuring.

"You wait until you see it in the day." Mariana gestured to the entrance. "The grounds in particular – they're a real tribute to Rua's green thumbs." Her eyes shone as she spoke, but Rua shook his head and waved his hand as if to swat away such praise. "Anyway, I have your room all made up, you're in 26B. At your request, we've put you in a garden suite, but let me know if you change your mind and would prefer an ocean view or a bungalow."

Hannah shook her head. Not happening. She had to put her foot down with Mike to get her way, but somewhat modest and away from the ocean was all she wanted.

"It'll be quiet around here tonight. You are the third party to arrive, the rest will come tomorrow," Mariana continued. "Rua will help you with your bags. If you need anything, dial *9 and your call will come straight through to me. You've got free Wi-Fi in your room. Here's the passcode." She handed a small card to Mike. "And your keys." She dropped two swipe cards into Mike's hand. "Breakfast is served from seven to ten in the Moonlight Bistro."

"Thank you. We don't want to keep you from Sam, so we'll hit the hay now and hope to see you tomorrow morning."

"Nice to meet you," Hannah said. She followed Mike and Rua through the lobby and out into a covered pathway which wove amongst lush vegetation illuminated by garden lights. The wheels of the suitcase clattered along the concrete path, and Hannah was grateful they had the place mostly to themselves.

They passed a two-storied block of resort rooms with balconies and beach chairs. Beside her came a rustle in the garden. Her eyes adjusted to the ambient light as a chicken and two little chicks wandered across her path for a late-night snack. The cackling of a rooster echoed through the grounds against the white-noise backdrop of the ocean in the distance.

She found it eerie being there at night, in grounds that were largely deserted. Holding back a shiver despite the warmth of the hour, she couldn't stop the flow of her thoughts. Her mind had switched to overdrive, thanks to Rua's suggestion of a curse.

Rua remained quiet the entire time, while Mike pointed out various landmarks, including paths leading to the Moonlight Bistro, the pools, the spa and the beach. Hannah shuddered. The beach was remarkably close.

After rounding the corner of another building block, they walked past a series of rooms to a flight of stairs that took them up to the second level. Here was a covered terrace with a balustrade on one side and room numbers on the other. The outdoor lights made it easy to find their room.

Mike gave the key card from his pocket a quick swipe in the card hole. The lock made a gentle click, and the door handle turned with ease in his hand. His fingers found the light switch, and the room blazed into life. No one moved.

"Would you like me to place this in your room for you?" Rua finally asked, with an air of hesitancy. He made no attempt to cross the threshold to their room.

"I've got it," Mike replied, setting his suitcase down to relieve Rua of his. "It's good to see you, man." He clapped Rua on the back.

Rua curved his lips into his broad smile again. "You too," he said.

Hannah wondered what he would have done if they had invited him in.

He nodded. "Mr O. Mrs O." Backing away, he took his leave.

Mike grabbed the suitcases and hurled them inside. Then he turned around and wrapped his arms around Hannah. She sank into his embrace. Finally, it was just the two of them. Husband and wife.

CHAPTER 5

Beside her, Mike slept like the dead. One leg stuck out at a weird angle from under the duvet. Golden curly hair shone in the sliver of early morning sunlight, which had stolen its way through a gap in the curtain. Lying on his back, he had one arm bent above his head and his face tilted to the side. He looked so peaceful. His long blond eyelashes brushed his upper cheek bones. With his lips gently parted, he made a gentle whistling sound with every breath. For a moment, Hannah's breath caught in her throat.

Nestling closer, she rested her face on the arm he had angled over his head. Her breath must have tickled his face. His eyelids fluttered and his lips curved into a gentle smile. Giving a soft moan, he shifted his body towards hers, wrapping an arm around her and pulling her closer.

"Morning, wife," he whispered, eyes still closed.

"Morning," Hannah replied, brushing a kiss across his lips. Holding her tight for a second, he opened his eyes, still heavy with sleep, then met her for a kiss that seemed to devour her. His warm tongue curled around hers with a deep sense of belonging. After Hannah's skin had flushed itself pink and her toes tingled, he broke away slightly, his eyes fully open now, and studied her. Lying curled together on their sides, cheeks on his pillow and their noses almost touching, Hannah felt safe.

Mike brushed an errant strand of hair from her cheek.

"What's the plan for today?" she asked.

He spoke between nuzzling her neck. "Wow. Raring to go, are you?"

Hannah smiled sheepishly. She couldn't help it. The night had been restless, full of fragmented dreams interrupted by the crowing of a rooster with no concept of time. But now, morning had come – the first actual day of their honeymoon – and Hannah felt a new sense of buoyancy about her. This was the beginning of their life together, and she desperately wanted to make the most of every moment they had. What had Edith said? Something about every second with your soulmate being a moment to treasure?

"Well, let's start with breakfast. Then I have a meeting at nine o'clock. Shouldn't be too long. I want to check in with Mariana about a few things."

Hannah's mood grew sombre.

A meeting.

Already.

"Then we can get ourselves set up with some scooters and go exploring."

By now Mike probably knew the island back to front, but for her, it was all new. Her spirits warmed again. She had to admit, she was looking forward to learning to ride a scooter too. She'd begrudge Mike an hour or so of business if it meant the rest of the day was theirs to spend together.

"Sounds good," she said. "I'll maybe go for a walk around the resort or something while you're in your meeting. But first … shower time!" She pushed away from him and hauled herself out of bed, tugging her tee-shirt over her hips.

Mike good naturedly threw a pillow at her, making Hannah jump and squeal. She thumbed her nose at him, wiggled her fingers and blew a raspberry.

She had taken in little of the hotel room when they first arrived the night before, mainly because she had been so tired and bed had been calling to her. But now, on the way to the bathroom, Hannah could appreciate its aesthetics.

The king-size bed, placed in the middle of the room, had a turquoise-and-white floral duvet and plump pillows, and faced large glass sliding doors and a balcony. Bright artwork of hibiscuses hung above the side tables. Above the headboard hung a massive painting of a lagoon at sunset. A spacious closet was on one wall, next to a built-in dresser. Attached to the room was the en suite, which was where she would head after her quick tour.

From there was another room with a jacuzzi positioned under a large skylight. The main entrance to their suite opened to a small kitchen area with a stovetop and mini fridge and all the minor conveniences. In the central living area, a glass-topped coffee table and two love seats in turquoise-and-grey striped fabric faced a television hung on the wall. A desk and a small dining table with two matching chairs offered working and eating options, and the balcony access linked to the bedroom. Tiled floors ran throughout the premises.

Everything was new, shiny and spotless. Hannah had to remind herself this was a hotel and not a permanent residence.

Mike was sitting upright in bed, his laptop open on his lap, as she made her way back to the en suite. She turned on the shower, allowing the room to steam up before stripping naked and getting in. She turned the shower pressure to maximum, feeling the water's needles dig into her skin, massaging and striping away the days and weeks before, the building stress of the wedding, the last of the travelling residue and her restless sleep. Her skin came alive under its sting, blushing pink. Another bubble of excitement rose within her. She had done it; she now had everything she had always wanted. She had found that much-coveted love all young girls dreamed of, her Disney prince. Just like her Mum before her. She'd found her soulmate.

The word stuck somewhere in her throat, and she had to take a hard swallow. Edith's words came unbidden. *And you love him?* Why would she even ask? Hannah wondered. They were on their honeymoon, weren't they?

Soulmates transcend death, but that doesn't mean you should seek it out. Hannah's thoughts flew to her parents. Is that what her father had done? Sought death?

The water chilled for a moment, as if her thoughts had manipulated its temperature to suit. With a shudder, Hannah moved out of the stream's way, shifting the dial further around to the warm markings.

Be careful, Edith had said.

Be careful of *what*? None of the conversation made sense to her. Edith and Henry had seemed like wonderful people, with Hannah instantly liking them. From all the evidence she could see, they were a loving couple celebrating a long lifetime together. She almost envied them. They looked happy. So why then the warning?

The water changed extremes again, and Hannah jumped as it turned searing hot. With a yelp, she slammed the dial off. Taken by surprise at the pain, she slumped against the tile, heart racing.

CHAPTER 6

fter drying herself off, she wrapped herself in one of the resort's fluffy emblemed dressing gowns. Normally she would have taken any excuse to forgo makeup, particularly on holiday, but today was different. There was a good chance she'd meet more of Mike's associates, and she wanted to make a good impression. She kept it to a minimum though: moisturiser, light foundation, eyeliner and a dash of mascara and lip balm.

Hannah pulled a comb through her chestnut hair, thankful for her mother-in-law's insistence to do away with her usual mousey brown. She liked it. It was a little more vibrant, a little less safe than she usually played it.

She took the time to dry it with the hotel's hair drier, doing her best to smooth and style it like she had seen it done at the hair stylists. By the knocking on the bathroom door, she had taken too long.

"Just wanted to see if you were still alive in here," Mike joked, pushing the door open. Hannah poked her tongue out at him.

"It's all yours now if you like." She stepped aside to let him in, giving him a quick kiss on the cheek as she left.

It wasn't long before they were both dressed and ready to head down to the Moonlight Bistro for breakfast.

"Come on, I want to show you something." Mike led Hannah out of their suite and paused on their terrace. Shocked, Hannah took in the long row of pots filled with pink, red, orange and yellow hibiscus flowers against the balustrade. It stretched in both directions, the length of the terrace. She let out a small gasp of appreciation. How had she missed them? They must have been lost in the shadows of the night's half-light.

Now she took the moment to appreciate their beauty, stroking the filigree of the locket around her neck, as she did so. The blooms were a lush mimicry of the tropical jungle stretching beyond their hotel block. Looking over the balustrade, Hannah felt she could see forever. Beautiful gardens were broken only by the tops of other hotel blocks. And beyond that, to her left, rose the hills of jungle. In the distance, to her right, the sea stretched out to the horizon. She supposed most of the pools and amenities were on the other side of their building.

"It's amazing," Hannah whispered, regretting how little justice her words gave the view.

Mike grinned.

As they made their way to the stairs, Mike pointed out a thatched roof, visible a little way off: the reception area. He was bouncing on the balls of his feet with excitement, taking a personal pride in the resort's beauty. And, Hannah thought, he should. Mike liked to be hands-on. He was detail oriented, and Hannah suspected he'd had more input than most in the finished product, even finding the right people to make his ideas reality. Like Rua and Mariana.

For a moment they stood side by side, admiring the view. Mike checked his watch and tugged her hand, leading her down the few stairs to the ground level. Rounding the corner of the building block, Mike brought them to a winding path past two swimming pools surrounded by stunning gardens. A rock garden complete with mini waterfall cascaded into one pool. Rua had outdone himself. Hannah made a mental note to tell him as much when she saw him again.

A sandwich board announced they had arrived at the Moonlight Bistro, an open-air restaurant with a thatched roof and surrounded by potted palms and yuccas. Wooden-backed chairs with cushions in grey and turquoise and a stripy splash of lime green to complement the tropical décor were placed invitingly around the patio. Inside, wooden beams ran across the roof.

From the corner of her eye, Hannah saw something scuttle across the ceiling and gave a small jolt. Mike followed her line of sight and gave a toothy grin. A small gecko stared back at them, unblinking. It took a moment before Hannah noticed at least another five were scampering around the ceiling. Looking for insects or something to eat, she assumed. As long as they stayed away from the human food, Hannah would chalk it up to island charm.

She thought back to the original plans Mike had shown her in the early days of their relationship. Rest Easy Resort had largely been a restoration project. They had made some changes; the original plans from the late 1980s were a little outdated in places. But to Hannah, so much had changed.

Mike had described the resort as a decaying skeleton overtaken by jungle and graffiti. He had even shown her some pictures. The resort had been eerily beautiful in a haunting and forlorn sort of way. But now, there could be no other emotion but awe.

What they had accomplished in three short years was amazing. Even with all the setbacks. The Rest Easy Resort had flourished almost in unison with her relationship with Mike. How strange, she thought. Coincidental.

Mike led her over to a table. As he always did, he pulled a chair out for her, and they seated themselves. A young woman dressed in a bright lime floral dress, with woven palm fronds making a crown in her hair, floated over to their table. In front of them, she placed a cold carafe of water and two glasses on a tray, and two menus.

"Kia orana," she welcomed them. "Welcome to Moonlight Bistro."

"Kia orana," Hannah and Mike replied in unison, adapting quickly to the island greeting.

"Can I interest you in our complimentary tropical breakfast buffet, or would you like to see the menus today?"

Hannah stole a glance in the buffet's direction. Two long table-clothed tables stood next to each other featuring a host of cereals, bowls of tropical fruit and yoghurt, a large shiny toaster machine and carafes of milk and various juices. Hannah's stomach gave an involuntary grumble, and heat rose on her cheeks.

"We'll look at the menu, thanks," Mike said, just as Hannah was about to agree to the buffet. He flashed white-teeth at the hostess who launched into the morning's specials. Minutes later, Mike was digging into his waffles with bananas and bacon, and Hannah nibbled at a shaved piece of coconut in a fruit salad that could have been just as easily and less expensively ordered from the buffet.

Mike's phone rang. It was an unwelcome intrusion. Hannah had noticed more and more over the last few weeks how she had grown to dislike, maybe even hate, his phone. It was the other person in their relationship.

After a lot of high energy greetings, questions about the caller's family, some "hm's" and "ha's", Hannah guessed she'd be losing him for more of the day than she'd hoped.

Finally, Mike put down his phone. Hannah pretended to be invested in her fruit salad.

"So, that was Graham," he said, giving Hannah a chance to skim through the Rolodex of names in her mind. From memory, Graham was a major stockholder in the resort.

"He's on his way with his family now. They've spent the last two nights at the Eventide so they'd have something to compare the Rest Easy to." His lips curved, and he didn't mention her dip in enthusiasm.

She returned a small smile.

"They should be here in the next twenty minutes or so. He wants to sit down with me when I meet with Mariana so we can go over some things."

Her stomach dropped further. No matter how much she prepared herself, the disappointment always stung. She doubted their meeting would stay within an hour now. Mike was a sociable being. Adding another person to the mix would only lengthen his time away from her.

"I'm sorry, babe," he said, finally catching on. "I'm still going to try to keep it to an hour. It's just … this is important." He tipped his head with boyish pleading and squeezed her hand across the table.

"It's fine," Hannah said. It had become a rote answer.

"When Graham gets here, I'll introduce you to his wife. Maybe the two of you could go exploring together?"

Hannah's stomach knotted at the thought. Did he not know

her at all? This was their *honeymoon*. The last thing she wanted – on any day, if she were honest – was to spend time with a stranger making forced small talk. A grimace flashed across her face, and she replaced it with what she hoped looked something like happiness.

"It's no problem," she repeated, this time making sure it sounded perky and real. "I kind of like exploring on my own, anyway." It wasn't a complete lie. Without Mike by her side, she was much happier in her own company than with other people.

"Okay," he said. "I'll make this up to you, I promise. We should still have plenty of time to get lunch and sort out scooters. Then we'll make a rock-solid plan for tomorrow, okay?"

"Sounds great," she said, meaning it. The wedding had been hectic, lots of people vying for their attention. The allure of the honeymoon for Hannah had been about them having some time together. Uninterrupted time alone. She knew she was naïve. It was always going to be a working holiday, but still...

She took a last sip of her iced water before placing the glass on the table.

"Ready?" Mike asked, pushing his chair back.

Hannah hummed a reply.

"I'm going to head to reception right away. Get in early with Mariana before Graham gets here. You sure you don't mind?"

"I'm fine. Honestly." She stood, and Mike raised an eyebrow. "But I am going to head back to the room first so I can put on some sunscreen and grab my hat."

"Alright then. You've got your key card?"

"I think you have it," she said, remembering Mike had

pocketed both of them when they had left the room.

He dug around, pulled out the swipe cards and gave one to her.

"Love you," he said. manoeuvring her towards him with one arm. He pushed a wayward strand of hair behind her ear.

"I love you too," she replied, closing her eyes and tiptoeing for a kiss.

Instead, he bent down and pressed his lips to her forehead, then turned his back and left.

CHAPTER 7

After smothering herself in oily sunscreen and grabbing her sun hat, Hannah headed back downstairs to explore the resort. Despite being so early in the day, it was already warm, and the hungry sun licked at her skin.

The resort was like nothing Hannah had ever experienced. It resembled a small community placed in a horseshoe around some of the largest leisure pools she had seen. Picturesque gardens gave those who swam or lounged by the pools some privacy. Palm trees were strewn throughout, with more growing along the beach. Some had white hammocks lazily hanging from them. She hoped the palms were not coconut trees. Hannah had heard about the high number of deaths by coconuts falling on people's heads. Although she couldn't remember the number, it still rattled her.

She headed towards the lagoon first. She wasn't sure what drew her there. Since her parents' accident, the sea, along with most bodies of water, had filled her with dread and grief. But here on an island, she couldn't escape it. Better to face her fears now, early on, and hope this would be the turning point. Maybe she would finally let go, even just a little, to the nightmares, the fears still holding her in their sway all these years later.

When Mike had first suggested their honeymoon at Kulani, Hannah had argued against it. She rarely spoke up for herself in such a way, but this had been different. In all of its intensity, she had felt what it was like to be back there, back to when she was six years old.

She had felt the undulation of the water beneath her as she stood in their living room. The past and present superimposing into one. That moment when, from nowhere, a giant rogue wave had hit their little aluminium boat.

Her father had thrown himself at her, noticing just in time. He wrapped her in his arms, Hannah in her bright orange, plumped up life vest, knocking her hard against the side of the boat which rocked mercilessly, threatening to overturn. The lyrics of a playground nursery rhyme flitted through her head: *Row, row, row your boat, gently down the stream...*

Then came an army of waves. An onslaught of them. One after the other. More and more. The sea had awoken, hammering against the thorn in its side that was their little boat.

Hannah remembered the rocking. How it hadn't overturned right then, she'd never know. Her mother, eyes wide, held onto the side of the boat across from her father and her. Though she was saying something, all Hannah could hear was a static roaring in her ears. Then the grandaddy of all waves hit them. The boat lifted over their heads, and Hannah and her father dropped into the sea.

The salt water burned her eyes and throat. Her dad's grip, never loosening, threatened to suffocate her. Her lifejacket forced her to the surface, while the weight of her father dragged her down.

There had been screaming, but she didn't know whose. For

a moment everything went dark. Had she closed her eyes? She wasn't sure, but she remembered the smack of her head against something hard and red dots floating amidst the dark. When she opened her eyes, the side of their little dinghy was smacking against her shoulder.

The swallowed sea water burned her throat. She cried out, coughing and choking at the same time. She heard yelling. It was her father, still not letting go of his own precious cargo. Without a life jacket of his own, he was half using her to buoy himself while struggling with one hand to get a grip of the boat which slammed into them with every new wave.

He was yelling for her mother too. "Annie! Annie!" he repeated between his own gagging mouthfuls of water.

No reply came.

The fury of the sea lessened enough for him to push Hannah's small body up on to the top of the overturned boat. She lay flat on her tummy, crying and gripping its slippery surface as smaller waves rocked it in a sadistic lullaby.

"Annie! Annie!" The words rasped from her father's mouth. Hannah raised her head. The sea stretched on forever. A plastic chilly bin housing their lunch floated in the distance. So did a life jacket, one of her parents'. One they hadn't thought to wear themselves.

The sea quietened. Her father's voice lost strength. He still clung to the side of the boat, one hand resting very near her ankle. Hannah gazed around again.

"Mum!" She was hoarse. "Mum!" She moved her head from side to side, searching for any glimpse of her. But her bright pink tee-shirt never broke the surface, nor did her long auburn hair reflect in the sunlight.

The temperature had dropped. A cool breeze chilled her

wet skin. Her father grew agitated. His calls rose into a high-pitched crescendo, using every bit of his breath to summon back his wife from the sea's depths. His voice broke with intermittent coughing spasms. His head jerked this way and that. He took a deep breath, puffing out his cheeks then diving under the water, under the boat. He was searching. Searching.

He would come up for air, moving further and further away from the boat. Over and over. His yells became whispers. He'd draw another breath and dive, again and again. Hannah watched hopelessly as his head dipped below the surface. She clutched tighter to the pleats on the boat's bottom, all her effort going into not sliding off, counting the seconds until her father's head resurfaced. He took longer and longer to come up for air.

His strokes slowed. He could no longer lift his arms.

One last breath.

Hannah waited.

She tried crying out, but no sound came. She was alone on the capsized corpse of a dinghy. The sun beat down, and the waves gave in to a new gentle undulation as if nothing had happened.

CHAPTER 8

Mike had empathised. Of course he had. But too much was tied up in the Rest Easy to not be there at the pre-opening. He suggested they put off their honeymoon, instead. Hannah was the one who had objected.

Besides, Mike had said, it would be good for her.

A warm, gentle breeze rocked the tops of the palm trees growing to the sides of the path as she neared the beach. Moisture streaked down her cheeks. She wiped her eyes with the back of her hand and surreptitiously touched the gold locket around her neck.

It had been a gift from her aunt. She had been lucky; her aunt said. Someone on shore had noticed the capsized boat and called the coastguard. Hannah had spent a few nights in the hospital as a Jane Doe, with a mild concussion and dehydration, refusing to talk. When her father's body washed up on shore, they had rung Wendy as next of kin. Her mother's body was never found.

She had been twelve when Wendy had given her the locket. A gold filigree heart that opened. On the inside, her aunt had glued two small photos of Hannah's mother and father, so she'd always have them close.

Hannah focussed on the view ahead of her, pushing back the unwelcome memories.

The lagoon was postcard perfect. Chilling, but beautiful all the same. Leaving the security of the solid path for the white sand beach, she took a big gulp of air. The crystalline blue water stretched out before her, dark shadows hinting at clusters of coral. Midway between her and the horizon, a thin line distinguished the lagoon from the sea.

Before her, the water was quiet, sleepy, lapping gently at the beach. She moved towards the water's edge, feeling the low thrum of her heart. The water was so clear she could see the rock pools underneath. Sea anemones, starfish and black sea cucumbers. Tiny little fish darting out from one rock to the next.

Feeling as if she were dragging herself through quicksand, she stepped closer. Small breakers in the distance sent flurries of white foam up where they broke on the reef. For a second, panic rose in her chest as she remembered the relentless waves that had stolen her parents from her. She tore her eyes away and focussed again on the sand at her feet. Perfect blond beige.

She steadied her breath.

Soft and fine and littered with sea shells.

Postcard perfect.

For a moment, she contemplated what it would be like to take off her sandals and walk barefoot along the beach, like they did in the movies. What would it be like to be free of fear?

But the shells could be sharp. There could be hidden glass and washed up coral, all perilous to soft city feet. Doctors and hospitals were not on her honeymooning agenda.

Instead, she forced herself to watch the waves crashing into the reef, telling herself repeatedly how beautiful it was, how lucky she was to be there in the hopes it would quell some panic and grief.

When she turned her back on the lagoon, relief flooded her. But as she returned to the main path, a mounting unease crawled up her spine and nestled at the base of her neck. Someone was watching her. She could feel it. Reluctantly, Hannah turned around, scanning the beach in both directions. Short of a woman and toddler collecting shells in a bucket much further down the beach, she was alone.

Completely alone.

She hurried along the path which soon snaked off in two directions. She could head back to the resort or take the path meandering off to her right. Stealing another glance over her shoulder, she veered off in that direction. With every step, her heart rate calmed and she could enjoy her surroundings again.

She couldn't get enough of the gardens. They were magical and seemed to go on forever. Green-thumbery had never been her thing, but she always admired gardens. It grieved her she'd never been able to grow more than a succulent.

The path continued through walls of lush greenery: ferns, grasses and broad-leaved plants with vibrantly coloured blooms. Hibiscuses, maybe? Gardenias, frangipani, yellow bells? She paused as a mama chicken and her three little babies stepped out from the undergrowth and ran across the path in front of her. It didn't bother them to be so close to a human.

The path changed direction, and Hannah thought she could hear voices, splashes from a nearby pool. The path curved again. Directions were not Hannah's strong suit, and she wondered if she'd be able to find her way back to the room, but she followed her trajectory anyway. Again, the path diverged into two, with one bearing right, likely circling around to the pools or the beach, she supposed. The other, a narrow gravel path branched to the left. More overgrown and not as heartily used by what she saw. This was the path that drew her attention.

The gravel crunched beneath her flip-flops, and the distant laughter of the people at the pool faded as she followed the path into denser overgrowth. The plants grew taller here, beginning at waist height and growing to head height. Hannah could no longer see any of the buildings, nor hear any resort noises, just birds and who knew what scuttling in the undergrowth.

Had she wandered off site completely? A small gecko ran across the gravel path in front of her, diving into a ferny bush on the other side.

The jungle grew thicker. Hannah thought back to the view from the terrace this morning. Did she remember such a dense section of plants? Not specifically, but that meant little. Everything reminded her of what she imagined the interior of the island would look like – dense jungle.

The gravel path gave way to a thin dirt track. She *had* said she wanted to go exploring. If she was trespassing, surely she would have seen a sign posted along the path.

After a few minutes, the gardens – if she could even call them that anymore – had thinned out. The flora on either side of her gave way to an opening. The plants turned to overgrown grass, almost knee-high, in ambers and spring greens, stalky and in desperate need of some TLC. The path had become a trampled grass and dirt track.

The path turned slightly again, and the shell of a large building complex came into view, half hidden by the languishing branches of overgrown trees. Their trunks were entangled with deep-green ivy. Hannah was awestruck. The building appeared old and forgotten. Moss had dirtied its once-pale walls, painting them a greenish-grey colour. Balconies, similar to her own room, wound around the second story. She saw hints of colour and the markings of graffiti.

Was this a part of the original building site? She had thought it had all been completed. However, when it came to business talk, she had to admit she wasn't always paying attention.

Mike had told her the Rest Easy was originally meant as a lavish Cooks Hotel Resort. Something had happened to its financial backing, she remembered. The development of the resort came to a halt part way through construction, leaving Kulani reeling in debt, the giant building complex marring the landscape. For years, it had remained forgotten, gradually taken over by tropical jungle. Until, of course, her father-in-law's company had come to its rescue, putting Mike at the helm of its revival.

A floating memory of Rua's comments about the resort being cursed, flitted through Hannah's mind. Superstitions, surely, but she couldn't help thinking how hauntingly beautiful the skeletal ruins were.

A strange shuffling sound came from her right. Hannah turned. The tall grass and overgrown jungle across the clearing were moving, rustling. Her heart skipped a beat. She wasn't as alone as she'd thought. What if she was trespassing? How much trouble would she be in?

The rustling drew closer. Part of her wanted to hide, but she stayed herself, convinced she could talk herself out of whatever trouble she might find herself in.

When it finally showed itself, Hannah was stunned. A dirty white cow with long curved horns stared back at her, unblinking. Its eyes were black holes. Its ribs were visible beneath its thin coat, and its hip bones stuck out at strange angles near its rump.

A cloud must have shifted in the sky. For a second, it was as if the sun reflected in its eyes, casting them a deep red. Then the poor creature bellowed a deep, mournful cry, which reverberated through Hannah's chest, chilling her skin and unsettling her thoughts. Terror swelled and her stomach clenched. And she ran.

She ran like the devil himself was after her.

CHAPTER 9

Sharp flax-like blades of grass whipped at her as she sprinted. Fear and adrenalin swept through her veins, unexpected and intense.

Just a cow, it was just a cow, Hannah repeated silently. Her lungs needed air, even as her rational mind sought sense for her fear.

She had ventured further than she had first thought, and it was with relief when the path turned to gravel underfoot. She forced herself to slow down, albeit into a fast walk.

Just a cow, just a cow, she repeated. Giggles built inside her. She feared a cow? The giggles bubbled out, and a wave of embarrassment swept over her.

The plants on both sides of her were more abundant now, and she allowed herself to walk at a regular pace. Whatever threat she had thought she was under, she was safe now.

Rounding a corner, Hannah noticed someone in long khaki shorts and a bright blue polo top kneeling further down the path. They were bent forward, face hidden from view by the vegetation.

At the crunch of gravel under her feet, the figure turned around.

"Ahh, kia orana, Mrs O'Connor. How are you this morning?"

"Morning, Rua." Hannah blew out a big breath, relieved to see a friendly and familiar face. "Please, call me Hannah."

"Ahh, Mrs O, it would be a hard habit for an old man to break," he said with a toothy grin and a wink.

Hannah wondered how old Rua was.

"How was your first night?" he asked.

"Oh, it was fine. We were both so exhausted from the travel, we slept like babies." A white lie, she thought. "Mike is in a meeting at the moment, so I decided to explore the resort a little," she continued, pre-empting the next question.

"Hmm," he murmured, furrowing his brows. "And what do you think so far?"

"It's beautiful. I don't think I've seen such lush gardens before. You really are a master of your craft."

Rua shook his head sadly.

"No, Mrs O. God made these gardens, I just tend them. Some things, I fear, even God won't touch."

She saw now what he had been focussed on – a low-lying shrub whose leaves had turned almost black. Standing about a foot high, it closely embraced a large grey stone. Fastened onto the front of the stone was a plaque inscribed with: "In commemoration of the breaking of ground of the Cooks Hotel Resort, May 11th 1989, Kulani Island, South Pacific." A long, jagged crack ran down the side of the rock closest to the plaque, not quite splitting the rock in half.

"Why's that still here?" she asked, pointing at the sign.

Rua paused, wiping his hands on his thighs. "Ahh, the infamous commemorative stone. Your husband's told you nothing, has he?" It was a rhetorical question.

"Well, it's for the previous resort. But why is it still here?

Especially since it's broken." Hannah tipped her head to the side. "Are they keeping it kind of like a … a memorial?"

"Aye," he stated. "But not quite."

Hannah drew her brows together, but sensed she didn't want to tread too deep. "What's happened to the plants?" she asked instead. The plants further back from the stone seemed unspoiled, but all leaned in, as if drawn to the rock.

"They were silly buggers," Rua said, half to himself. "They should have had the stone blessed again. And this time, *removed*. It might not have lifted the curse, but it might have weakened it at least. I tried to tell them, but they thought the history of the stone might draw people here. A tourist attraction. Silly buggers," he said again, shaking his head.

"What do you mean? What history?" She couldn't stop herself, despite the cold tickle along the back of her neck.

"They don't understand it's like a cancer, this curse. And this rock, it's a focal point for it. It does more than draw things to it – it kills." Rua rubbed one of the blackened leaves between his fingers. It turned to ash and fell onto the rock. Rua brought his fingers up to his nose to sniff, pulling a face as he did so.

Hannah suppressed a shiver, unsure whether to press for more details. "I didn't realise there are some original buildings still on site," Hannah said in what she hoped was a gentle change of subject. Rua stared back at her blankly for a second.

"Most of them are original," he said, narrowing his eyes.

"Oh, I meant I just saw some incomplete buildings on site. I had thought they were all renovated?"

Rua's eyes focussed intently on hers. A small bubble of saliva formed at the corner of his mouth. His lips pressed into a thin steely line. "They have been," he said, eyes not leaving her face.

"No, I mean, the one back there." She pointed down the path where she had come from. "At least, I had thought it was part of the original complex. It looked similar to the building I'm staying in." The words fell from her mouth faster than she expected as she tried to explain herself. Her nervousness grew. Something wasn't right. She could feel it.

"I'm sorry if I wasn't supposed to go there. I followed the path and it led me there. And then I saw this cow--" She took a quick breath. The words had toppled out ungoverned. "And this cow, it just looked at me and—"

"A cow?" Rua interrupted.

Hannah shuffled from foot to foot. Was she in trouble? "Yeah, this white cow with horns. I'm sorry if I wasn't supposed to be walking there," Hannah said again.

Rua sighed. "Ahh, this place. It will do you no favours, Mrs O." His lips turned down, and he averted his gaze.

Fear spiked Hannah's heart rate. She brought her hands to her chest to steady herself.

Clearing his throat, Rua brought his eyes back to her face. "This is your honeymoon. You should spend it away from Mr O's work. Take some time and explore the rest of the island. Ah, *there* you'll see real beauty, Mrs O. But this place – this place is not for exploring." Pausing, he gave a shrug, seeming at a loss for words. "This place is not for you," he finished.

Hannah shrunk back, hurt by his words. But despite the disconcerting conversation, Hannah felt, without a sliver of doubt, Rua was wrong about one thing. This place was exactly where she needed to be. She didn't know why, but she could feel it. It had a hold on her. A yearning to be heard.

Recognition flitted across Rua's face. His eyes grew sad. His shoulders slumped with a flash of defeat.

"Be careful, Mrs O," he said, looking as if he wanted to say more, but hesitating, shaking his head as if to shake it from his mind.

"Well, I should head back," Hannah said, eager to put distance between them, to end the awkward conversation. "Mike will be waiting for me."

She gave Rua a quick smile, a peace offering, *nothing unusual going on here*, as if to pretend the conversation had been nothing out of the normal. Then she turned away and continued back towards the resort.

"God speed," he muttered, just in earshot.

Refusing to turn around, Hannah straightened her shoulders and headed back.

CHAPTER 10

Not long after Hannah arrived, Mike returned to their room. The meeting had gone well, although a few minor things needing tweaking. A bathroom tap in one room kept turning on automatically. The industrial dishwasher in the Moonlight Bistro had broken down twice and was being repaired. And a stock-take of inventory had shown that a few of the monographed towels and robes had disappeared from the storage room. Souvenirs taken by staff? Hannah wondered.

Minor teething problems, Mike called them. All things to be expected with a new resort.

They didn't seem too minor to Hannah. They seemed like things waiting to take their cut of Mike's time. Like Graham, the stockholder Mike had just met with, suggesting they have dinner together with his family at Moonlight Bistro that night. Hannah involuntarily cringed. Mike might be happy playing a social butterfly, but she preferred to avoid it.

"It's one meal," Mike said.

He rested his hands on her shoulders and gave her wide puppy-dog eyes while sticking out his lower lip. The corners of his mouth hinted a grin. He was so frustrating. Part of her wanted to be angry with him, but she couldn't.

"Okay," she said, resisting the temptation to stamp her foot like a child. Mike beamed. He'd won again, she thought.

Had her mother ever felt this way? Had she ever felt jealous of … what? Her father's job? Not enough time spent together? Not likely. As a six-year-old, she had thought the three of them did everything together. Hannah winced.

"Fine," she said. "It'll be fun." Even to her, the words sounded hollow, petulant.

"How was your morning, anyway?" he asked. "What do you think of the resort?" Mike opened the small fridge and pulled out two bottles of water, offering one to Hannah.

She took it, biting her lip. How much should she tell? "It was good." Simple was best. She pulled off the cap and took a sip before sitting on a loveseat. "I went for a walk down to the beach and explored the gardens. They're beautiful."

For a second, Mike's eyes widened. "The beach, huh?"

"Yeah. I just … wanted to see, I guess…" She wasn't sure how to finish the sentence, so she took another sip of water.

"And?" he said, plonking himself down on the other loveseat and leaning towards her.

"It was hard," she said, feeling the tears rise unbidden. She turned away for a moment, blinking back the threat of waterworks. "But the gardens really were beautiful," she said again, once she'd regained some composure."I knew you'd love them," Mike said, the corners of his mouth curling upwards. "Rua's got a special knack with the plants around here."

"He really does," Hannah agreed. She paused, wondering if she should tell him about her conversation with Rua. She decided it would be best. "I saw Rua today," she said cautiously. "He was working in the garden, by this old commemorative stone…"

"Ahh, yes. And I bet he couldn't wait to tell you more about the curse, huh?" Giving a chuckle, Mike leant back in his chair. He crossed his ankle over his knee as if he were settling in for a good story. "That man is so superstitious." He shook his head. "Don't let it get to you."

"I came across part of the old resort today too." Hannah said, testing him, hoping Mike wouldn't dismiss it as easily as Rua. "I didn't realise some parts of the resort still hadn't been developed?"

Confusion swept across Mike's face, just as it had Rua's.

"What do you mean?" he asked. "The resort's finished."

"When I was out walking, I came across an overgrown clearing with a building a lot like this one, only it was all mossy and graffitied and stuff. I assumed it was an unrenovated part of the original resort."

"Where did you go walking exactly?" One eyebrow arched upward.

Hannah wiggled in her seat. She knew what she'd seen.

"There's lots of abandoned houses further off the main road, but far from the Rest Easy. You must have walked further than you thought."

"I didn't see any main road," Hannah said, feeling her skin chill. "I followed a path leading through Rua's gardens before it turned into a gravel path. I definitely didn't see or hear any roads around."

"Well, you would have had to have crossed it. The road follows the contours of the resort. It used to cut straight through along where the beach is, but we got it moved to go around the back of the resort when we took on this project. All the buildings on site are newly renovated though." His face was still perplexed like Hannah was talking gibberish. It was painful.

Not even she was so oblivious that she could have crossed a major road without noticing. And the ruins themselves were so expansive, no one would describe them as an abandoned house. What worried her was that this was the second time she had mentioned what she had seen, and both Mike's and Rua's reactions made her feel as if maybe she had imagined it. Sun stroke, maybe? Involuntarily, she shook her head. No way.

"Well, like you said, I must've wandered further than I thought and not noticed I was crossing the main road," Hannah said, hoping to drop the matter and smooth over the strange look on Mike's face.

"Too much sun already, wifey?" he teased, pushing himself up off the loveseat. "Let's go get this scooter thing sorted, shall we, unless you've changed your mind?" He winked.

CHAPTER 11

As soon as Hannah had heard most tourists and locals used scooters to get around the island, she had decided she wanted to do the same. Mike had been pining for something flashier to see the sights, but she had won out. In this instance at least, Mike had taken Henry's words into consideration – happy wife, happy life.

Mike had let Mariana know they would rent scooters during their stay. She had organised to have a few brought over to the resort so they could choose which ones suited them. Hannah smiled. Finally, she was getting some time alone with her husband. She'd worry about the ruins and Rua's strange warnings later.

Mariana met the two of them outside the reception with a young man who appeared no older than eighteen. His skin was pink and freckly, and his face was heavily pocked with acne. Tall and skinny, his arms hung limply at his sides as if he wasn't sure what to do with them. A flash of red hair poked out from under his baseball cap.

"This is Rob," Mariana introduced them to the young man. "He's the son of a friend of mine who owns Barrak's Bikes just down the road from us. They are our go-to scooter rental company," Marilyn told them. "Rob will take good care of you and get you set up." She excused herself and hurried back to the front desk where a phone was ringing.

"Either of you ridden before?" Rob asked by greeting, displaying more confidence and a deeper voice than his first appearance suggested.

"I have," Mike said. "My wife, not so much." He gave Hannah a lopsided grin.

"No problem," Rob responded deadpan. "Come over to the bikes, and I'll give you a run through."

Hannah and Mike followed him to where four scooters stood lined up against the berm between the gardens and the driveway to the resort. Two black, one red and one blue scooter waited, with a range of helmets sitting in a box beside them. He took Hannah and Mike over to the box first and had them try on the astronaut-like white helmets until they found ones that fit. Wearing them promised a bad hair day, but Hannah shrugged it off.

Rob then went about giving them an overview of the scooters. He showed them the seat compartment to store the helmets and where the gas cap was. How to hold the front brake tight in one hand while hitting the ignition to get the engine to start. How to check the lights were working, how to accelerate, and how to brake without throwing oneself over the handlebars.

Finally, they were given their bikes. Rob had already chosen the blue for Mike and the red for Hannah. Hannah's stomach fluttered as she turned the ignition on. Nerves and excitement played for power.

Rob mounted a black scooter and took off down the driveway, expecting them to follow. As it was a large circular driveway, it allowed space for the three of them to do a few circuits, practising tight U-turns as they changed from going clockwise to anticlockwise around the course. They practised slowing and speeding up a little until Rob was satisfied Hannah and Mike could handle themselves on the road.

They parked near the berm, and the party moved inside to the reception desk, where Rob had already laid out the paperwork. There, they signed their lives away and noted all the usual fine print for hiring scooters. Finally, Rob took an imprint of Mike's credit card using one of the old manual swipe machines Hannah hadn't seen since her retail days prior to teaching.

Not long after, having thanked the unsmiling Rob who promptly disappeared, Hannah and Mike were left to their own devices, scooter keys in hand and ugly helmets on their heads.

"Alright," Mike said. "Shall we do this, then?"

"Yes, let's," Hannah said, trying to tame the wide grin that threatened to give away how excited she really was. "You lead ahead, and I'll follow."

They turned right onto the main road from the Rest Easy driveway. Immediately, they were flanked by rich jungle and hills on their left, and palm trees and a teaser of Rua's gardens on their right. A few minutes along, Hannah saw the ruins of a few old houses nestled amongst overgrown vegetation on her left. They were definitely not the ruins she had stumbled upon. And nothing on her right – where she expected them to be – proved she had earlier stumbled upon the unrenovated resort. Before long, the road curved back towards the lagoon and followed the shoreline, ending any hope of being able to show Mike he was wrong about what she had seen.

Palm trees framed the view of the azure lagoon and reef, where small white frothy waves crashed. Mostly, Hannah kept her eyes on the road ahead and Mike's back. He remained about twenty meters ahead of her.

They passed a supermarket and gas station on the left. It was not large in relation to the supermarkets back home, yet here it seemed of a significant size. A couple of cars passed them from the opposite direction, and except for a few other tourists on scooters, the roads were quiet.

A scrawny dog lazed on the side of the road, and Hannah slowed, in case it surprised her by jumping out in front of them. Further along on their left, they passed a sign stating they had arrived at the halfway mark around the island. Mike had told her it would take about thirty minutes to ride all the way around, yet it baffled Hannah thinking how small the island actually was. They passed lots of resorts and houses and chickens roaming free before Mike indicated and pulled over to the left, stopping his scooter on the grass verge. He turned around, waiting for Hannah to pull up behind him.

"We're here," he said, pointing across the road at a small shack with picnic tables in the car park and a large sign, reading: "Charlie's Café". Checking no traffic was coming from either direction, the two of them pulled across the road into the small car park. After stashing their helmets under the bike seats, they made their way to the decked area, which looked through palm trees down to the white sand beach and lagoon. Mike put his hand on Hannah's lower back. "What did you think of the ride?"

"It was amazing," she said, beaming at him. She had loved it. The thrill of riding the bike and the scenery had combined into magic.

Mike smiled back at her and gave her a quick peck on the forehead as they climbed the few steps up to where other patrons enjoyed their lunch.

They ordered burgers, with Cokes and fries to share, finding a table that looked out over the beach and lagoon. The sky was unbelievably blue, unblemished by even a hint of cloud. Against it, the azure sea was almost indistinguishable.

"This is beautiful," Hannah whispered. She could even appreciate the sea from this distance without her stomach clenching.

"It is," Mike breathed in agreement, following her line of sight.

"Could you imagine," she asked, "living here? Do you think the people here end up taking it all for granted?"

"Probably," he replied, wiping a drip of aioli mayo from the side of his mouth. "Internet here is sketchy and expensive; I think we'd tire of that real fast. No Netflix, Spotify … Would you consider it, though?" he asked, taking her by surprise.

"I think I could survive without the Netflix and what not, but you know I wouldn't want to live here. No matter how beautiful it might be at this moment, I just—" She stalled, not entirely sure what to say. "I just couldn't," she finished, watching Mike, hoping he understood. She swallowed a lump. Was he disappointed?

"I understand," he said. "We'll enjoy paradise while we're here. Stay too long, and it probably won't feel so much like paradise. Can you imagine waking up to that damn rooster every morning?" His snort lightened the mood.

"Well, if my arm ever needed twisting to leave," she said, "the rooster will do it."

Mike laughed, then popped another fry into his mouth, a

ringlet of hair falling into his eye.

"I love you," she said, catching Mike by surprise. His eyes widened slightly and sparkled. The dimple in his left cheek showed.

"Shall we head off then?" he said, grabbing the last fry.

"Okay, Mr O'Connor." Noting the bedroom gleam in his eyes, this time she gave him her own teasing smile.

Standing up, he tugged at her hand, getting her to follow. Then he pulled her to him for a deep, lingering kiss. Heat flooded Hannah's body, his need more than clear.

It didn't take them long to get back to the resort. Hannah's confidence riding the scooter increased by the moment, and she could focus more on the scenery this time.

Pulling into the Rest Easy's entrance, it shocked Hannah to see the driveway clogged with three big utes and four or so bikes and scooters. Mike pulled onto the berm and motioned for Hannah to do the same.

A small crowd of at least a dozen people, some holding signs and one with a megaphone, gathered outside the reception. Hannah saw Mariana through the throng, a phone to her ear. Another couple of women wearing the Rest Easy uniform shifted nervously beside her while she gestured frantically. Hannah killed the engine and pulled off her helmet.

"Let devils lie," a woman's voice thundered through the megaphone.

"Give us back our land," a few of the crowd shouted.

"Stay here," Mike said, turning to Hannah before pushing his way towards Mariana.

Hannah did as she was told, reluctant to leave the side of her bike.

What the *hell* was happening? she wondered.

CHAPTER 12

Hannah tracked the back of Mike's head with her eyes as he fought his way to the front of the mob where he stood beside Mariana. Mariana looked to be filling him in on what was happening. The two young Rest Easy employees took that moment to disappear into the lobby.

"Give us back our land," voices chanted again.

Hannah's insides slid. First curses, now land disputes? Seriously, what the hell was going on?

A gap in the horde allowed for Hannah to make out the woman at the front.

"You have stolen the land of my forefathers and risked the curse enacted by Mama and Rawiri Tangaroa. You play with fire here on our island! You curse this resort by opening your doors, and you curse yourselves by your own stupidity," her voice rang out.

A roar of approval spread through the crowd.

She was young, Hannah noticed, as she turned to face her entourage. Close to her own age, with long dark hair falling in waves down her back, her wild eyes seemed to narrow in on Hannah. She snarled, and Hannah recoiled. Despite her slight build, she had an intimidating presence.

"Let devils lie!" another voice called out across the audience. "Leave this land!"

A gathering crowd pooled behind Mike and Mariana. A few curious hotel guests and staff watched from doorways.

"The police have been summoned. You need to leave," Mike called out above the noise. The woman spun around, facing him, as Rua joined him.

"Awhina!" His voice rang out. "Leave well enough alone! What's done is done!" For an older man, Rua's voice carried well across the crowd.

"This is not your concern, Papa. If it was, you would stand over here with us demanding recompense for what they are doing!" Another roar rose from the crowd.

"These people have done nothing, Awhina. You are angry with people long since dead," he countered, his tone reprimanding her in a way familiarity allowed.

"How can you say that?" the woman, Awhina argued. She had dropped her megaphone down by her hip and addressed Rua as if he were the only one there.

"This land is cursed, and these people – these people—" She vehemently gestured towards Mike. "They come and they disturb things that should be left alone, things they have no right to, and you know what happens..." She pointed at Rua.

Hannah half expected to see sparks flying from it. The crowd took a step backwards and quietened. Rua took a step forward and met Awhina eye to eye.

Hannah's heart strained against her chest with the weight of the tension in the air. She hated conflict, and suddenly she felt vulnerable watching alone by the scooters. She was likely one of "these people"; a foreigner, an intruder. Hannah searched for Mike's eyes over the crowd. His locked on hers.

His mouth stretched into a thin line. He wanted Hannah to stay where she was, she could read it on his face.

"Awhina…" Rua growled in warning.

"People die," she said. "*Our* people die." Her voice dropped.

Mixed emotions stormed across both of their faces while Mike stood stoic as if a bodyguard to Rua, although she doubted Rua needed one. For a second, she swore Awhina trembled, but then she straightened her shoulders and spat on the ground. When she turned on her heel and stormed down the drive, her eyes landed on Hannah again. She snarled and hawked, spit hitting the ground metres from Hannah's feet, but making its point all the same.

The others, the sign holders and followers, seemed unsure what to do. Disorganised now, they eyed each other, then stumbled after her, almost as if they were afraid to be the last one remaining.

As soon as the crowd passed, Hannah swiftly joined Mike, who was already closing the gap between them.

"Are you okay?" he asked.

"Yeah," Hannah said, trying to hide the trembling in her hands and legs. Mike gave her a quick kiss on the forehead, and with an arm around her waist, he led her towards Rua and Mariana. In the background, she heard the revving of engines and the squeal of tyres as the utes and scooters left.

A red rash had spread its way up Mariana's chest and throat, flushing her cheeks. She was also visibly shaking. Hannah wondered if this had been the first time she had had to entertain such guests.

"What was that about?" Hannah asked no one in particular.

"Just a misunderstanding," Mike was quick to answer, though it appeared Rua wished to add more. He turned to

Mariana. "Are the police coming?"

"No… No," she answered, fluttering her hand. "The police aren't interested, I learnt that the first time."

"The first time?" Hannah's eyebrows climbed.

Rua stared after where the protesters had left. He stood silent; his mouth frozen in a grimace.

"Rua?" She placed a hand on his arm, thinking he knew more than any of them. The woman, Awhina, had called him Papa for starters.

"They are right," he said. "This land is cursed. We are messing with things we…" His voice petered off. He pulled back his arm, turned on his heel and pushed back through the reception, likely to wherever he had come from.

A look passed between Mariana and Mike, and Hannah wondered when someone was going to bother telling her the truth.

CHAPTER 13

Mariana, Mike and Hannah sat in the back room off of the office. One of the young women Hannah had seen earlier was manning the front desk. Mike had called the police again to reinstate what had happened, emphasising he wanted it on file in case it happened again or escalated. Mike and Mariana had a hot cup of coffee in their hands, while Hannah sipped on a glass of sparkling water. She had never gained a taste for coffee.

The three of them had been sitting there pretty much in silence for the past ten minutes. Hannah had spent the time taking in her surroundings. The room was cosy, the perfect size for private meetings. Seating was provided by a small two-person sofa, which Mariana was sitting on, and two single arm chairs occupied by Mike and herself, with cane arms and soft stripy cushions in the themed aqua and grey.

A coffee table held a large, glossy photography book of Kulani Island, and a side table sported a lamp. On one wall hung a picture of the resort and its staff. Another wall had a window looking straight into the lush greenery of the garden. The one door led back into the main office area, which led to the reception.

Hannah studied Mariana's hands. They had finally stopped

shaking.

Mike took a loud breath and put his coffee mug down on the table. "I think maybe you should tell us what's been happening," he said to Mariana.

Hannah bit her lip. She'd taken little interest in the business side of the resort before and felt like she was eavesdropping now. Mike had suggested she go back to their room, but startling even her, she had insisted she wanted to hear what had happened. The experience had unnerved her.

"They just arrived. A few minutes before the two of you." Mariana shrugged. "That woman – Awhina? She started yelling about how the land was cursed, and we needed to close the doors on the whole resort and give the land back. I told her they needed to leave, or I'd be calling the cops, but they didn't seem to care. We open our doors in less than a week, Mike. I can't have them scaring off the guests." Mariana's hands were shaking again. Hannah could tell this went beyond terrible publicity for the resort. They had rattled her.

"You said it had happened before?" Hannah asked, not able to restrain herself. How long, she wondered, had this been going on? Why hadn't Mike told her anything? This was serious and went beyond any lack of business knowledge on her part and even the frustration of a working honeymoon.

"This is the fourth time," Mariana answered.

Hannah took in a sharp breath. "Fourth?" The words slipped from her tongue without thought. She shot a glance at Mike, who closed his eyes and exhaled loudly, as if he had been willing Mariana not to answer that question.

He had known. He had known and not told me, Hannah thought. He'd deliberately kept this secret from her. Why? Because she couldn't handle it? Would have put the kibosh on spending their honeymoon here?

"The fourth time?" Hannah asked again, her voice pitching a little. "Why didn't I know about this?" She directed her gaze at Mike.

"The locals…" Mike began. "I've told you, they've got some strange ideas. The government signed off. The land's legally ours, it's just the land has a bit of a past, is all, and there are lots of superstitions about it." He paused, leaning back a bit in his armchair.

"So Rua was right?" Hannah asked. "The land *is* cursed?"

"Of course not." Mike's voice was sharp.

Mariana wrung her hands and focussed on the tabletop, a flush climbing her cheeks again. Hannah touched her locket. She wasn't used to Mike using this tone with her.

"Look," he said, running his hand through his hair. "The locals have these ideas, and we've tried to be respectful, but at some point, they have to realise the Rest Easy isn't going anywhere. The land was up for public sale, so we purchased it. There's no paperwork to claim any validity to past land claims. Everything was done by the book."

Who's book? Hannah wondered. From the small amount she knew, land claims were tricky. "By the book" could mean different things to different people.

"What is it they want, exactly?" Hannah asked.

Mike opened his mouth to answer, but Mariana got in first.

"They want us to leave." Marian sighed. "Awhina believes the land belongs in her family, and we are trespassers. And until the land is returned to her family, the curse can't be lifted." Mariana paused, an internal conflict playing out with the twitching lines on her face. "And I—" She swallowed hard and pressed her lips together when Mike passed his hands over his face.

"There are no curses, no angry spirits and no overlooked land claim," Mike said, exasperation lacing his words. "There's just an amazing resort suffering a few small harassments from locals who have nothing better to do with their time but superstitious fear-mongering and dwelling on past resentments. Give it a few weeks, and I'm sure they'll tire of it and move on to something else."

"And if they don't?" Hannah asked.

Mike frowned at her, plainly wanting to put an end to the conversation. "Look, we have to head to the police station tomorrow anyway to get our scooter licenses. I'll have another talk to the officers there and see if maybe they can tighten their surveillance of the resort for the next little while and take these protests a little more seriously." He shot them both a pinched smile. It worked on Mariana. She exhaled deeply and took another sip of coffee.

"You are probably right," Mariana said. "It's all nonsense, and I don't really believe Awhina and her crew would do any of us injury. They'd have Rua to deal with, for starters. I think I've been a little on edge. We all have. Getting this resort up and running for our opening week has been hard work, but I'm sure they'll lose interest shortly and move on to someone else."

Mike laughed. "I pity them already." He turned on a full one-hundred watt in Mariana's direction. "Anyway, that's enough adventure for today. I'm thinking a swim and drink by the pool might be what I need. What do you think, Hannah? Bring a book down to the poolside?"

"Sounds good," Hannah said, her mind still preoccupied by the protestors, land claims and curse. As blasé as Mike had been, Awhina and her crew were pretty riled up. In the less than twenty-four hours since they'd been there, Hannah had heard more about curses than she ever had in the rest of her life altogether. But curse or not, people were unhappy, and *that* was unsettling.

Mike stood up from his chair and gave Mariana a quick pat on the shoulder. For the moment at least, the conversation was over. Hannah followed suit and stood. She told Mariana she should call them if any more problems cropped up. Mariana, regaining her composure, waved them off as if they were children, and she was more than capable of handling anything coming her way. She believed her.

CHAPTER 14

Avoiding all resort-focussed conversation, they went back to their room. Hannah could tell Mike was itching to jump on his laptop or make some phone calls, but, for whatever reason, he restrained himself. She was glad.

Mike had suggested they, meaning he, go for a swim while she enjoyed a book poolside. She could do that. Although swimming was not something she enjoyed, pools held less anxiety for her than the sea. Now, to her surprise, he suggested taking their snorkelling gear and books to spend some time down on the beach.

The snorkelling gear had been a wedding gift from a member of Mike's family, unaware of Hannah's past. When Mike had mentioned bringing the equipment on their honeymoon, it had stunned Hannah. She tried to tell him she wasn't able to get in the water, but Mike had insisted. She might change her mind, he said.

"I'm still not snorkelling though," she said, arms crossed.

Mike let out a sharp exhalation of breath.

Taken aback, Hannah wondered what had gotten into him. One thing that drew her to Mike – drew *everyone* to Mike—was his easy-going, optimistic attitude. The hint of annoyance that had etched its way into his brow was not the Mike she thought she knew. She had thought he understood…

"I'm happy to take my book and wait in the hammock while you go exploring," she said, hoping to dispel any rising tension between them.

"You could just give it a go," Mike mumbled. "I know it's hard but … it happened so long ago."

Hannah turned her back to him, her eyes welling. He didn't know. How could he?

"I thought this could be good for us," he continued. "You could face your fears and make fresh memories. Happy memories."

Mike took a step closer to her, his breath tickling her neck as he wrapped his arms around her waist. She chewed on her lip, giving herself a moment to collect herself. She would not spoil their honeymoon by breaking down in tears.

"I'm not ready," she said in a half whisper, pleading he'd understand and not ask it of her again.

He turned her around in his arms. She stared down at his sandal clad feet.

"We've time," he said before tilting her face up to his. "Promise me you'll think about it. While we're here…" He leaned in and gave her a light kiss on the lips.

She turned away again to stem the emotion gathering below the surface. To steady herself, she picked up the sunblock and applied another coat.

Mike went about gathering towels for them, a tote, two bottles of water and his snorkelling equipment alone. For the moment at least, Hannah could immerse herself in her book and try to forget about the sea being mere metres away from her.

The beach was as she had remembered it from that morning. Other than a couple of people collecting shells further along the way, it was empty. Giant hammocks strung between palm trees waited for them. In the distance, Hannah could make out the voices of children or young teenagers laughing and enjoying one of the resort's pools.

Hannah and Mike each chose a nearby hammock and got settled in. It was Hannah's first time and as relaxing as they might look; she found it a little uncomfortable. Every movement had her wonder how long before she fell to the ground. Mike relaxed into his immediately, and it didn't take long before he seemed fully immersed in his book. Hannah took a moment to observe her surroundings again.

The sun filtered through the jungle of palm leaves overhead, and it was with relief she noticed no coconuts hanging precariously above her. She spent a few minutes observing the water too. It was perfectly calm in the lagoon, sparkling with the sun's reflection, and even she had to admit it was beautiful. Calming. Her usual buzz of anxiety lay dormant. Maybe this honeymoon *would* heal her.

She switched her gaze to Mike. Hat pulled low over his sunglasses. Curls of blond hair poking out from under his hat's brim. His sun-burnished skin glistening with sunscreen. He looked so at peace, so at home here. Other than the distant echo of the kids arguing near the pool, and the gentle murmur of the palm leaves in the breeze, it was quiet.

The stumbling upon strange ruins, the warnings from Rua, and the protest drama almost seemed like another lifetime ago. It was fading into a hazy waking dream. Something that had happened but held no weight. No need to mention it again.

"I think I'm going to take a dip," Mike said, swinging his legs out of the hammock and onto the sand. "Will you be alright on your own?"

Hannah gave him a big smile in reply and held her Kindle up for him to see. Her heart chattered under her breastbone, the beginnings of a nervous vibrating.

Mike took his snorkelling gear down to the water's edge. Putting on his flippers and face mask, he barely paused before slipping into the clear blue water. Hannah tried to tear her eyes away from where he went under. Twisting her neck where she lay, she could follow him by the faint red hue of his swimming trunks that now and then broke through the surface of the water. As much as she didn't like being in the water, she did not enjoy seeing her loved ones in it either.

She tried to focus on her book, re-reading the same paragraph over and over as her distraction forced her to seek Mike's form again and again. Her heart did a slow gallop. Mike was a skilled swimmer. He'd been snorkelling many times all around the world. She had seen pictures. But knowing this did nothing to subdue her rising panic.

Hannah took a few deep breaths. In. Out. In. Out. And tried again to focus on her surroundings, this time choosing the trunk of the palm nearest her feet. She traced the texture of its brown-grey bark, following its lines with her eyes, feeling herself calm slightly. She noticed some marks, indentations in the bark that were out of place, like someone had carved something. Interest piqued, she gingerly rolled herself out of the hammock and onto her feet.

Even in the shade, the sand was hot. After finding and quickly donning her flip-flops, she moved closer to the tree trunk. As if reading braille, she traced her fingertips over what she quickly realised were words.

Row, row, row your boat.

It took Hannah a second to realise what she was reading. Her fingers had already reached for the safety of her locket when the weight of it hit her, and a tsunami of panic rose within, sending her heart into a canter.

Mike!

CHAPTER 15

Hannah's feet hit the sand as she raced down to the shoreline, her eyes frantically searching for her husband's form. It took her a moment to see the red of his swimming trunks floating near the surface. Hannah held her breath, willing him to stand up so she could see he was still alive.

"Please," she whispered. She had lost both of her parents to the sea. She couldn't bear the thought of losing Mike too.

Maybe sensing her desperation, the red-trunked form moved closer into shore, and Hannah let out a breath of relief. Her locket stamped patterns on the flesh of her palm as she clutched it, waiting for the moment Mike brought his head above water. When he finally did, she almost collapsed to her knees.

Mike waved out to her and pulled away the mouthpiece, beaming at her. Hannah waved back, stifling the flood of emotion gripping her. Mike made his way onto shore.

She had overreacted. Caught out by a whimsical nursery rhyme carved into a tree. Why? Because it had reminded her of her parents drowning? A threat? Hannah shook her head to dislodge the absurdity of her actions.

Of course, he was fine. The lagoon was one of the safest

places to snorkel – curses and land disputes aside, she thought with a grimace.

Back at their room, Hannah showered and dressed, readying herself for an evening spent with Mike's colleagues. It had been a rollercoaster of a first day, and combined with the sea air, Hannah felt exhausted. She wasn't optimistic she'd make it past nine.

"You're beautiful," Mike complimented her as they walked hand in hand down the path from their room to the restaurant. Hannah had tried for a casual evening feel, with wedge heels and an off-the-shoulder blue dress covered in small white flowers. Her hair hung loose down her back.

"You don't look so bad yourself," she said, dropping his hand to draw her arm through his, giving him a quick kiss on his shoulder where her mouth naturally reached.

When they arrived at the restaurant, a few people were already sitting at tables. Almost immediately, a middle-aged couple on the other side of the dining area honed in on Mike. The gentleman stood and waved Hannah and Mike over. Hannah forced a smile.

"Graham," Mike said, shaking the man's hand.

Graham appeared somewhere in his early fifties. A little shorter than Mike, he was apple-shaped with a prominent widow's peak and jowls almost touching the collar of his shirt. His face was flushed red, and his nose glowed with broken capillaries. Beads of sweat clung to the sides of his face and his hairline.

"This is my wife, Hannah," Mike said, directing Graham's attention to her.

"Ah, nice to meet you. Mike's told me a lot about you," Graham said in a booming voice, clasping her hand in his and giving it a shake. "This is my wife, Sheryl."

Sheryl rose from her seat. With a short blonde bob angled at her chin and heavy makeup settling into the many fine lines on her face, her age was hard to guess. Dressed immaculately, she had gold bangles on both wrists and an assortment of large rings adorning her fingers. She wore three-quarter-length Capri's with high heels and a long flowing tunic in greens, blues and golds, reminding Hannah of a petite peacock.

"Nice to meet you," Hannah said, giving her hand a shake.

"Nice to meet you too," she answered in a small voice at odds with her husband's.

"You're as lovely as ever," Mike announced, giving Sheryl a quick peck on the cheek.

She blushed, showing a hint of discomfort at the attention.

"Come, come, join us," Graham's deep voice bellowed as he pulled out a chair for Hannah to sit on.

"Where are the children today?" Mike asked as they settled themselves at the table.

"Oh, they've been goofing around the pool most the day. They should be here soon," Graham answered.

"Well, should we move to another table, so we've room for when they arrive?" Mike went to stand up.

"No, no," Graham insisted, gesticulating for Mike to remain seated. "The kids can fend for themselves."

Mike shot Hannah a private look, the corner of his mouth quirking upwards, while Sheryl stared down at the table.

"I heard there was an *incident* today?" Graham continued, this time in a stage whisper.

Hannah glanced around them. A young couple stood down the other end of the bar. Except for the few restaurant staff, no one else could overhear.

"So what happened?" he asked, eager for gossip. Hannah willed a small smile onto her face to disguise the threatening grimace. Talking about the protesters was one thing Hannah had no desire to do over dinner. Stealing a glance at Sheryl, Hannah sensed she was thinking the same thing.

Shrugging his shoulders in resignation, Mike readjusted himself in his seat and gave a brief recount of what had happened earlier that afternoon. It was punctuated with small sounds of empathy from Sheryl, and noisier guffaws from Graham.

"Lunatics!" Graham bellowed, making the other patrons and waiting staff balk and turn their heads in his direction. Heat rose to Hannah's cheeks. She hated being the centre of attention, and Graham had moved all eyes onto their little party.

"We need to talk to the mayor about this. We can't let them get away with it. They will lose us business, they will. And after all we have done for these people." His voice echoed around the restaurant.

Hannah recoiled from his words as if slapped. *All we have done for these people?* Good God, he's a *racist!* The thoughts burned through her mind. She widened her eyes at Sheryl, who shifted uneasily in her chair, as if she wanted to disappear under her table.

Mike tried to placate Graham by pointing out he'd been in touch with the police and they would deal with it. A new fire crawled up her spine, warming the back of her neck. She collected her thoughts before finding her voice.

"I'm sorry," she said, "but who are *these people*, and what exactly have *we* done for them?"

Mike cringed at her words and narrowed his eyes in

warning. Hannah waited, heart hammering, to hear Graham's response.

"Oh, no, no, no. I didn't mean it like *that*," he said, quickly relenting, jowls shaking as he shook his head side to side, the broken capillaries on his cheeks burning red in what Hannah hoped was equal parts alcohol and embarrassment.

"It's all about the money, you see. This resort has already created hundreds of jobs for the locals, not to mention all the tourism it'll add to the island. They just don't see it. Stuck in their own little worlds, they are. You wait – before long, Kulani's economy is going to be booming, and you know they won't be complaining about some ancient land claims and curses then, will they?"

Sheryl wrung her hands and still said nothing. He hadn't made a better case for himself.

Hannah considered the dining area, noticing some staff getting twitchy, muttering behind hands and shooting sharp looks in their direction. She wanted to give him the benefit of the doubt that he meant well, but her insides somersaulted over him being so callous about the whole thing. Who were they, as outsiders, to tell the locals what was in their best interests?

"Sheryl, Graham's been telling me your new jewellery line has been taking off. Going international now, I hear," Mike said, changing the subject.

Sheryl opened her mouth to answer but was interrupted by her husband answering in her place. It was obvious Graham liked to dominate the conversation. Hannah didn't like him very much at all.

From there the conversation cycled through thoughts about the resort, future investment plans, other places Graham and

Sheryl had travelled to. It seemed they were avid travellers. Hannah zoned out to parts of the conversation, instead focussing on her meal and the wine glass in her hand. Food had already arrived by the time Jake and Bethany, Graham and Sheryl's offspring, finally showed their faces. They came in like a whirlwind, loud voices, bickering, and with no obvious concern for those around them. Much like their father, Hannah thought.

Jake was tall with lanky limbs and a mop of brown hair falling into his eyes. His face was pimply and red. In one of the few instances Sheryl was allowed to talk, she told them he was in his last year of high school.

His sister, Bethany, was about two feet shorter and fourteen years old. She had long brown hair tied into a single plait and small squinty eyes that seemed to flash one way or the next. Her voice was probably her most defining feature. Loud and whiny. Hannah had heard them coming minutes before they had even arrived.

They crowded poor Sheryl and started a ruckus, complaining about and pushing each other roughly, while Sheryl quietly tried to calm them. Hannah stole a look at Mike, who shrugged his shoulders while Graham continued undeterred with the point he was trying to make. The noise from his offspring didn't seem to bother him in the slightest.

Hannah swallowed another mouthful of her fish. The noise was getting to her, and her inner teacher hungered for release. But it was not the time or place. She bit back the sharp words brewing inside her and focussed on willing everyone to eat faster so they could say their goodbyes and she and Mike could retreat to their room.

Finally, Graham must have noticed his less than avid

audience and turned his attention to his kids.

"That's enough, kids!" he said, his voice thunderous. Jake and Bethany turned to him and opened their mouth to whine, but one glare shut them down fast.

"Go find yourselves a table and order something to eat, the adults are busy here. Keep the noise down, or you can go back to the room." Knowing not to bother arguing with their father, they stomped over to a nearby table, muttering under their breath. A server quickly met them and took their order, a tight smile on her face as they argued over who was going to order first and what they were going to eat. How Sheryl appeared so put together with two tornadoes like that, let alone her husband, Hannah had no idea.

From there, dinner was largely uneventful. Graham roared at his progenies a couple of times to keep the noise down and when a bread roll came flying across to their table.

It made Hannah thankful she didn't have kids. She loved kids. She was a teacher, so it went without saying, but still. Jake and Bethany were effective contraception. A small giggle escaped, but fortunately went unnoticed. Too much sun and too much wine, she thought.

It had been a long night, a long day in fact, when Hannah and Mike could finally say their goodbyes to Graham and Sheryl and their two hurricanes. The sky was dark and speckled with a few stars. The garden lighting made it easy for them to find their way back to their room.

When they eventually fell into bed Hannah's eyes were already heavy with sleep. She had so many questions fighting for space in her mind about the hotel, the protesters and the history of the land, but now they had all scrambled together into a foggy mess too hard to untangle. Mike lay on his back, his arm outstretched. Hannah snuggled closer, nuzzled into his chest.

"I'm sorry about tonight," he whispered into the top of her head. "We'll make tomorrow about us, okay? No protesters, no meals with others, unless you want to." Hannah made a noise in agreement, liking the sound of that very much, but even in her sleepy state, sceptical. Hadn't he promised something similar today?

"I love you, wifey," he said, his eyes already closed

"I love you too, my husband," she murmured before sleep took over.

CHAPTER 16

A loud bang reverberated through the room.

Hannah's eyes flew open, trying to make sense of the shadows. Her heart pounded against her ribcage.

"What the hell?" Mike cursed, fumbling around for the light on the bedside table. The alarm clock read 2:18 a.m. They had only been asleep for a handful of hours.

"What *was* that?" Hannah sat up, wiping sleep from her eyes.

"I don't know," Mike said, already pulling on a pair of shorts he had left discarded on the floor. Hannah clasped the thin duvet to her chest as Mike made his way across the room, opened the sliding door out to the balcony and disappeared from view. Hannah could hear voices coming from outside. She grabbed her robe hanging on the bathroom door and joined Mike.

"Hey!" a voice called up from down below. "Did you hear that?"

"Yeah. Any idea what it was?" Mike leaned over the balcony.

Hannah followed his line of sight. A young man stood on the pavement outside a room opposite theirs. Their hotel blocks were separated by one of the resort's pools, and yet their voices carried easily in the still night. Hannah wondered who he was. Could he be a member of staff? This late? Or a guest, one of the early invitees to the resort's opening?

"It sounded like a gunshot," the young man below called back.

Hannah shivered despite the warmth of the night. He wasn't wrong. It had sounded exactly what she imagined a gunshot would sound like. The air seemed to vibrate from its echo.

Have we been shot at? She wondered. Were the protesters back, causing mischief?

From their balcony, Hannah could see a good portion of the resort. A few lights had turned on in other rooms too. Hannah wondered if Graham and his family had woken as well. They were in one of the beach view villas out of her line of sight.

Another man arrived to join the one down below. He was larger than the first and carried a flashlight.

"It's nothing to worry about," he shouted up at Mike. "Probably a car or bike backfiring". Hannah suspected both men were staff. The man with the flashlight held himself like he might even be security. It made sense after the resort's run in with the protestors.

"Not bloody likely," another voice called out. Hannah recognised Graham right away, even if she couldn't see him. "That noise could've woken the dead."

Hannah hugged her arms around her waist.

"Go back to bed, folks. There are alarms in place if it were anything to worry about," Mike called out.

The man with the flashlight waved his hand at Mike in thanks. "Yeah, it's nothing to worry about," the man with the flashlight reiterated before heading off down the path, no doubt continuing with his security rounds.

Mike turned heel and headed back to the room, and Hannah followed suit.

"What do you think it was?" Hannah asked, returning to bed.

"Not sure. Tama could have been right, thinking it was just a car backfiring."

"But it was so loud," she countered.

"Yeah, but all sounds carry further at night, plus we've those hills back there for the sound to reflect off," Mike added, looking none too worried. He plumped up his pillow with his fist before laying down, ready to fall straight back asleep.

Hannah remained sitting for a while. So far, there seemed very little to rest easy about at the Rest Easy resort. Mike could be right. She hoped he was. But the noise left her feeling like someone had walked over her grave.

She slept fitfully for the rest of the night. The top sheet kept wrapping itself around her legs, and she'd wake feeling bound up, her heart racing and sweat pasting the fabric to her skin. While she wrestled to free herself, Mike slept like the dead.

The rooster from the previous night, or at least one like it, started its incessant crowing from about four in the morning. Mike still slept soundlessly beside her. At some point Hannah must have fallen back asleep because she woke to an empty bed. It took her a moment to register the sound of the shower running. Her head felt foggy and headachy, almost like a hangover.

She lay there staring at the ceiling for a moment, forcing her mind back through the events of the previous night and day. This had not been the start to the honeymoon she had envisioned.

A sound came from the bathroom, and the shower turned

off. Seconds later, Mike walked in, a white towel around his waist. For a man who spent so much of his time on the phone or computer—or sitting at a desk—he was in great shape. His stomach was taut and well-defined and his hips narrow. Something inside her warmed.

He grinned on seeing her awake and made his way over to the bed, sliding in beside her while sitting against the wall. "Good morning," he said. "How'd you sleep?"

"Before or after the weird noise last night?" she asked.

He gave her another toothy grin, running his fingers through his damp curls. "Ah, well, we'll have a chill day today. I thought maybe we could spend it on site. Go for another snorkel. You could join me this time?" he said cautiously. Hannah said nothing. "Or we could relax by the pool. Read. That kind of thing."

"Sounds great," she said, shrugging away the niggling thought that maybe he had an ulterior motive. Was he wanting to wait and see if Awhina and her crew of protesters came back? "Didn't you want to get to the police station today?" Hannah asked, remembering his promise to Mariana.

"It can wait one more day. Plus, if we're on site, I can deal with it right away if anything happens."

Hannah had been right. Her stomach sank. Why he thought he'd be better to deal with it than the police, Hannah didn't know.

"You know, you really are beautiful," he said, catching her completely off guard.

She blushed. "Thanks," she said, not knowing what else to say. Beautiful wasn't on the spectrum of how she was feeling now. But before she had time to say anything else, Mike dropped his towel and slipped under the covers beside her and kissed her, his lips warm and moist against her own. The scent of his aftershave and body wash fresh and slightly overpowering. Moving his body over hers, he straddled her, pinning her to the bed.

"It is our honeymoon," he said. His tongue traced a trail from the base of Hannah's ear to her jawline. Her body warmed and responded to the weight of him pressing down on her. A small groan slipped from her lips as he stripped away the singlet top and underwear she had been sleeping in. His need was urgent. She could feel him hard against the base of her stomach, making her blood bubble with lust. Her hand traced the muscles of his back, and she teased his desire further by gently pressing her nails into his shoulder blades.

"I need you," he murmured and pushed her thighs apart with his leg, sinking lower and deeper into her, filling her completely. Hannah let out a groan, her own desire building as his gentle rocking became more and more urgent, until his pelvis was slamming into hers and her hips arched of their own accord to meet him, not wanting him to stop, dreading the fact he might finish before her.

With a shudder, he stiffened, a low guttural sound escaping his lips. Hannah pressed herself up closer to him, clenching her thighs, trying to savour those last moments as she teetered on the cusp, but then he pulled away. The loss was all-encompassing. It was over too soon and she felt empty without him. Unsatisfied. Lost.

Mike had already turned his back to her. Hannah watched, waiting for her breath to steady as he disappeared into the bathroom again. She wondered if she could finish herself off in the time it took him to clean up. Something akin to shame stopped her. She didn't want to be caught. Didn't want him to know she wasn't satisfied. That she was too shy to ask for what she wanted.

The yearning between her legs waned. Hannah pulled the edge of the duvet over herself, feeling self-conscious, as if someone were watching. Mike came back with a box of tissues, holding them out for her. She took them as he bent down and kissed her. Making her way to the bathroom for her own ablutions, she tried to shake the whisper of disappointment clinging to her skin.

CHAPTER 17

It was already late in the morning when they arrived at the Moonlight Bistro, and most of the patrons had left. Thankfully, of the few people remaining, Hannah recognised none, and Mike seemed blissfully unaware of anyone else's presence.

Whether from lack of sleep or the dramas of the day before, Hannah still didn't feel well. This time she opted for the continental breakfast without waiting for Mike to decide otherwise.

"So what did you want to do first?" Mike asked, spooning a big mouthful of muesli and yoghurt into his mouth.

"Hmm … I'm not sure." That wasn't true. She'd had the growing urge to seek out Rua again. She wanted to hear more about the curse and the land dispute. More about his connection to Awhina. If Hannah was going to be a part of the Rest Easy, even if just by marriage, she wanted to make sure she was on the right side of things. And Mike seemed to be slow in giving her answers.

Instead she said, "We could go for a walk along the beach? I didn't get very far yesterday."

"Sounds great," Mike said, "Are you sure you're up for it though?"

"Sure," she said. "New memories and all." She gave Mike a half smile.

"A romantic walk along the beach, just like real honeymooners," he teased.

We *are* real honeymooners, Hannah reminded herself.

Hannah heard voices shouting before they even made it down to the beach. She recognised them immediately.

"Jake! Jake! Jake!" Bethany, Graham and Sheryl's daughter, was yelling at the top of her lungs, apparently trying to get her brother's attention. It was a whiny yell. A "Look at me! Look at me!" type of yell. Now and then, a muffled reply or a spasm of laughter followed. At least they were having fun, she thought, although being in their sphere seemed to be much less relaxing for everyone else.

The sea was smooth again today, with small breakers out further where the reef was. A couple of translucent clouds drifted across an otherwise perfect blue sky, and the sand sparkled from the sun. It wasn't long before all Hannah noticed was the hollering.

Two figures stood in the distance, one tall and lanky and the other a few heads shorted with long dark hair plaited down her back. They had already donned snorkelling equipment and were bounding in and out of the water like excited dolphins. Bethany paused every few minutes to pull her mask away and scream about her latest find to her brother. There was no sign of Graham and Sheryl, who were probably right now enjoying a needed reprieve from their offspring.

Hannah and Mike continued their walk along the beach which stretched out into a similar view in both directions. With every step, Hannah relaxed a little more. Was it possible she was getting more comfortable being close to the sea? It helped that Mike's fingers gently intertwined with her own.

Hannah made sure to avoid stepping on the coral and shells littering the beach. Every so often, small legs stretched out from under a shell and moved across their path.

It didn't take long before Bethany's, and Jake's incessant noise got the better of them. Every time Hannah heard Bethany scream her brother's name, she felt a clawing behind her eyes. Wanting to put some distance between them and the kids, they headed back towards the resort, stopping when they came across some loungers perched beside one of the smaller kidney-shaped pools. Water cascaded down a miniature rock waterfall, while more lush gardens surrounded them, offering a hint of privacy.

The loungers Hannah and Mike chose were sheltered by large canvas umbrellas. A small wooden table sat between them. They had come well prepared with their usual tote: towels, water and Kindles. Hannah had opted to wear her swimsuit under her clothes – for sunbathing, she told herself. Mike's swimsuit seconded for shorts.

She lay back in the lounger and let the sun melt away her stress. Part of her was buying in to the whole tropical paradise thing.

They spent an hour or so lounging there, invested in their books, occasionally making small talk about their surroundings. Since arriving in Kulani, Hannah had done away with her watch, but she suspected it was around the hour mark when the familiar jingle of Mike's phone went off. The clawing sensation flared behind her eyes again, and she cringed. Mike had it to his ear by the third ring.

With little luck, Hannah tried to ignore the one-sided conversation.

When Mike hung up, she pretended she was too absorbed in her book to notice.

"So," he started, pausing for effect and waiting for her attention. "One of the big freezing units in the Moonlight Bistro has stopped working.

"Oh, that's too bad," she answered. She tried to show nonchalance, briefly making eye contact and then pretending to go back to reading her book. Now was his chance to choose her or the resort.

"Mariana's having problems getting the repair guy in. He says he's too busy, but she thinks some locals might have got to him and had him swear off this place, so she needs me to talk to him."

Hannah looked up. Anger flared in her stomach. Her mind swirled with a torrent of emotions, thoughts, accusations, but she settled with, "Why you?" It came out more biting than she had intended. "Don't they have a restaurant manager or someone else to do it? Mariana's husband, even?" She bit her tongue. She knew Mariana's husband was unwell.

Mike's brow crinkled.

"It's just that … it's not your job to fix things like this or to soothe the locals." Nothing in her tone softened things.

"Hannah." Mike paused, as if struggling to find the right words. "You know this resort is important to me. To *us*," he corrected. "Mariana's husband is really ill, and it's a conversation that might be best coming from another man."

Hannah prickled at the sexism.

"The amount of money my family … *we* have invested in this place—" He swiped his hand over his hair. "I'm good at these things, talking people into doing things. We are less than a week away from the official opening, and the Moonlight needs to be up and running."

"But it's our honeymoon," Hannah said, realising too late how whiny it sounded.

"Look, it won't be long. Give me an hour at tops. By then, it'll be nearing lunchtime, and we can go get some lunch together. Besides, you can enjoy your book, make the most of this time."

She wasn't enjoying her book; she had been finding it hard to get into and their conversation had turned her completely off it, but she couldn't really argue with him. He shouldn't take too long. They still had plenty of honeymoon time together, plus it had been only a few hours earlier that she had been wanting an opportunity to talk to Rua. And here he was providing ample opportunity.

He must have seen her faltering because he swung his legs off the beach recliner, planted both feet on the concrete and levered himself to standing. After a stretch, he bent over, pressing a kiss on the top of her head. "You know I love you," he said, the corner of his mouth quirking upwards.

How would the freezer fix-it guy resist? she thought.

"I won't be long, promise. You have your key to the room, right?"

"Yeah," she said, still a little peeved.

"Good. Relax. Have fun, and I'll see you in an hour if not less." He blew her a kiss, leaving her with his towel, water bottle and book.

She bit her lip. He would not ruin her morning. Until then, it had been wonderful. Now he had given her an excuse to find Rua, so she might as well use it. Maybe she could retrace her steps back to the overgrown ruins. It had unnerved her that Mike hadn't believed her when she told him about it. She knew what she had seen.

Hannah gathered up her their belongings and put them in her tote before swinging it over her shoulder. Maybe today she'd get some answers.

CHAPTER 18

I t turned out he wasn't hard to find. He was kneeling on the path in front of the commemorative stone again. He wasn't moving, just staring, his back to her. His trowel and gardening gloves lay on the path beside him. He was so still Hannah felt self-conscious standing there. She hadn't thought through what she wanted to say. And was any of it her business?

"Kia orana, Mrs O," he said without turning, sparing her the trouble of interrupting.

"Good morning," Hannah replied. "Is everything okay, Rua?" she asked, moving closer. She still couldn't see what it was he was looking at. As she got closer, she could see over his shoulder. More of the plant growing around the rock had turned an ugly black colour and seemed to be curling in upon itself and dying.

"Oh no," she said, not able to restrain herself. "What's happened to it? It's gotten worse."

"*We* have happened to it, Mrs O," he answered cryptically, still not bothering to turn around.

She leaned in closer to the plant to see it better. Rua had outstretched his hand, tracing a giant crack running all the way through the stone. Yesterday the crack had just marred its surface, but today the rock was near completely split in half. At the top, the distance between the two pieces was about two centimetres.

"How did this happen?" she asked, bending over to get a better look.

"We woke it."

"Woke what?" Hannah asked, standing up properly again. "The curse?"

This was not how she had imagined their conversation going. "Does this have something to do with the protesters yesterday?" she asked, trying to make sense of the two incidents.

"No," he replied, finally turning his head to her. "And yes. They are only the messengers of what most of us already know. You need to be careful, Mrs O, they know you are here."

"The protesters?" She raised her eyebrows. "How do they know me? What does this even have to do with me?"

"Oh no, not the protesters, although they won't be thrilled either." He paused, and Hannah's head pounded again. She was going around in circles. "This Resort, this land," he said. "It knows you are here and that you have the gift."

"The gift?" she asked. Gentle fingers plucked at the flesh at the base of her neck.

"The knowing," he said. "You see things … feel things others can't."

Hannah shivered. She had always thought she was good at reading people, knowing what they were feeling, but surely lots of people were like that. Her aunt had always called her sensitive. Mike called it her Spidey-senses.

"Places like this … they feed on it."

She wasn't sure she wanted to know what that meant, so

she changed tact.

"The woman yesterday … Awhina? Is she your daughter?"

It was personal, but it did the trick; Rua's whole demeanour changed. He chuckled and shook his head as if to dispel the moment's heaviness.

"No, Mrs O, she is not my daughter, and I think she'd be shocked to hear you ask."

"I'm sorry. I heard her call you Papa, so I assumed…"

"Ahh," he said, drawing it out. "That is a term for one's elders. I am her great-uncle, so we *are* family. But she's not always happy to be reminded of it." He rocked back on his heels.

"What happened to the stone and plants?" Hannah asked, backtracking and hoping now she'd get a more solid answer.

"This resort was never meant to open its doors to guests. It was never meant to be anything more than the rotten unfinished carcass you saw yesterday," his tone grew serious again.

"So that was part of the resort?" she asked, confused.

"Yes and no. What you saw was the Cooks Hotel Resort. All those years it was left to slumber, but now … now nothing rests easy. Fitting name for a resort, eh?"

Hannah was still confused. It was the same resort. It was not the same resort. Which was it? She had to agree on one point, though. Rest Easy Resort was a stupid name. It reminded her of something you said when someone had died.

Trying to get straight answers seemed near impossible.

"You have the sight, Mrs O. Keep Mr O close if you can. Your love might be what keeps you safe." He peered closely at her, his deep muddy eyes searching hers. "I am sorry, Mrs O. I've always believed the best weapon against evil is love." He spread his hands wide. "I am sure you'll be fine."

Hannah didn't buy it. It was as if he was trying to convince himself, not her.

"I have some supplies I need to get from the shed, see if I can resurrect this plant." Slowly, he pulled himself to his feet.

"Before you go—" Another question had sprung to mind. "Do you know what made that sound last night? Like a gunshot or something."

"You're looking at it," he said, waving his hand towards the cracked stone. Then he turned his back and walked down the path.

Hannah stood there, unsure what to do. Should she follow him, remain where she was, or take off on her own, despite Rua's warning not to do so? She couldn't wrap her head around how one stone could make as much noise as what she'd heard last night. The sound had reverberated through their room, woken both Mike and her from a deep sleep – and most of the other guests, it seemed. How did a stone spontaneously crack? Something was definitely off about the resort, but she wasn't sold on the whole "curse" thing.

Hannah bent down and followed the crack in the rock's surface with her fingertips. At that moment, the sun slipped behind a cloud, and Hannah shivered at the unnerving dip in temperature. Then came a prickling on the back of her neck. The feeling of being watched.

Hannah stood and slowly turned around. As she half expected, no one was there. When she double checked up and down the path, a flash of movement caught her attention. It rounded a corner and disappeared into the trees and gardens. Strange. She hadn't seen any intersecting paths when she had walked it yesterday, and if someone was there, they couldn't have walked past Rua and her unnoticed. The path had been too narrow, with both of them taking up most of it.

Again, a curiosity she had not known before, a driving force, pulled her towards the movement. Maybe there was another path she had been unaware of, she wondered, or maybe, better yet, someone else had also seen the abandoned hotel remains that she had stumbled on yesterday. Then she could prove it to Mike and push the curse explanation aside.

CHAPTER 19

The path was exactly as it had been yesterday. It continued for some time, weaving through beautifully landscaped gardens until almost unexpectedly the gardens became unkempt, overgrown by weeds and grasses, and the path gave way to gravel, then a dirt trail.

She saw no more signs of anyone ahead of her. No person. No cow, like she half expected.

Eventually, the skeletal form of forgotten hotel blocks appeared before her. Exactly where she knew they'd be. Next time, she'd try to bring Mike, or at least try to remember her phone to take pictures. Then she could prove she hadn't imagined the whole thing.

Before venturing too close, Hannah took the time to take in her surroundings. The place looked deserted. She sighed with relief.

It was eerily quiet. Hannah hadn't noticed last time. There was no sign of Jake and Bethany. No cars or scooters or sounds of other guests. No annoying crowing of roosters or chirping of birds. Only the gentle rustling of palm leaves in the slight breeze.

Now that she was here and alone, she thought she would take advantage of the moment and explore.

The grass was almost knee high in places. Hannah kept close to the side of one of the building blocks. It had the same terraces with low railings like that of her room back at the Rest Easy. It was a two-story concrete block, with green mould growing on its walls. The roof was pitched and was made of an apricot-rust-coloured corrugated iron. Hannah followed along the edge of the building until she found the entranceway. For many people, she guessed the building would have looked spooky. To her, it seemed sad and lonely, but also intriguing. For that reason, she was pulled to it, and fear took a backseat. Even the cliché graffiti on the wall beside the entrance, declaring "Keep Out", did nothing to dissuade her.

The entrance was an open hallway with rooms coming off one side. Hannah noticed right away how the layout was near identical to her own hotel block. In many of the rooms, the French doors that would have faced beautiful gardens and pools had been smashed or were missing altogether. Everything was still concrete. The only paint on the walls was graffiti, much of which she couldn't read even with a teacher's brain. The ceilings were marked out with white grids and dots marking where there might have been panelling or other fixtures. Exposed wires hung down where lights would have been. The floor was covered in a thick layer of dirt and vines and rotting fern and palm leaves that had blown in from outside. Someone had etched a heart on one wall with the initials "CM + RT", which suggested the place was an adolescent haunt.

For a second, Hannah checked herself. Exploring an abandoned hotel on her own, that wasn't supposed to exist, in an unfamiliar country, may not be the choicest of ideas.

It had obviously not been completely abandoned. Left to the elements, yes, but there was a lot of evidence of human destruction too. Hannah moved into a second attached room where a jacuzzi was installed. They'd cut away part of the wall, leaving the jacuzzi visible to what might have been the main bedroom. Small intact tiles still surrounded the jacuzzi. Larger floor tiles were cracked or smashed on the floor. The jacuzzi itself was covered in a thick layer of dirt and green algae or mould. Someone had taken a sharp object and carved more graffiti on the concrete wall above it.

It was a haunting sight, mainly because it was so familiar. What a waste, Hannah thought.

Leaving the room, Hannah continued down the hallway. Now and then, she came to a room that still had a door, its sterling door handle and key card slot waiting expectantly. Following a staircase upward, she came to a landing or terrace similar to the one outside her room back at the Rest Easy. Entering one room, she made her way towards the balcony, careful not to stand on it, and sure enough, saw a near replica of the Rest Easy's grounds, minus Rua's gardens.

Several building complexes were arranged in a half circle, all in a similar state to the one she was walking through. Tall trees and overgrowth took over what would have been perfectly manicured gardens, trees and pools. This was the Rest Easy, she thought. Even as her mind fought to register how it was possible, she felt it within her, a gentle knowing. This was Rest Easy Resort.

In the distance, she could see the lagoon and further out the reef. This was the same beach she had walked on only a few hours prior with Mike. It made no sense, but this was what she knew.

Then she heard it. A voice or human-type sound. Her heart started an erratic canter in her chest. Someone was here; she wasn't alone. She scoured the view but couldn't see anyone. Was it teens back to vandalise and create general mayhem? Awhina and her mob?

Hannah shook her head, trying again to integrate the two realities. This place couldn't exist, so how could anyone be here? How could *she* be here?

Cautiously, she stepped onto the balcony. Not knowing how long it had been left to the mercy of the elements, she wanted to be careful. Leaning out over the balcony, she scanned the ground for anything out of place or unusual. Through the long grass and overbearing trees, she saw a small building like a shed a little further off. From this vantage point, it was hard to see, with columns opening it up to the elements and a small pitched roof in a similar style to the rest of the buildings.

But it was there that Hannah saw a flash of movement and heard a child's laugh. Who would let a child wander around such a dangerous and neglected space? she wondered before she caught herself. How could a child be here?

Scanning the horizon further, she saw no sign of anyone else. Damn it, she thought, not sure whether she was cursing because she felt obligated to make sure the child was okay or because she wasn't alone.

Hannah heard it again, the laughter of a child carrying its way up to her on the balcony. Moving with some determination and urgency, she traced her way back down the stairs and out of the building. From there, she followed the wall of the building, rounding a corner so she stood under the vicinity of the balcony she had seen the child from. Because of the cluster of palms and other trees blocking the view, she couldn't make out the small building. But she made a beeline for that area, keeping her ears open for the sound of the child again, and fighting through knee-high grass. As she neared the outcropping of trees, the top of a roof peeked out from behind some palm fronds.

She heard it again, the high-pitched laughter of a child. She couldn't place where it was coming from. It seemed to surround her. She continued weaving through the trees and tall grass until she saw the building.

It wasn't really a building at all. Instead, it was more like a pergola with a stone column at each corner. It oversaw what once might have been a swimming pool. Something clicked inside her brain. She had seen this earlier, yesterday in fact, when she had gone exploring around the real Rest Easy Resort. Her Rest Easy Resort. Only, it looked different then – more like a small pool house stacked with fresh turquoise-and-white striped towels, snorkels and flippers. Here, unpainted concrete was covered in a film of dirt and mould, with dead palm fronds littering the ground and no benches to store the towels and snorkels. A concrete deck met a dark murky green swamp of water where the shadows from the palm trees lay black on its surface. The graduating steps on the other side were unpainted concrete, peeking out from grass and dirt that had somehow found adherence there. This was not the pool Hannah had seen the day before, where the water had been clear and crystalline blue. White loungers and canvas beach chairs had sat amongst Rua's perfectly landscaped garden with bursts of pink flowers. Not here.

Hannah took a step closer to the pool, drawn for no reason she could think of. Almost afraid to peek inside it, she was appalled by how dark and harrowing it was. Her reflection, drawn and confused, bounced off its dark surface.

A peal of laughter made her jump out of her skin. She spun around, trying to spot the culprit, but saw no one. A burst of footsteps made her whirl around again. Still no one.

A humming hung in the air. It took her a moment to recognise the tune. *Row, row, row your boat.* Her heart leapt into her throat, and Hannah instinctively grasped her locket.

A shadow darted from behind one pillar to the next.

"Hello?" Hannah called; her voice thick. "Who's there?" She scanned all around her. Nobody.

But someone was there. She knew it. A noise from the other side of the pool made her spin around again. Then came a childlike voice, echoing as if from inside her head: *Throw your teacher overboard, and listen to her scream.*

Two small hands slammed into her lower back, sending Hannah tottering on the edge of the pool. Her arms waved wildly as she tried to regain her balance. Her reflection, mouth wide with horror, was mirrored back to her in the black, inky liquid. She screamed, and a shriek of laughter followed her as she hit the water.

CHAPTER 20

The thickness of the water engulfed her, instantly filling her mouth and nose and chilling her skin. Unknown hands tugged at her legs and dragged her down.

Hannah kicked and frantically tried to claw her way to the surface. Briefly, she broke through to gasp a small lungful of air, seeing for the first time a young boy, eight or nine. His hands rested on his knees as he bent over, his face peering down at hers. He wore cut-off jean shorts and nothing else. His teeth were big and white in his copper-toned face. His eyes, black holes. He was laughing. The same sound Hannah had heard before, only now it was directed at her. Something grabbed her ankle again, pulling her back under the water.

Hannah kicked out with her legs but couldn't seem to loosen herself from whatever was holding her grounded to the bottom of the pool. A thick weed wrapped itself around her arms, and its viscous tentacles brushed against her face. Her chest burned, lungs on fire.

Her mother's face flashed before hers. Was this what it felt like, was this what had happened? Hannah wanted to scream, but held her lips tight against the invasive water. In desperation, Hannah's hands clawed through the water, stretching with everything she had to bridge the gap between herself and the surface, or at least the side of the pool. Where the hell was the side of the pool?

The water was dark, near impossible to see through. Hannah's lungs felt close to bursting. Her head spun with panic spurred on by the muffled laughter. And the words swirling around in her head as she fought for survival. *Row, row, row your boat, gently down the stream...*

Then, almost as suddenly, an instant calm came over her, and she let her limbs go limp. Somewhere in her mind she heard a voice tell her to let go. Let go. Give in. This was how it was going to end. It was always going to end this way, like her mother and father before her.

I'm so sorry, Mike, she thought. All it would take would be for her to open her mouth and breathe in and then ... darkness? She'd disappear? The roaring in her head, the burning in her chest, it would all disappear.

Give in. Let go, the voice told her. She opened her mouth, and thick, viscous water flooded past her lips.

Something tightened around her wrist and tugged. Fingers. They pressed into her skin.

Mike.

Somehow, he had found her. Rescued her. But then everything went black.

Hannah woke coughing and heaving onto the hard, mouldy concrete. She half lay in a puddle of water, her clothes heavy and sticking to her body. Hannah's chest and throat felt like shattered glass, and her head throbbed even harder than before. A long sliver of swamp weed wound around her leg and ankle, making her convulse again into another coughing fit.

After a while, her coughs dissipated, and her memories rushed back.

In an instant she saw it all play out again. Following the little boy, hearing his laugh, feeling his hands on her lower back as he pushed her in. Feeling hands around her ankles, pulling her under, then breaking the surface to see the boy laughing hysterically as she drowned.

Her fear spiked again. Where the hell was he now? Hannah looked around wildly, trying to push herself up onto her knees, but she wobbled and folded over in another coughing fit, every breath scraping and heaving in her chest. Tears streamed down her face.

Finally, she could fully open her eyes again, and she saw him. Only it wasn't the boy. This was a man. A dark-skinned man, standing a few metres from her, watching her as if he had seen nothing like her before.

Hannah panicked. Who was he? What was he doing here? Where was Mike? She glanced around, but they were alone.

She tried again to lift herself to her feet, shaking as she did so. He kept staring. His dark amber eyes holding Hannah's as she steadied herself on two feet.

"Who … are … you?" Hannah asked between breaths, unable to keep the raw panic from her voice. She had to bend over with her hands on her knees to keep the dizziness from overwhelming her. Closing her eyes for a second, she willed the growing nausea to dissipate. Next thing she knew, hands were around her shoulders, trying to steady her. Her first instinct was to recoil, but something about their warmth, their strength made her relax as they held her upright, grounded.

"How can you see me?" a voice whispered. Both deep and musical, it tugged at something inside of her, unleashing a torrent of emotions. Confusion, fear, and gratitude for being alive; great big sobs welled up from somewhere deep in the pit of her stomach, wracking her body. Hannah slid to her knees, his hands still on her shoulders, almost guiding her so she did not fall.

And Hannah wept.

Giant, fat tears rolled down her cheeks while she sobbed, as if she'd been holding them in for a lifetime. And maybe she had. They broke free and finally found their escape. Amongst it all, she pitied the poor stranger whose hands had not yet left her shoulders, holding her together as he knelt beside her. Hannah continued to cry, and he let her. She couldn't remember ever feeling so thankful for anyone in her life.

CHAPTER 21

After a while, her sobs subsided. Hannah's head pounded, and her eyes were swollen and sore. Her nose was runny, and she was ashamed at how many times she had used her hands to wipe away its wetness. The man was sitting down beside her now on the wet concrete. A part of her cringed at the mess she was in, the rest of her was too exhausted to care.

"I'm so sorry." She hiccoughed. "I don't know why I'm crying like this."

"You almost drowned," the stranger said. "I think it's understandable." He dropped his hands to his side.

From under her tear-clumped lashes, she observed her rescuer. He had similar warm brown skin as Rua's, and the way his eyes crinkled at the corners as he gave her a half grin also reminded her of the old man. But he was somewhere around her age. Short-cropped jet hair. Deep amber eyes peered out from under long dark eyelashes. His tee-shirt and shorts as equally wet as hers.

Warmth flushed her cheeks. Even in her sorry state, she could see her rescuer was attractive. It should have been Mike, a voice in her head said, and she quickly sought her locket with her fingers.

"Thank you," Hannah squeaked, her vocal cords raw and tight. Thank you barely seemed enough. This man had saved her life.

"What were you doing here?" he asked. "You almost drowned."

She thought she *had* drowned. She had definitely lost consciousness for a little while.

He had moved his body away from her a little and scanned her from head to toe. "Are you okay?"

"Yes. Thank you. I – I…" Hannah didn't know what to say. What was she doing here? Chasing a strange child in a place that wasn't supposed to exist?

"I'm Amiri," the stranger said, breaking the silence. He held out a hand, all serious, ready to shake Hannah's. It seemed so comical, this man who had just saved her life, wanting to introduce himself by shaking her hand.

Hannah burst out laughing amidst coughs, and his entire face lit up, eyes sparkling. A dimple appeared on his left cheek.

Finally composing herself, she reached for his hand. "I'm sorry," she said. "I'm Hannah."

Nothing could have prepared her for the moment their hands touched.

An electrical charge zipped through her body, making her squeal out loud. The force pushed her backwards.

"What the hell?" Amiri said, eyes huge as he shook out his hand.

"I – I don't know," she said, completely at a loss

"Are you okay?" he asked.

"Yeah. It just surprised me." She shook her head. It made little sense. It hadn't hurt but … she felt it, like a current suspended between them, waking every molecule in her body.

Pins and needles prickled her limbs.

They sat there, staring at each other without speaking, until he broke the silence.

"You're staying at the resort." A statement rather than a question.

"Yeah," Hannah said, wondering if she should mention her new family's role in its resurrection.

"I thought I had seen you around," he said.

Hannah tilted her head to the side, eyes narrowed. It was true she wasn't always good at noticing details, but she was sure she would have noticed him if they'd crossed paths. Embarrassed, she filed through her memories. Was he a staff member? An acquaintance of Mike's? "Are you staying there?" she asked, cringing at her lack of knowledge.

"Not exactly." He rubbed his jawline. "I used to work there."

Used to? Hannah was confused. This was the first week the resort had been in action. Maybe he had helped with the renovations. It would explain why he had the physique of someone who worked with his hands. He was muscular in the way of someone who came about it naturally and not by the gym. She compared him to Mike.

He offered no more explanation, so she didn't push him on it.

Despite the sun being high in the sky, Hannah shivered. Her wet clothes were getting uncomfortable.

Amiri pulled himself up onto his feet, then reached a hand down to her. "If you want to risk it," he said with another half-smile.

She grinned in returned. Surely it had been static electricity. This time when she took his hand, she experienced a wave of warmth and familiarity. It almost had the same effect. She felt as if she had known him all her life.

He pulled her up to her feet. As weak as she felt, she found she could hold her own but was loath to let go of his hand. He must have felt the same. They stayed like that a second longer than comfortable until Hannah blushed again and let go to play with the locket around her neck.

"Thank you." She focussed on her feet.

"No problem," he said. An inexplicable awkwardness hung between them.

"I should get back." Hannah's feet felt like lead, unable to move. With an enormous effort, she turned around, searching for where she had entered the complex. She could just make out where the thin trail began. She took a step towards it, then stopped, turning back to Amiri, not yet ready to leave.

"Did you see a little boy?" she asked, her voice a little shaky.

"Boy?" Amiri's eyes narrowed and his brows knitted together.

Hannah took a deep breath. "He was running around the resort, and I followed him out here; then, he snuck up on me and—" Hannah's coughed again, her throat and chest still raw.

"He pushed you?" Amiri's voice was tight, and the muscles in his neck tensed.

"I'm sure it was just a joke. He was laughing and—" And what? It hadn't seemed like a joke. "I'm sure he meant as a game," she said while a voice in her head reprimanded her. "Anyway, did you see him?"

Face grim, Amiri shook his head. "You should get back." His lips thinned.

Had she upset him? She tried to push aside the pang of hurt in her chest.

"It's not safe here," he said. "And I'm sure you'll be wanting to get changed out of your wet clothes." His half smile never reached his eyes.

Suddenly Hannah felt exhausted, all her energy leaving her body. She couldn't very well fault his observations, though. "You're right," she said, hiding her bizarre overwhelming disappointment. "Are you heading back to the resort too?"

Confusion flitted across his face. "Maybe later."

"Oh. Okay." Hannah turned back in the path's direction she'd followed into the complex.

"It was nice to meet you, Hannah."

Something inside her moved, hearing her name on his tongue, and her legs felt weak again. Taking a deep breath, she gave him a nod over her shoulder, aware of how flushed her cheeks must look. Then, she headed back to the Rest Easy Resort, the *real* resort.

Hannah sensed his eyes following her for a while, heat on the back of her neck. She did not dare turn around until she came to the side of the building. Once there, she took one last look at the strange man who had saved her life. Only, he wasn't there. Why would he have been?

CHAPTER 22

"Sorry I'm so late," Mike said, apologising as he walked into the room.

"No problem," Hannah said, meaning it. Had he arrived any earlier, he would have seen a whole different Hannah. Thank God for the miracles of showers and makeup.

"How was your morning?" He kicked off his flip-flops and slumped onto a sofa.

Hannah grabbed them both a bottle of water from the mini fridge. "It was fine," Hannah said, turning around to hand him a drink. "Crap! what happened to your hand?" She blanched. Mike's left hand was heavily wrapped with a white bandage.

"Oh," Mike said, grimacing. "There was a *thing* … and I got cut." He held his other hand out for the bottle of water Hannah still held. "It's fine. Really."

"A thing?" Hannah repeated. "What kind of thing?"

Mike sighed. "Well … we got the freezer guy in to check out the freezer. We were right. Some locals had got to him, so he was pretty on edge. As was our chef, I guess. And …" Mike sipped his water, an obvious stall tactic. He was reluctant to tell her whatever had happened. "They had an argument and … a fight broke out."

"What?" Hannah interrupted, incredulous.

"It was fine, no big deal, but I guess I stepped in, and accidents happen, eh?"

"How?" Hannah asked, not believing how innocent he was trying to make it sound.

"The chef had a knife." He shrugged.

Hannah's jaw dropped. For a moment she didn't know what to say.

"And I guess I got in the way."

"What the—"

"No, it's fine. It's all sorted now. It was an accident," Mike interrupted.

"It doesn't sound like an accident. Do we need to get you a doctor?"

"No, no." Mike grinned. "Mariana's looked at it. She's got her first aid certificate. It's all good." He waved his bandaged hand in the air as if to prove his point.

Hannah cringed. These things were not supposed to be happening. Not on a honeymoon. Not at a luxury resort.

"Anyway, I wanted to hear how *your* morning was." Mike interrupted her thoughts, and flashed her a smile.

How much did she want to tell him? Not about her near-drowning. Not yet, anyway. And Amiri could wait. "I bumped into Rua again, by the stone …" While she fiddled with the cap on her bottle, she tried to gauge what his reaction would be. Mike watched her and took another gulp of water.

She'd almost forgotten her interaction with Rua, what with everything else that had gone on.

"The commemorative stone has cracked," Hannah said, carefully.

"It's always had a crack," Mike replied, with a shrug of his shoulders.

"Hmm," Hannah agreed. "It's really cracked now, like almost right through. Rua thinks it was the noise we heard last night."

Mike let out a hearty laugh and shook his head. "Look, I love Rua and all, but there's no way a stone would make that much noise."

Hannah's hackles rose.

"Why not?" she asked, feeling the bite in her tone. Something wasn't right with this place, and if she had ever been in doubt before, the events of the morning had changed everything.

Mike raised an eyebrow. "I'm sure it was someone hunting or something up in the hills. It was probably an echo from a gun; nothing to worry about. I can't see how a rock splitting in half would have made the amount of noise we heard last night. How would it have cracked, anyway?"

"I don't know." She stared down at the rings on her fingers and exhaled. "I'm sorry, I just have a bit of a headache."

"Well, come here, then," he said, thumping the seat cushion beside him. Hannah sat down, and he pulled her towards him so her head was leaning on his chest. He stroked her head and forehead. Any other time she would have melted. Part of her wanted to.

She closed her eyes, willing herself to shake the unsettled feeling clinging to her skin. She could feel his heart beating through his shirt. This is my husband, she thought. He is the man I love.

But it was Amiri's face she saw; the deep pull of his amber eyes and the ripple of electricity that flooded her body when he'd held out his hand.

"I'm sorry." She pulled away, aware she was repeating herself. "I just need some paracetamol, and I'll be fine. I think I have some in the bathroom." Hannah pushed herself up off the sofa and shut herself in the bathroom. Leaning on the counter, she glared at herself in the mirror. Her eyes were pink and dams of tears threatened to burst their banks at any moment. Now was not the time to cry.

Hannah took a few deep breaths and ran some water as if she was taking a pill. She had already taken two, not even half an hour before, so she had no intention of taking any more.

Psyching herself up, she blinked back the tears and forced a smile. It was already 1:00 p.m., and she could feel the dull ache of hunger in her belly. It would do her no harm to eat something, and maybe it would even help to balance her emotions a little. She took one more deep breath to centre herself and turned off the basin tap.

Mike already had his cell phone to his ear and was in conversation with someone.

"Uh hmm," he said, sending her an apologetic expression.

A flash of anger seared Hannah's bones, and she willed it away. She walked over to the balcony, listening to the murmurings from Mike on his phone. Leaning against the railing, Hannah looked out over the resort. Everything was postcard perfect.

One of the swimming pools caught her eye. Two people were enjoying the sun on the loungers. Even from this distance, she was sure they were Graham and Sheryl. No sign of their noisy offspring.

Towards the left, Hannah could see the scattering of palm tree tops and the azure of the lagoon. Except for Mike on his phone and the gentle sea breeze playing with the trees, the resort was soundless.

And then, as if the gods had read her thoughts and dared

to play a mean joke, she heard yelling. The words were nondescript, but Hannah could taste the fear that travelled with them across the resort. The shouting came from the beach and etched a mean scar in what had been peaceful tranquillity. Stomach clenched, Hannah strained out against the railing, trying to see who was making the noise.

She thought she heard a call for help but wasn't sure. A tall, gangly figure dressed only in board shorts stumbled up the path from the beach. His cries were louder now. His voice thick with fear.

"Help," he yelled. "My sister."

Hannah felt the colour drain from her face. It was Jake.

Graham and Sheryl must have simultaneously recognised the voice too. Sheryl gave a high-pitched start and both of them sprung from their loungers, racing to their son's cries. Paralysed, Hannah watched, her heart tight in her chest. Something bad had happened. Again.

Someone else yelled out and rushed towards them. The small group turned their backs to her and ran back towards the beach. Sheryl's cover-up floated behind her like angel wings as she ran. Graham moved faster than Hannah could have imagined.

She needed to get down there. The thought tore through Hannah's skull, spurring her to action. Ignoring a startled cry from Mike, she sped out of the room, down the hallway, down the steps. Footsteps pounded behind her. Mike. She heard his breath as they raced down the path to the beach.

A group was already gathering, forming a crowd around someone down on the beach. One woman stood off to the side, cell phone to her ear making frantic gestures. Hannah knew what they would see before they even arrived. Like a snapshot, a picture flashed through her mind.

Mike arrived before she did, having overtaken her. He pushed the crowd aside until he could get to the centre. Hannah followed in his wake. A high-pitched wail from Sheryl made Hannah flinch. Sheryl sobbed over the prone figure of her daughter.

Bethany lay there in her swimsuit. Eyes closed. Wet and pale. The blue tinge of her skin making her appear almost translucent. Ghostly. Her dark hair lay in snakes around her head. Graham knelt beside her, compressing her chest.

"Breathe," he begged, "Breathe," before bending over to puff oxygen into her small body. Sheryl swiped at the hair around Bethany's face, her tears rolling down her daughter's cheeks. Jake was being held back by another woman who was holding him as he sobbed and looked ready to collapse.

"Get back!" Mike yelled at the crowd, taking charge of the situation. "Let me," he said to Graham, moving him aside. Graham was already pink in the face and wheezing from the physical exertion. Mike took over the CPR and compressions while Graham grabbed hold of his wife, holding her to his chest as if by clutching her he could bring his child back to life.

Hannah stood motionless, watching the scene before her unravel, removed as if she were a nosey spectator watching a scene on a midday soap opera. Unsure what to do or how to help, but transfixed in horror.

How could this be happening?

Someone else echoed her thoughts. "How did it happen?" they asked. "Drowning," another said, not answering the question. Someone else was crying. "The ambulance is on the way," the first voice said. Hannah spun around on her feet until the panicked faces melted into one. She could hear Mike counting, "One … two … three … four …" as he pressed down on the child's chest.

She hadn't known she was looking for him until her eyes locked on his. Amiri. Half hidden by a couple of resort staff, he stood off to one side. His lips a thin line, his forehead creased with concern. He went to mouth something to her, but the sound of choking and coughing tore her attention away.

Hannah turned to see Mike putting Bethany on her side as she vomited water. Sheryl, sobbing louder now, dropped to her knees and grabbed her child. Jake and Graham ran forward to join her.

A sigh of relief and a few cheers rippled through the small crowd.

Hannah turned back, but Amiri was gone.

Her eyes found Mike's. Before she could even give him a small smile, someone slapped him on the back in praise, taking his attention away. Mike's face was red from exertion and sweat dripped down his forehead. Blood had seeped through his bandage on his hand, turning it red. Hannah stood there stunned, trying to process what had happened, until she heard the distant wail of an ambulance.

The following moments were a blur. The ambulance arrived. Two young men carried a stretcher between them and an oxygen mask. Mike had wrapped his arms around Hannah's waist, his chin resting on her shoulder. The crowd had grown even larger, joined by more of the resort staff, including Mariana, but all respectfully kept their distance to allow the medics to do what they needed to do.

The two young men lifted poor Bethany onto the stretcher.

Taking in her frailness, Hannah felt a pang of guilt for all the bad thoughts she had previously had about the girl.

Sheryl refused to let go of her daughter's hand. Graham had his arm around his son's shoulders. He followed, pausing for a moment to clasp Mike's hand with both of his own. He whispered a thank you in a strangled voice, wiping the tears from his eyes, then followed his wife and daughter to the ambulance. A hand touched her back, and she turned to see the concerned face of Mariana. She looked close to breaking into tears herself, and without thinking, Hannah leant forward and embraced her in a hug.

"How did it happen?" Mariana choked out.

"Not sure," Mike answered.

The crowd dispersed with the waning sound of the ambulance, leaving the three of them to linger before walking back to the resort. Hannah had barely said a word throughout the entire incident. What were the chances that two near-drownings would happen in one day at the same resort? What were the chances of Amiri being at both of them?

Mike kept his arm around Hannah's waist as they followed Mariana. This man had saved Bethany's life. He was a hero. Her husband; she reminded herself again. Her soulmate.

She pushed down the small sense of doubt prickling at the back of her mind.

CHAPTER 23

Hannah and Mike never made it out for lunch that day. By the time they arrived back at their room, they were both exhausted, and it was already well into late afternoon. Mike's face was pinched with worry. He had barely said a word since the incident, and Hannah – with no idea what to say – had done no better. She had wanted to tell him how amazing he was, taking charge and saving Bethany's life, but all she managed was, "How do you think it happened?"

"I don't know. Could have been anything, I guess. Cramp, getting stuck on the coral. God, I hope she didn't go out past the reef."

The lagoon was said to be safe for swimming except for cutting yourself on coral or standing on a scorpion fish. From what Hannah had seen, albeit from the beach, it had seemed relatively shallow too. Past the reef were strong currents and rips.

Hannah assumed Jake had been the one to pull her from the water. The poor boy. She could only imagine what he was going through. What any of them were. Hannah wrapped her arms around Mike's waist, hugging him to her while she rested her head on his heart.

"I'm so sorry, Mike," she kept saying, not knowing what she was apologising for. He kissed the top of her head.

"It's okay," he said. "She's going to be alright, that's all that matters."

Neither of them really knew that. But they could hope. They wouldn't know until they heard from Graham and Sheryl. How long she had been lying there without breathing was anyone's guess. Hannah didn't want to think about it too much. Remembering how angry she had been at Mike for taking his phone call seemed so ridiculous right now. For the moment, she never wanted to let him go. His warmth fed into her own chest, as if it kept her heart ticking. Part of her felt that if she pulled away, she'd shatter. But it was Mike who withdrew first. His face was white and drawn.

"I'm going to have a shower," he said. "Then maybe we can go to the hospital."

"Sure," Hannah said. As much as she hated hospitals, it was the right thing to do. Besides, Mike needed it, she could tell. Poor Graham and Sheryl, Hannah thought, almost losing a child like that.

The room was warm. Almost stifling. They had forgotten to put on the air conditioner, so Hannah picked up the remote and turned the unit on, then went back out to the balcony. She took stock of the resort. Everything looked the same as it always did. It was eerily quiet again, with a heaviness to the air. A lingering sense of melancholy and something else. She couldn't put her finger on it. The memory of a small child laughing at her as she fought against drowning flickered in her mind. She shivered. Was that what it was? The resort was laughing at them? The curse?

It took Hannah a moment to realise she was scanning the

resort for Amiri. How strange he should have been down on the beach too. Hannah's mind sorted through all the events from the past two days. She felt more emotionally exhausted and high-strung than before she had left home. Thank God, she thought, that Awhina and her protesters hadn't come back today to create more drama. She doubted anyone would react kindly to an appearance after what they'd been through.

Hannah sat on a lounger, tucking her legs up under herself. She leaned back on the head cushion and closed her eyes. Just resting them, she told herself, but an overwhelming cloak of sleepiness fell over her. She woke to Mike whispering her name and shaking her shoulder. Dressed in clean shorts and a dress shirt, he smelt of soap and freshly applied deodorant. With some of his usual composure, he smiled at her and she returned it.

"Almost ready to go?" he asked.

"Yeah," she said. "Let me re-do your bandage and brush my teeth and freshen up."

He held out his good hand to help her up, pulling her into him and pressing his lips hard against hers. "Seem fresh enough to me," he said, eyes sparkling.

Hannah gave him a playful punch in the arm before heading off to the bathroom. Minutes later, they were both ready to leave.

"We're taking a car," he said, leaving no room for negotiation. She wouldn't have argued, anyway. She had no desire, and really no energy to be riding. She was emotionally and physically spent. What with her own near drowning and then the most recent drama, she gave herself kudos for being able to stay upright.

Mariana had offered them the use of her car for the trip.

Mike drove while Hannah watched out the window, enjoying the scenery. Strings of shops, houses and resorts, followed by stretches of palm trees and beach and lagoon.

The hospital, a simple white building, hardly looked like a hospital. It might have been mistaken for a hall, had it not been for the two parked ambulances and the large blue signs stating otherwise. A large woman sat at the reception desk, smiling from cheek to cheek. After asking what room they'd find Bethany and her family in, and Hannah inquiring about Mike having the cut on his hand seen to, they were given a general direction to walk in. On their way, they bumped into Graham wandering the hall with two paper coffee cups in his hands. His face was strained, but he recognised them right away and gave them a nod. The two men regarded each other awkwardly.

"How is Bethany?" Hannah asked, breaking the strained silence.

"She's good, thanks to this man." Graham clapped Mike on the shoulder. "I owe you my life," he said with utter sincerity.

Mike rubbed the back of his neck with his good hand. "Sheryl and Jake are with her now. She'll be spending the night for observation, but otherwise we got lucky." He choked up on the last few words and cleared his throat. "They're this way if you want to say hi."

"I'm so glad she's okay," Mike said.

Hannah followed Graham down the hallway with Mike close behind, his hand resting on the hollow of her back. They turned into a room on the left. Bethany was half sitting up in the bed, propped by a bunch of pillows. Jake was immersed in a magazine in a chair under the window, relaxed now it seemed the immediate danger had passed.

On seeing Hannah and Mike, Sheryl sprung from her perch on the side of the bed and flung herself at Mike in a big embrace. "Thank you, thank you, thank you," she whispered, choking back tears.

"I'm glad she's okay," Mike answered.

Turning her attention to Hannah, she embraced her in a quick hug, "So good of you to come."

"Of course," Hannah said. "We wanted to check you were alright."

"Mum, I'm hungry," a raw whiny voice broke the moment. Despite the drip in her hand and the dark circles under her eyes, Bethany seemed to have recovered well.

Jake looked up from his magazine. "Me too, Mum. Can I go to the cafeteria?"

"Only if I can go too," Bethany demanded.

"You can't! Mum, I need some money," Jake added his whine to his sisters.

Hannah cringed inside.

"I can too, go! I can walk, you know!"

"No, I don't want you walking just yet. You can take the wheelchair. Jake, you can push her."

Jake let out a drawn-out moan in response.

"Remember the drip!" Sheryl squealed as her daughter yelped at the pinch of her forgotten drip-line. "Alright, I'm coming with you. I can't trust you two not to kill each other." Sheryl said, rolling her eyes at Hannah and Mike.

Hannah could tell Sheryl was thrilled her kids were well enough to be arguing and demanding food again.

"I'll be back soon," she said, turning to Graham as she took over for Jake at the wheelchair. It didn't take long before the chorus of complaints had disappeared down the hall.

"How did it happen?" Hannah asked, trying to imbue as much sensitivity as she could into her tone.

Mike raised an eyebrow in her direction.

"It's the strangest thing." Graham rubbed his jowls. "Jake said everything was normal. They'd been goofing around and snorkelling and stuff, and no doubt arguing like the little rotters they are." Positioning himself on the edge of the hospital bed, he gestured for Hannah and Mike to take a seat in the two chairs under the window.

"Jake said he was snorkelling a little further way and came up for air, looked around and couldn't see her for a moment. He called out, then saw her arms thrashing around out of the water, but her head was still under. Like something was holding her down. When he swam closer, he saw her face mask floating in the water, and he panicked. Lost sight of her for a while and when he got to her, she wasn't moving. He dragged her back to shore, then went running for help."

"I'm so sorry," Hannah said, feeling guilty for making him relive it. It was too real. Too familiar. She still hadn't got over her shock from the morning. Her stomach churned, and she swallowed. Though she wanted fresh air, she had to hear more.

"Was there no one else on the beach?" *Like a small child?* Hannah wondered.

"No one, apparently. Sheryl and I were lounging by the pool when we heard Jake charging up the path in a panic, and then you two arrived and you know the rest." He paused; an internal struggle clear on his face. "There was one thing…" He let it hang in the air for a moment. "Bethany thought she saw someone under the water, holding her by the ankle, dragging her down…."

Hannah flinched.

"… but Jake was incessant no one else was around. I suppose she got her flipper caught under some coral or something." He shrugged his broad shoulders. "Doesn't matter now, anyhow. I'm just glad she's okay."

Mike and Hannah nodded in agreement. Graham shook his head, eyes downcast, batting away the emotion.

Mike stood up and patted him on the shoulder. "She's alright, mate. She's going to be fine." As if to punctuate his sentence, an argumentative chorus sang down the hallway, getting closer. Hannah willed Mike to read her mind. Time to leave, she tried telling him with her eyes. There was no need. He had the same idea.

"Well, we better get going, give you guys some family time. Let us know if there is anything we can do."

"It's all good." Graham leveraged himself off the hospital bed. "Thanks for coming."

Hannah turned her head slightly when he kissed her on her cheek, trying to avoid the sour smell of cigar smoke clinging to his breath. They said their goodbyes and passed the convoy on the way out.

A man wearing a casual business shirt and a name badge reading Dr Heta stopped them in the hallway. "Mr O'Connor?" he asked.

"Yeah, I'm Mike."

"I've a quick minute to look at your hand if you're available?"

"Great. Hannah, do you want to wait in the car?"

A wave of relief passed through her. Hospitals and doctors made her uneasy at the best of times, and what she needed was some fresh air to think things over. "Thanks," she said, as Mike handed her the car keys. He followed the doctor around the corner while Hannah headed for the exit.

Hannah opened the front car doors to let in the slightly cooler air. Outside was humid, but better than a cooking vehicle. Leaning on the bonnet, she gathered her thoughts. Was it possible Bethany had experienced the same thing she had? Being pulled under by invisible hands?

The heaviness of everything weighed on Hannah. She wanted nothing more than to crawl into bed and forget the entire day had happened.

"How is your hand?" Hannah asked when Mike returned, another fresh bandage in place.

"It's fine. A fresh dressing and some antibiotics. No need for stitches and the cut missed anything important."

"Good," Hannah answered, relieved. When she had re-bandaged it back in their room, it had appeared angry and red to her, and nothing as minor as Mike had made it out to be. But then, she was no doctor.

"What was with all the questions?" Mike asked as he slid into the driver's seat.

"I don't know," Hannah said. "I guess I wanted to know in case there was something dangerous we needed to know about if you go snorkelling again."

"If? Of course I'll go again. Sounds like it was a fluke accident." He turned on the car's ignition and AC. "It was bad luck getting a flipper caught under a rock or something."

It didn't sit right with Hannah, but she let it go. "Mike," Hannah said. "How are you doing?" The enormity of what he had been through hadn't escaped her. Thankfully, there had been a positive outcome, but what if there hadn't been? The thought played itself round and round her head like a carousel, the creepy kind: abandoned structure, haunting music, cracked horse faces from a horror movie. What if Bethany had died? It *must* have crossed his mind.

Mike stayed silent for a moment, staring ahead. Finally, he turned to her.

"I did what I had to do," he said. "What I would have done for you, for *our* daughter, if we had one. Graham was tiring, so I stepped in."

Hannah took his hand, careful not to hurt him. Her fingers gently wrapped around his, and her eyelashes beat back tears. Bringing his hand to her lips, she gave it a small kiss.

"I love you," she whispered. It was all she could think to say.

"I love you too," he replied.

Hannah yawned; she couldn't hold back anymore. "I'm sorry," she said, embarrassed.

He laughed loudly. "Alright," he said. "I'll get you to bed, but first, I'm starving." As he voiced this, Hannah's stomach gave a long, deep growl. She grimaced.

"Right, definitely food first!" He grinned, gently squeezing her hand back.

CHAPTER 24

When they finally arrived back at the resort, they were both satiated and full. Hannah and Mike had stopped off at the first eatery they came across. Hannah was now beyond tired, and looking at Mike, he felt the same. It was all she could do to not fall asleep on the drive home.

"How about a glass of wine and a soak in the hot tub," Mike suggested as he slipped out of his sandals and pushed them aside. Hannah's eyes welled up with pure gratitude. Exhaustion always made her more emotional than normal.

"Sounds amazing," she said, slumping down on the edge of the bed. As amazing as a soak sounded, she couldn't imagine mustering the energy to run the bath. Mike disappeared into the kitchen, returning with a glass of sav. He handed it to her.

"Are you okay?" he asked. Concern in his eyes.

"I'm fine," she said, "just wiped out. I don't think I'm used to so much sun, and then with the drama of this afternoon…" She left the sentence hanging. Not to mention her own near-death experience earlier in the morning, she thought. Something caught in her throat. If Amiri hadn't been there… Hannah took another swallow of wine.

Mike went and poured himself a rum and Coke, then came

over and gave her a kiss on the head. Hannah forced a small smile his way. A pang of guilt shot through her. He saved someone's life today. She should pamper him. And definitely not be thinking of someone else.

Mike disappeared into the room with the jacuzzi. Hannah could hear the water running and went to join him. She suppressed a shiver. It was so like the room she had seen this morning.

Shaking the image from her head, she placed her glass down on the side of the tub. Mike had already added bubble bath courtesy of the resort, a sweet floral bouquet filling the air. She sat down on the side of the tub and watched the water and bubbles rise.

Mike periodically dipped his hand in to test the water and mix the bubble bath around. Finally, he turned off the water and gave the bubbles a final thrash before moving over to Hannah. He pulled her up to standing, gently, as if she were made of porcelain. Gripping the bottom of her shirt, he carefully pulled it up over her head. Too tired to resist, Hannah lifted her arms and let him pull it off her. He leant in and traced small kisses from the bottom of her ear down her throat. A small groan escaped her lips as her eyes fluttered shut. His fingers ran down to the pull string on her shorts. She let him pull them off so they fell to the ground. Then he kissed her on the lips, gently at first, then harder, deeper, until she felt like they were one.

Gently sliding her underwear down her thighs, she meekly stepped out of them. Her fingers undid the clasp of her bra. She slid it over both arms and let it also fall to the ground. Mike slipped his hand into hers and led her the few steps to the tub, gesturing for her to get in. Hannah stepped over the side. The water was the perfect temperature. Richly warm. Her limbs turned to jelly as her tension evaporated.

The bubbles clung to her skin, and she played with them with gentle movements of her hands as she waited for Mike to join her. Pulling off his own shirt and pants, he slipped in behind her, wrapping his legs around her. Hannah leant back, resting her head on his chest. His arms crossed over her body, holding her to him. Right here, right now, was complete perfection, she thought. With the warmth of the water and the warmth of his chest, all the day's tension ebbed away.

Hannah felt the flutter of his lips against the crown of her head and closed her eyes. She just needed a moment to rest them, she told herself. Instead, she was lulled to sleep by the rise and fall of Mike's chest.

In the dark, behind closed eyelids, she saw him. He arrived unbidden before her. Amiri.

His dark amber eyes reflected a light that rose from unknown depths. Windows to his soul, she thought. His brow was furrowed as if concerned or worried. Staring right at her, through her, maybe. His mouth was moving. Hannah followed the movement of the rose-blush pink of his lips. They made no noise. Feeling almost drugged, she lost herself in their movements. For a second, she wondered what they would taste like.

Finally, his voice broke through with great urgency.

"Wake up, Hannah. You need to leave!" She started. She hadn't expected such harshness, such loudness. Her eyes flung open. Her arms thrashed, hitting the soft body of the man who held her. Mike. His arms still wrapped tight around her.

"It's okay," he breathed. "It's okay."

The water had cooled. Hannah gathered her bearings.

She must have fallen asleep, she told herself, then blushed, remembering how real it had seemed. Here in this bathtub, while she was in the embrace of her husband. Good God, Hannah, she chastised herself. What was wrong with her?

CHAPTER 25

How long had she been sleeping? she wondered.

"Are you alright? You were having a bad dream, so I thought it best to wake you."

"It gave me a fright, is all," she said.

"I tried to be gentle," Mike said, smiling sheepishly. "Anyway, the water's getting cold. Time to get out and get you into bed."

Hannah held up her hands. Her skin had puckered into wrinkles while goosebumps stood to attention on her arms. She wasn't sure whether that was from the water or her strange dream. A strange thing, dreams. She could have sworn she'd heard Amiri's voice, not Mikes. She levered herself out of the tub and wrapped herself in a towel. The cold of the tile flooring reminded her of the smashed tiles she had seen in the abandoned hotel only that morning.

Moving to the bedroom, she dried herself off and pulled a singlet top over her head as makeshift sleepwear. In the bathroom, Hannah stared at herself in the mirror. Having cleaned her face, the dark circles under her eyes were back and her eyelids were a little puffy. Maybe Mike wouldn't notice, she hoped.

If Mike did, he said nothing. When she left the bathroom, he was already in bed, sitting up, pillows propped behind him, with the TV on. She slipped in beside him, lying on her side facing him and puffing the pillows under her head. Mike switched off the TV and snuggled down, facing her.

"Hey," he said. Hannah followed his lips with her eyes. They were thinner than Amiri's, a pinker colour. They moved differently. Sharper, maybe.

"Hey," she replied. Silence strung out between them for a moment. "You really were amazing today," she whispered. Meaning it. This man had saved a young girl's life.

Mike said nothing. He leant forward and planted a kiss on her forehead between her eyes.

"Sleep well," he said.

Hannah smiled and closed her eyes, praying for a visionless sleep.

It was anything but. Strange shapes and colours tangled into confusing images until a scene sharpened and unfolded.

Hannah was amongst a crowd of people. Drained of colour, everything was in black and white. The crowd faced an open space where beautiful island women and men danced to a chorus of drums.

The women wore grass skirts and coconut bras and leis that swished against their stomachs as they swayed their hips. The men pounded their feet on the earth, the muscles on their legs tight and well defined – their skin, dark and shiny. Ornate headdresses sat as crowns on their heads.

Hannah was as mesmerised as the crowd. The drums built up to a heart-racing crescendo. They pulsed in time to the blood in her veins and vibrated through her bones. Faster and faster, the dancers moved until suddenly everything came to an orgasmic standstill. Silence. Then clapping as the performers dispersed into the crowd and an older man took centre place.

Balding and portly, his face glistened from exertion without looking as if he'd ever exerted himself. He pushed his glasses up to the bridge of his nose and addressed the crowd. Words danced around Hannah, but none landed. Though standing with the crowd, she seemed to be just out of hearing distance.

Two well-dressed white men continued the conversation. Again, the words were nothing but meaningless static, but she noticed the crowd grow restless around her.

The men at the front pointed to something on the ground. Hannah pushed herself closer and saw a decorative cloth covering a small mound.

From somewhere in the crowd, a child let out a sharp cry. Hannah swivelled to see where it had come from. A woman further away from her held up a little girl in a floral print dress. The child's eyes locked on Hannah's; scrutinising her as if she were much older than she was.

The crowd moved, parting as if it were being pulled in two separate directions. An uneasy quietness silenced the static. An elderly man dressed in ceremonial garb, headdress and tapa cloth, using a gnarled wooden staff as a walking stick, made his way to the front where the two men stood. They backed away from him, confused, fearful even, as he took his place behind the mound. The air fizzed with electricity.

The man removed the covering from the mound, throwing it aside and laying bare the commemorative stone Hannah had seen in Rua's garden. Intact. Unharmed.

Hannah glanced around. Could it be? The jungled hills rose in the background. Through the crowd, she could see the sea. A few palm tree outcroppings rose here and there. She could have been on any part of the island, but she knew, could feel it, deep inside her. This was the land they built the Rest Easy on. No. The Cooks Hotel Resort.

This was cursed land. The old man's voice rang out across the crowd. She knew what he was saying, even if she couldn't quite touch the words.

He held his staff up for the crowd to see, pausing as if time stood still. Then, in one swift motion, he thrusted it downwards, stabbing the surface of the rock. A sharp inhale from the crowd told her something horrible had happened. Hannah pushed forward to see. A thin jagged line now marred the rock's surface. Someone far back in the audience cried.

The man, the priest, whoever he was, swung his eyes back and forth over the crowd, eventually resting on Hannah. For a second, it was as if a flame flared behind them. A sharp pain seared through her head. She stumbled backward a couple of paces before losing her balance completely. Her arms flailed, and it was as if she were drowning all over again, fighting to reach the surface before her breath ran out.

"You're safe. It's okay; I'm here." She woke for the second time to Mike trying to console her. "Another dream?" he asked.

Hannah nodded her head, blinking as her eyes adjusted to the harsh light from the lamp. Her heart thrashed against her ribcage as if trying to escape. Taking a few staggered gulps of air, she tried to centre herself, trying to ground herself back in the room away from the man with the painful eyes.

Her singlet top had stuck to her body, soaked through with sweat, and her hair was plastered to the back of her neck. Hannah rarely had dreams like this. In fact, other than when she dreamt about her parents, she rarely remembered her dreams. And now she'd had two in one night.

"Are you okay?" Mike asked.

"Yeah," Hannah replied, not knowing what else to say.

"About today?"

Hannah cycled through her mind, trying to remember what had happened earlier that day. Working backwards, the images came back to her: Mike resuscitating Bethany on the beach, meeting Amiri as he pulled her from a sludgy pool where she almost drowned, and a strange little child laughing hysterically as he pushed her into the water. Then there was Rua and his cryptic warnings.

"I think so," Hannah said. Who wouldn't have had nightmares after the day she'd had?

"I need to get a drink." Hannah said, "and maybe wash up again." She was scared if she wrung out her top it would leave a visible puddle.

"Okay," Mike said, unconvinced. He looked worried.

She wasn't used to seeing him like this. Hannah's heart ached. What had happened to them? There had been so much excitement, to be married, to be husband and wife, to go on their honeymoon. But then … Mike still had a job to do. And mostly, their time at the Rest Easy Resort had been anything but relaxing.

At the kitchenette, Hannah poured herself a glass of water. She gulped it down, feeling its coolness trickle down her throat, bringing her a little more back into her body.

Afterward, she went into the bathroom and ran the shower. The lukewarm water washed over her, and she imagined it cleansing her of any remnants of sweat and bad dreams.

This wasn't the vacation she had wanted it to be. Part of her wanted to call it quits. Return home and get back to their everyday lives, putting the Rest Easy Resort well behind them.

But part of her was curious.

If the resort ruins didn't exist, there must be a reason she was seeing them. Either Rua was right and she had a special gift; a second sight, or else she was crazy. And if they didn't exist, how was it she nearly drowned? Or had she imagined that too? And if that was the case, what else had she imagined? The child who pushed her? Amiri?

Maybe she *was* crazy. Closing her eyes, Hannah let the water trickle over her, feeling it make trails down her face.

What a tragic love story her life would make, she thought. She could see the headlines now: Newlywed millionaire developer discovers his wife is insane, commits her to asylum on return from honeymoon at a cursed resort.

Hannah stifled a chuckle. It was a good sign. If she could laugh, maybe it meant everything was going to be alright.

Mike was snoring softly as she climbed into bed beside him. The air conditioner was blowing, a gentle breeze cooling the room nicely. The shower had helped get rid of some of her anxiety. She was feeling better about things. Morning would bring a new day. And this new day would be different. Top priority was to relax and spend time with Mike, to treat this holiday like an actual honeymoon. Two people in love. No curses, no near-death situations, just a honeymoon on a tropical island, please and thanks. Hannah smiled to herself as she closed her eyes. Admitting to herself that she might have been temporarily losing her mind was enough to make her think there was hope for her yet.

CHAPTER 26

Hannah had no idea how long the damn rooster had been crowing, but she suspected it had been a while. She was thankful for being so exhausted that she had been oblivious to it until now.

Mike was already up, humming in the shower. Fragments from the night before filtered back into her consciousness. Today was a new day, she reminded herself.

First on the to do list was to get their scooter licenses. It was day three of them being on the island, and Hannah didn't want to risk going any longer without the proper legalities. Also, she suspected Mike might want to follow up with the police about the protestors.

Hannah was glad to be getting away from the resort. As gorgeous as it was, it seemed to attract drama, and more than anything, she wanted today to be drama free. Mike's aunt had booked the two of them tickets to a cultural show and dinner for the night as a honeymoon gift, so she had that to look forward to too.

After another buffet breakfast at the Moonlight Bistro, they headed back to their room to get ready for their outing. Mike seemed unaffected from the events of the day before, back to his normal self and, surprising Hannah, happy to oblige when she asked that he turn his phone off for the day. At first, she had suggested he leave it in the hotel room, but he said it was a bit of a safety thing. So he'd agreed to turn it off, though they'd have it with them should an emergency crop up. She could hardly argue with that. Mike even told reception he'd be incommunicado for the day. All her previous misgivings vanished. Today was going to be a good day, she told herself.

They hit the road, heading their scooters in the direction of the hospital and airport again. It took two trips through the town centre before they found the police station. The building was an unassuming concrete box, painted white with blue trim. Out the front stood a sign stating, "Police". Climbing the few stairs and walking through the glass doors, she was relieved only four other people sat on plastic chairs in the waiting room.

The entire licensing process was easy enough. A few forms to fill in and money to pay, then a theory test they took with another couple there for the same reason. It wasn't a hard test, but when one of them stumbled on an answer, it surprised Hannah to see the policeman whispering correct answers to that person.

The practical test took place outside along the side of the building. A squawking rooster and a makeshift course of evenly spaced orange cones sat waiting for them. The officer's instructions were simple; drive down one side of the cones, indicate to turn right, slow down to give way, turn a hard right without putting your feet on the ground and come back up the other side of the cones. The second test required them to weave in and out of the cones.

A small bubble of nervousness stirred in Hannah's stomach. Her confidence on the scooters had been increasing, but the added pressure of being watched was a little unsettling. Fortunately, Mike went first. Hannah grimaced as he took the turn too wide, momentarily disappearing behind the building before coming back out to follow the cones back to the starting point. The officer made some notes on his piece of paper.

"You disappeared," was all he said.

Nerves well and truly tingling, Hannah set out on her turn. Just breathe, she told herself. The turning point came up ahead of her. Flustered, she indicated left, pulling out wide to U-turn right, quickly flicking the indicator that way, realising at that moment what a mess she had made.

The turn was so sharp she got the wobbles, and her legs went out, tempted to touch the ground and steady herself. She willed herself not to, but as she faced putting her foot down or hitting the corner of the brick building, she put her foot down as gentle guidance, regained her composure and continued on straight, following the lane of the cones. Hannah's first impulse on seeing the officer was to apologise and beg for a do-over. Mike had disappeared inside to chat to someone about the protestors, so she was at least saved the embarrassment of being seen. The officer scribbled on his piece of paper and handed it to her. His grimace matched her own.

"Well," he said. "I'm assuming you probably have better things to do with your time, so I've signed you off." He shook his head, his disappointment all too clear. Hannah was speechless. Though pained by her ridiculous riding skills, he had not only passed her but let her off doing the second test. Heat roasted her cheeks. She slowly rode her bike back around to the front of the building where she saw Mike waiting for her, grinning.

"How did you do?" he asked.

"Appalling," she said, "but he passed me all the same. What about you?"

"A clean pass," he said.

"A clean pass, huh?" she teased. "You seemed to have disappeared around the back of the building there for a moment. We were wondering whether we were ever going to see you again." Hannah chuckled at him and he joined in.

"Yeah, not my best effort," he said, shrugging his shoulders. Parking up the bikes for the last time, the two of them went inside again, passing their pieces of paper over the counter to the receptionist. A couple of photos later and they had their new scooter licenses.

"How did it go with talking to someone about the protestors?" Hannah asked.

"Fine," Mike said, dodging the question. "Anyway, what now?"

Hannah would not pressure him. "Well, now, we go exploring," She answered. She was enjoying this time with just the two of them.

After pulling the dumpy, white helmets back on their heads, they started up the scooters and followed the road out of the town. Mike led the way. Hannah drove at a leisurely pace behind him, taking in as much of the scenery as she could while keeping her eyes on the road. Past coconut trees and imposing concrete churches, past stretches of signs showing fancy resorts and hotels, and past old, boxy houses with concrete gravestones in the front yards. Past derelict buildings and inhabited houses with brightly covered fabric hanging in the windows as makeshift curtains. Past a three-legged dog waddling along the side of the road near a sign showing an Animal Rescue.

Stresses momentarily put aside, she felt free and relaxed. A gust of wind whipped through, and Hannah struggled to keep on the road. Her heart beat faster, and the memory of seeing the scooter accident on the way to the resort on their first night flashed in her mind, but she was able to keep going.

Mike pulled over, giving Hannah time to take a multitude of photos. She wanted to savour every piece of beauty in a place she was reluctantly falling in love with.

They took lunch at a roadside café. The food was none too exciting, but the simple act of drinking an ice-cold Coke was satisfying enough in the tropical island sun. They talked about silly things, admiring the surroundings, mainly, and imagining what it would be like to live a life like many of the locals. It seemed so simple, so uncorrupted. But then, the grass was always greener.

They made no mention of the resort.

"So." Mike folded his hands on the table, letting the word sit ominously in the air. "I've been thinking about the kid thing."

Hannah spluttered on her Coke as a little of it went down the wrong way. Eyes watering, she tried to gain composure. It was not where she thought the conversation was going.

Mike knew how she felt about kids. She loved them, but that didn't mean she was ready to be a mother.

"Seeing Bethany nearly drown like that, and the way Graham and Sheryl just … well, it was like their heart was being torn out…" he said.

Hannah's heart picked up pace again. Where could he possibly be going with this? Seeing Graham and Sheryl's pain had added to her growing list of reasons not to have children.

"Bethany and Jake, they're their…" He tipped his head, his eyes going somewhere she couldn't follow. "They're their legacies. Their purpose. Their reason for getting up in the morning."

Something heavy dropped in Hannah's stomach.

"Well, I think I want that," he said. He turned back to Hannah, obviously waiting for her to say something.

She tried taking another sip of Coke, without choking this time, stalling for time. His words startled her mind into a racing, twisting frenzy. She had no idea what to say.

"Someone to look after us when we're old," Mike filled in Hannah's silence. "To take over the company when I'm gone. Something we can be proud of creating, you and me together," he elaborated.

Hannah wondered if he'd glimpsed terror or something similar on her face. It wasn't often Mike got flustered.

"Just think about it," he said. "I'm not saying it has to be right away, but soon maybe. We're not getting any younger and" – he shrugged – "God knows we could afford it."

The heaviness in her gut worsened. No women of any age wanted to be reminded of their biological clock ticking. And something about his mention of money made her cringe inside. Not everything should be about money.

"I don't know," she said, her voice strained. She toyed with her locket. It was true. She wished she had a better excuse, but for the moment she didn't. She just didn't feel ready.

Mike reached across the table and stroked her hand. "Think about it, okay? Don't write it off yet?"

Pressure mounted in Hannah's head. She had thought they had sorted this and had hoped to have longer before it was brought up again. The pressure built behind her left eye. It hadn't been brought up for months. Why now?

"I'll … yes, I'll think about it," she said, mentally kicking herself. Just not now. Not on a day when everything was going so well.

"That's all I want," Mike said, giving her hand a pat. "Shall we hit the road again?" he asked.

"Sure," Hannah said, relieved for a topic change. She took her last sip of Coke. "Can we stop somewhere and pick up some snacks on the way?" Hannah asked.

Mike raised an eyebrow. The corner of his mouth curled upwards. He could judge all he liked. She felt a killer chocolate craving coming on.

CHAPTER 27

The supermarket was only a few minutes away. Except for a few cars getting gas at the attached fill up station, it was quiet. They parked the scooters close to the front door beside a forest-green jeep.

"Why don't I wait here?" Mike asked.

Hannah suspected it was so he could take a quick peek at his phone for missed calls or messages, but shrugged it off. "Do you need anything?" she asked.

"Actually, we could probably use more sunblock if you don't mind."

"No problem," she said.

The supermarket was small. A handful of cash registers faced towards the filling dock. Narrow aisles stocked most of the essentials. A large folding table at the entrance held homemade baked goods. A row of fridges extended down one wall, the first of which held Hannah's sought-after chocolate bars. She grabbed a few and continued down the aisle past the chips and snack foods, until she got to the end of the store, then she turned right, peering down each aisle, searching for the one with toiletries. The sun care items were down the farthest end.

Mid-way down the aisle, a woman was bent over, peering

through the hair care products. Seeing her from the back, Hannah admired how beautiful her hair already was. Thick, almost black, and nearing her waist with a natural wave. In contrast, Hannah's had always been mousy brown, until her mother-in-law stepped in. Hers hung below her shoulders but lacked volume or movement. She ran a hand through it-consciously.

Boxes of product were stacked against the shelves behind her, making it impossible to squeeze past the woman.

"Excuse me," Hannah said, hoping the woman might stand or shuffle over more to allow her to pass.

The woman stood up, pivoting with a polite smile. Her eyes, when they landed on her, flashed steel. An almost feral growl emanated from the back of her throat.

Hannah took a step back, surprised. She recognised the woman right away. Awhina. Rua's great-niece, the woman who had led the protest back at the resort. Awhina's expression told Hannah she recognised her too.

"Sorry," Hannah whispered, giving her a half-smile as she edged past her, unsure what exactly she was sorry for. The heat of her eyes burned into the back of her neck.

"That resort is not for you. If you knew what was best for you, you'd leave." Awhina's tone was sharp.

Hannah's ears burnt, but she continued walking, refusing to turn around or engage. She grabbed the first bottle of sunscreen she found and headed straight to the counter. After paying for the items, she re-joined Mike at their scooters.

"Is everything alright?" Mike asked, obviously reading her demeanour.

"I'm fine," Hannah muttered, lifting the seat of her scooter and putting in the grocery bag with its few items. More than anything, she just wanted to leave to avoid crossing paths with Awhina again. Mike kept staring at her but said nothing. Hannah pulled on her helmet and started her bike. Taking that as a hint, Mike started his own, and she followed him as they pulled onto the road again, heading back to the resort.

Hannah's mood slipped a little on the way back to their room. The "kid" conversation and then crossing paths with Awhina had gotten under her skin. To Mike's credit, he didn't bring the kid thing up again that afternoon or question her about the supermarket.

They spent a few hours sitting by the pool, savouring the strange quietness that had permeated the resort. Possibly Bethany was still not back from the hospital or else Graham and Sheryl had taken their family out for a day trip, as had everyone else. It was eerie yet strangely pleasant to feel as if the two of them had the resort to themselves.

Mike took a dip in the water. Hannah watched him as he dived in, then freestyled to the other end of the pool. His broad shoulders cut through the water. His back muscles and shoulder blades were well defined. Mike turned around and headed back towards her end of the pool, sculling the water when it got too deep to stand. "You coming in?" he asked, a toothy grin lighting up his face.

"No, thanks," Hannah said, smiling back at him.

"Come in," he begged, pulling his lower lip down into a pretend pout.

"No, thanks," she repeated, blowing him a kiss then pretending to return to her book. Suddenly, large droplets of water splattered from the pool over her legs and wet the pages of her book.

"Mike!" Hannah yelped. "My book!"

"Then put it down and join me," he held his palm ready to send another shower of water her way.

"Grrr," she growled, folding over a corner of the page and putting it down on the table beside her. "You know how I feel about water…" She tried a gentler tone.

"But you're safe, and you're here with me. I won't let anything happen to you," he said, resting his arms on the edge of the pool and pleading with big mock puppy dog eyes.

"Fine," she said, giving in. Standing up, Hannah slowly began stripping off her cover up. She could trust him. Right? Regardless, small pins and needles of dread fluttered in her stomach. She eased herself down into a sitting position on the edge of the pool, her feet slipping into the lukewarm water. A thought flashed through her mind; could this be the same pool? The one she'd nearly drowned in?

No. There was no pergola. And no slime or sludge.

The water was pristine. Clear. She could easily see to the bottom: no water weed, no hands tugging on her legs. Mike shuffled himself along the side of the pool where she sat. He held onto the edge either side of her legs.

"I've got you," he said, showing she should get in.

She scoured her surroundings, stalling for time. When nothing showed itself as out of place, Hannah rested her hands on Mike's shoulders, using him as a brace while she slipped into the water. Her head was the only thing not submerged. An inkling of panic rose all the way up her chest to her throat. She tried to will it away. *Don't spoil this*, she told herself. This was her time with Mike. She automatically kicked to help keep afloat, trying to squash the thought of fingers wrapping around her ankles.

"Not so bad now, is it?" Mike said, locking eyes with her, a smile playing on his lips.

"It's nice," she said, trying again to hide her feelings of fear and anxiety. Mike gently backed Hannah up against the pool wall. Taking one hand off Mike's shoulder, she propped it up over the edge to keep her better afloat.

He placed both his hands on either side of her shoulders on the pool edge. "You are beautiful," he said before pressing his body into hers and encapsulating her mouth with his own. It was a needy kiss. Desperate. Hannah linked one of her arms around his neck and returned the kiss, feeling some fear and anxiety ebb.

"You can let go of the wall, you know. I've got you." And he did. One of his arms slid against Hannah's lower back and was pressing her to him. She knew he wouldn't let her sink.

The sun beat down on her head, warming her from the shoulders up. Hannah gingerly let go, threading her other arm around the back of his neck so she was staying afloat by holding on to him. He kissed her deeply again, and she savoured the kiss, remembering again why she had married him. *This* man, not Amiri, the thought seared through her mind.

CHAPTER 28

Overall, it had been a relaxing day, an example of what their honeymoon should be like, Hannah thought. Now it was time to get ready for the cultural show. Hannah spent extra time dressing for the occasion, excited for a night of music and good food, and more time alone with her husband.

She slipped her phone into her purse, hoping to get some photos of the night's entertainment. But when Mike slipped his into his pocket, she cringed. Please, not tonight, she thought. Don't let it ring tonight.

A shuttle collected them from outside the Rest Easy, dropping them off outside the event in a queue behind other tourist buses and shuttles.

It was the most people Hannah had seen in one place on the island. She joined an excited flurry of visitors signing in at the booking table. Then she and Mike trailed a procession of people following a gravel path through beautiful gardens.

Mike took hold of her hand, and she smiled. It was getting dark, but many of the plants on both sides of them were lit up with coloured garden lights, making their surroundings magical. They walked past an ornate stone waterfall framed with tropical greenery. Tall palm trees sheltered them on one side, leading them towards an open-view restaurant on the other side.

A waitress greeted them, wearing a lei around her neck and a flower behind her ear. After getting their names, she led them through the restaurant to a large table with a few guests already seated.

"Look, Edie. It's the couple from the plane!" a familiar voice boomed.

"Shh, Henry!"

"Edith. Henry. Nice to see you both," Mike exclaimed.

The waitress had moved out the way, allowing a glimpse of who they would share their table with. Hannah smiled and said hello. What were the chances? She and Mike shuffled along the benches beside them, Mike sitting beside Henry, across from Hannah and Edith.

Minus the bit of awkwardness when Edith had joined her to wash up after the flight, they had seemed like lovely people.

"How has your anniversary been?" Hannah asked, as the waitress poured them water.

"Oh, any day with this fair maiden is a happy day on Earth." Henry beamed, making Edith grimace and blush at the same time.

Hannah couldn't help but notice the way they gazed at each other. Thinking back to her conversation with Edith in the washrooms, she understood completely why Edith believed them to be soulmates.

"It was lovely, dear," Edith said, turning to Hannah and smiling. No hint of ominous warnings now.

"And how about you two lovebirds?" Henry asked.

The man exuded warmth, and Hannah was genuinely thankful they had bumped into the two of them.

"Oh, we've been having a great time, haven't we, Han?" Mike turned to her and gave her a wink. Hannah laughed. With today being the exception, it wasn't exactly how she would have described it. Edith's eyebrow arched and she passed a look at Henry.

Hannah took a moment to take in her surroundings.

The room had a bar at one end, with several other large wooden tables placed in rows parallel to theirs. On the other side of the room, the buffet was set up on white-clothed tables. A circular table held an enormous cauldron filled with soup and baskets full of fresh bread. It was already busy, and most tables were at least half full. The servers ushered in more people as they arrived.

Their seats looked out over a beautiful pond, where a floating stage with canopy sat, awaiting the performances to begin. On the opposite side of the stage was a near-identical restaurant, and at the farthest end another one; three identical restaurants set up for optimum viewing of the stage.

A buzz of excitement surged through her, and she grinned without even meaning to. A trio of men had already set themselves up on the corner of the stage with a ukulele, drum and keyboard and were playing background music to start off the night. After their drink orders arrived two more couples joined their table.

Hannah had never been a fan of small talk, but the others seemed to do fine, introducing themselves, asking the usual questions of where they were from and where they were staying. Hannah only half-listened, preferring to people watch and enjoy the ambient music.

"How are you liking your resort?" Henry asked, pulling Hannah from her reverie. The question was directed at Mike.

She waited for his reply, noticing the movement of Edith's leg under the table next to her.

"Ouch," Henry grunted, wrinkling his brow in his wife's direction.

Hannah's skin prickled.

"Oh, you know. We've been ironing out some usual birthing pains, but it's all coming together," Mike said, brushing it off.

"Oh, good, good," Henry said, continuing the charade. He was digging for something, Hannah could tell.

"We'd heard there was an incident yesterday? A near drowning…" Hannah and Edith both shifted in their seats, and Hannah fiddled with her locket.

Intent on downplaying everything, Mike shrugged it off. "Yeah. One of those things, I guess. Could have happened anywhere. What's important is everyone's okay."

"And your hand?" Henry asked. There was another movement under the table and an *oomph* from Henry. Hannah stole a glance at Edith, who was giving nothing less than the evil eye to her husband. Soulmates or not, she suspected Henry was going to be in a lot of trouble by the end of the night.

"Oh, it's nothing," Mike said, his joviality a little more forced this time. "Just an accident in the kitchen."

"Ah, ha," Henry mumbled, nodding his head.

Please don't mention the protests, Hannah was secretly praying as she chewed on her lip. She could write a list of all the weird things that had happened since arriving at the Rest Easy, but tonight, she wanted to put it all from her mind.

Fortunately, she was saved by the performance beginning. The lights dimmed and the trio on stage stopped playing. A lady with a microphone appeared on stage. She introduced herself as Mama and shared the history of the restaurant and cultural performance. A brief break before the main performance allowed them to join the line at the buffet.

The food was impressive. Lots of salads and barbecued meats and fun island delicacies: seafood, mango chutney, plantains and fried bananas. As was usually the way with buffets, Hannah over-filled her plate, but she was happy with the distraction. Conversation turned to the food; a much less polarising topic. It wasn't long after starting on her meal she realised she had been optimistic about what she could eat.

The show was spectacular, leaving Hannah spellbound. She clicked away on her phone camera, knowing there was no way it could do justice to the scene in front of her.

A love story at its core, the performance was about the marriage between the son and daughter of two chiefs of warring tribes. Their union brought peace to the land.

The dancers were amazing. Drums beat in an orchestrated frenzy as dancers gyrated on the stage. Gorgeous women swung their hips, their fingers weaving patterns in the air. The men, shining with sweat, pounded the stage with their feet. They had toned thighs and calves with taut tendons. The dancer's bodies shone under the coloured lights and tiki torches.

The chiefs, dressed in elaborate headdresses, paddled around the stage on wooden rafts. Fire dancers wove flames through the air as it licked at their limbs. And the drums – the drums pulsated like blood through veins. Hannah could feel them in her bones, separating the worlds of reality and other. As they increased in crescendo Hannah was sure her heart was doing the same.

It was all so otherworldly, yet so familiar. Everything

around her melted away until it was just her and the people on stage. At moments, scenes from her dream from the night before flashed through her mind. Those dancers transposing over the ones in front of her. Other times, she would follow the movements of one man on stage and Amiri's face would flicker to mind, her heart racing a little faster every time.

"It's wonderful, isn't it?" Edith whispered in her ear.

"It's amazing," Hannah said, knowing no actual words could express what it was.

She stole a glance at Mike. He was staring down at his phone on his lap. Hannah's stomach fell. He was missing it. Missing it *all*. For what? A sting of resentment built in her chest. She eyed Henry. He appeared as absorbed in the performance as everyone else. She caught Edith considering her and knew right away she'd witnessed all of Hannah's emotions play out on her face. Hannah's cheeks warmed, and she turned away.

The show ended to a loud chorus of applause. Hannah was sure she clapped the loudest. Something had changed inside her. She was vibrating slightly differently, slightly disconnected from reality – as if she were separate from everything and connected at the same time. She sat in silence for a moment, unable to move. Mike broke her trance. He reached for her hand and she pulled away.

They made small talk for a while with their companions before all four of them headed back towards the carpark where buses and shuttles awaited.

"The offer still stands if you want to join us at the Eventide," Henry mentioned as they said their goodbyes, his gaze lingering on Hannah for a moment longer than necessary.

Mike put an arm around her shoulder and pulled her close "I think we're fine right where we are," Mike said, good-naturedly. He let her go to shake Henry's hand and give Edith a kiss on the cheek.

"It's good to see you again," Edith whispered in Hannah's ear as they embraced a goodbye.

"You too," Hannah said.

"Please stay safe," she said. "And remember what I said last time." Edith held Hannah at arm's length. Her eyes shone as if holding back tears.

Acting reluctant to let her go, Edith at last was guided away by Henry's hands on her shoulders.

"Stay safe, you two!" he added as they turned away to get on their bus.

"And you!" Mike said, waving at the two of them.

Hannah bit down on her lip. She remembered what Edith had said. Or the gist of it, anyway. It made as much sense to her now as it had then.

"Shall we go?" Mike turned to her.

"Did you like it?" Hannah asked.

"Of course," Mike said, automatically.

"No. I mean, did you *really* like it? The performance? The music? The dancers?"

"Yeah, it was great," he said, guiding them towards where their shuttle waited for them.

"What about you?" he asked. "Did you enjoy it?"

"Yeah, it was great," she said, feeling something die inside her.

CHAPTER 29

Swirling red, blue and yellow lights welcomed them back to the resort. The shuttle pulled up on the road, opening its doors for Hannah and Mike to disembark, but made no rush to leave. Hannah knew all passenger eyes were on the scene in front of them. More drama than a small island was used to, Hannah thought.

Beside her, Mike swore under his breath. Funny, how his words made her blood run cold, rather than the flashing lights of the police cars.

Hannah followed Mike down the steps, surprised by the strength of the breeze. Raised voices reached her, the words indiscernible thanks to the palm fronds dancing on the wind. She had noticed nothing of the sort on leaving the cultural centre. In fact, the night had seemed perfectly calm, sky clear and littered with stars. Now the air felt heavy, the sky a concrete blue with few stars. Hannah wasn't certain whether the feeling came from the weather or the drama unfolding before them.

Mike strode ahead, ready to charge into the fold of things, and Hannah wondered for a moment if he even remembered she was there. Something had changed between them. She could feel it with a niggling sense of unease.

Two police cars blocked the driveway to the resort. A few scooters and the old blue ute Hannah remembered from the few days before, were all parked haphazardly on the grass. The red and blue flashing lights sent an eerie glow over the scene and made gnarly finger-like shadows from the palm fronds.

"What's going on?" Mike call out over the din. Hannah saw people now. A man was struggling against a police officer, his hands handcuffed behind his back, a heavy hand on his shoulder as he twisted this way and that. A female police officer was yelling into a microphone at a small group of people flashing flaming torches at the reception of the resort, telling them to extinguish their torches. Hannah recognised Awhina right away at the centre of the brawl. Her hair whipping around her face with the fury of the breeze. Hannah wondered how it was it hadn't caught fire from the flames lashing towards her from the torches.

"This is our land," she yelled. Another police officer struggled with a young man who took exception to him. He threw his torch on the ground in the scuffle as the officer grabbed him from behind. A third officer spoke into his radio. Chanting from the group of protestors rose in chorus with the wind.

"Leave this land! Let devils lie! Leave this land! Let devils lie!" Awhina whipped her own torch around as an officer got too close. There must have been twelve to fifteen protestors, shaking their torches or fists in the air. A few of the resort's staff formed a human chain in front of the entry to the reception area. The red and blue lights and flames from the torches illuminated their fear and distorted their features. Mike marched ahead, unperturbed by the chaos ahead of him.

"Mike!" Hannah called out, hoping to get his attention. What the hell was he doing, walking into the fray? Hannah didn't know what to do. She stood further back on the gravel road, unsure where to turn. The shuttle of tourists with gaping mouths continued to watch the scene in front of her.

"Leave this land! Let devils lie! Leave this land! Let devils lie!" The words lashed at Hannah with a fury she wasn't prepared for. She kept her eyes on Mike, bringing her hand up to her locket to calm her nerves.

One protestor noticed him – a young man, maybe in his twenties, shaking his fist and chanting. He must have sensed Mike behind him because he turned around. She couldn't catch the words between the two of them, just the look of surprise from the man as Mike pulled back his arm and punched him full force in the stomach, sending him doubled over. The man stumbled backwards into one of his comrades before landing hard on his butt.

Someone yelled out. The chanting momentarily quietened as faces turned back towards Mike. An officer moved towards him but got caught sideways by another protestor, going to his friend's defence, shoulder barging him. The officer went sprawling to the ground and Mike turned on his new target.

Hannah had never seen Mike like this. This wasn't the man she knew. *Her* Mike wasn't violent, wouldn't hurt anyone, especially unprovoked.

Fear and adrenalin crashed through her body. What the hell was going on?

Pushing and shoving, the small group now became one moving, breathing entity. Awhina continued yelling, lashing out at those who bumped into her. Her back was now to the resort as she and her supporters fought for some control.

Mike turned and helped the fallen officer back onto his feet. Another officer had joined his side, battens drawn and ready to strike if needed.

"Put your torches down," a voice called out.

The high-pitched scream of sirens drew closer. She turned. The bus slowly pulled away to make room for further law enforcement. Hannah stood alone at the entrance of the driveway, remaining in the shadows, mouth agape.

Do something, she told herself. Move or get out of the way, but *do* something. Another police vehicle pulled up; a screech of tyres followed by two policemen on bikes. Hannah backed away, leaning against the trunk of a palm. When the new police officers joined the skirmish, the chaos seemed to settle down. Two protestors were thrown to the ground and handcuffed. An officer shook his head, as if recognising the person he was arresting.

They probably all knew each other. It was a small island.

Mike moved through to the front reception where a few of the resort staff stood uneasily. Gradually the protestors dispersed, put into vehicles or sent home. As they left, Hannah could see a small gathering of spectators from the resort. Some in what appeared to be sleepwear, as if they had pulled themselves out of bed to watch the excitement.

The voices had largely died down while the wind continued to build. Hannah still made no effort to move. Discarded torches lay on the gravel drive, kerosene scenting the air. One of the resort staff came around the corner with a bucket of water, dousing a few of the smouldering torches, sending up plumes of grey smoke into the air.

Awhina was the only one making noise now. An officer touched her arm. Awhina shrugged her off, sharp words making the young officer flinch. She marched herself towards one of the police vehicles; the officer following close but cautiously behind, letting Awhina lead the way. When she put herself into the back of the vehicle, Hannah suspected this wasn't Awhina's first run in with the law.

A cold gust of wind howled through, and Hannah shivered. Overhead came a low rumble, and the first few fat drops of rain hit her. Something held her in place as she watched Mike give a statement or something to a police officer. Not once had he searched for her.

That's not your husband, a voice said in her mind. Hannah jumped with fear. It wasn't her voice; it was Amiri's. Somehow. Inside her head.

The curse is like a cancer. Be careful.

Hannah wrapped her arms around her body. Her legs felt heavy, but she made them move anyway. More fat droplets of rain hit her, soaking through her flimsy shawl. She wished she had brought something warmer with her.

Hannah tried to avert her eyes from Awhina as she passed by the police car, but something made her look up. Through the open door, Awhina glared at her. Her hair was wild and untamed around her face, while her eyes burned with fury. Her lips were pulled back in a sneer.

"You'll be as cursed as this place if you stay here," she yelled at Hannah.

The words were like a punch to the chest. Hannah shrank back. Awhina spat on the ground before turning back and closing the car door.

A hand grabbed Hannah's arm, and she turned around, startled, fight mode ready to kick in. It was an officer. But before Hannah could do anything, Mike had crossed the distance between him and her in a few quick strides.

"She's with me," he said to the officer, who dropped his hand from her arm.

"Mike," she said. "What the hell happened?"

"It's okay. We're okay. It's all over now." His face looked different. Worn. The rain fell with increasing density, and streams rolled down his face. She took in the rest of him.

"Your hand!" she said, startled. Even in the poor lighting, she could see a dark stain through the bandage again.

"I'm fine." He glanced down at it. Surprise crossed his face as if he hadn't noticed. He grimaced in pain.

Hannah grabbed his wrist. "No, it's not," she said, going into nurse mode. "We need to get this checked out, or at the very least get some ice on it."

The police officer Mike had been talking to interrupted them. "We're all done, if you want to head off. If you can come down to the police station tomorrow morning for a few more questions, we'd appreciate it."

"Sure," Mike said.

"Ma'am," the officer said, nodding to Hannah before turning his back on them both and heading over to one of his colleagues.

The area had cleared out with few vehicles remaining. Hannah supposed they'd be there until the morning, their owners having received lifts in the back of the cop cars. The wind rallied, and the rainfall grew heavier.

Graham and Sheryl stood in the foyer. Graham gave a loud shout out in greeting and waved to the two of them before putting his arm around his wife's shoulders and heading inside.

A few of the hotel attendants were still rushing around

picking up the discarded torches or talking in hushed tones to each other, anxiety written all over their faces. There was no sign of Mariana. Of course not, Hannah thought. She couldn't be there every moment of every day.

Mike put an arm around Hannah, who shook so much her teeth chattered, equal parts from the chilly rain and the adrenalin rush. They moved towards the reception area for shelter as the last police vehicle pulled out of the drive, followed by one officer on a motorbike. Hannah watched as their lights disappeared around the bend. The resort was eerily quiet but for the heavy splattering of rain and the angry lashing of the palm trees. It was a wonder they hadn't added flying debris to the drama of the night.

Turning around, Hannah made eye contact with the girl behind the reception desk. She must have been in her early twenties. Her skin was pale, and her hand noticeably wobbled as she doodled on the pad in front of her. To her credit, she mustered a smile in their direction.

"Are you okay?" Hannah asked.

"Yes, yes, I'm fine," she said, her lower lip trembling and eyes shining with unshed tears.

"They're gone now," Mike said, taking a step towards her. "They won't be back tonight, if ever. You don't need to worry about them."

The girl nodded and straightened her shoulders. "Of course not," she said. "I'm not worried about them at all."

"If you want us to stay or call someone, we can," Hannah said.

"No, no. I'm fine. Just a shock," she said, forcing an even wider smile.

"Okay," Mike replied. "We're in room 26B. If you need

anything.

The girl gave a small nod.

With Mike's arm still around her shoulder, they headed to their room. Hannah believed the girl. She didn't think she was worried about the protestors at all. She *was* worried about something, though. The feeling sat heavy in the pit of Hannah's stomach. No. It was the curse that had the girl scared.

CHAPTER 30

"I think we should leave." Hannah sat perched on the end of the sofa. Her hands dug into the seat cushions to stop them from shaking. She needed to get out of her wet clothes. With the air conditioner running, it chilled her to the bone. But for the moment, she just needed to sit. She was in shock.

Mike was getting a drink out of the minibar fridge, back to her. His hand had been re-bandaged; Hannah had seen to it. An icepack sat on the counter ready to be applied once he had got his drink. He pulled out a bottle of sparkling water and slowly stood up and turned to face her. His expression was stony.

"What do you mean?" he said, enunciating each word as if it caused him pain to do so.

"I think we should leave," Hannah said again, swallowing hard on a lump in her throat. She hadn't seen this expression before. Maybe the voice had been right; this wasn't her husband.

This wasn't the Mike she knew. The Mike she knew was easy going, ready to listen – and with a grin not too far under the surface even in the worst of circumstances. This Mike, the one who was staring at her with a hardness to his jawline, this was a different man.

Hannah summoned a smile, hoping to see it reflected in Mike's face. She didn't know where to start but knew, for the first time with him, she would need to choose her words carefully.

"It doesn't feel safe anymore." She held still as he placed the bottle of water down on the bench and dragged his good hand across his face. She imagined him trying to physically manipulate his face into an expression of calm. Lines Hannah hadn't seen before were etched into his forehead.

"With the protestors and—"

"That's been dealt with." Mike's voice was sharp.

"So much has been going wrong. What with Bethany nearly drowning, and you being called away every five minutes to fix something …" She hadn't meant to say the second part. As soon as she did, remorse flooded her. It would hit a nerve.

"Are you kidding me?" Mike said in a low growl, taking a step towards her. "Are you bloody *kidding* me?" His face had grown red.

Hannah flinched.

"The money we've put into this place – like I'm just going to sit back and let this place go to hell? I have a responsibility, Hannah. I thought you got that. I thought you understood. We're in fucking *paradise*, and it's still not good enough for you?" He took another step towards her, and both rage and fear fought for control of her body.

She stood up to meet him at his level. Heat flared across her clavicle. "This was supposed to be our honeymoon. This was supposed to be *our* time together." She fought to keep her emotions in control. She was both furious at him and horrified.

His bandaged hand curled into a fist by his side.

Hannah took a breath, calming herself before she spoke again, noticing her nails were now digging into the palms of her hands. "I know this resort's important to you." She kept her voice low, breathy, trying to appeal to him.

"Well, it should be important to you too. This here is our future."

"I get it," Hannah said. "But I married *you*. Not this resort. I want our honeymoon to be about us, not some stupid curse."

"So that's what this is about?" His tone was mocking. "You fear some stupid, superstitious bullshit riled up by the locals. There's no curse, Hannah." He almost spat it at her.

"Something *is* wrong with this place," she fired back. *That's not your husband. That's not your husband.* The words circled around her mind. She reached for her locket, willing herself to steady her breath, steady her shaking. But she felt it, deep within her chest. Something was wrong, and he was the fool if he couldn't see for himself.

They were almost eye to eye now. A vein throbbed in Mike's neck. For a moment, complete confusion coursed through her body, staying her tongue. How the hell had things got to this point where they were actually having a faceoff?

"Look, I'm sorry," she countered, trying to deescalate things. "It's been a tough night. I thought maybe we could talk about it. This place will be fine without you. We could go home, have a staycation of sorts, or even spend a weekend in the country or something, just you and I. No responsibilities."

"You're serious?" he said, his tone icy again. "It's a few days until the grand opening and you want me to pack up and head back home, to hell with our investment, all because you're a little scared of some protestors and a made-up curse. God,

Hannah! When are you going to grow up? Is there anything you're not bloody scared of?"

It felt like a slap. Right away, Hannah knew he was getting at her fear of water. It was bad enough he didn't care how she felt about things, but now he was calling her out on her parents' death.

For a moment, something shifted behind his eyes, a grain of remorse maybe. Then he seemed to shake it off, as he shook his shoulders too.

"If you've got such a problem with this place, maybe *you* should leave." The words hung heavy in the air.

Her bottom lip trembled. He would really allow her to leave midway through their honeymoon? She blinked hard, willing the building tears away. "Screw you," she whispered, setting the first tear free to roll down her face, feeling the distaste of the words as she said them.

A low animalistic growl escaped from Mike as he swung around, his back to her. He slammed his bandaged hand against his thigh.

"Fuck!" he growled.

Hannah stared at his back. He was shaking. What the hell had just happened? She had to get out. Had to get away. The air vibrated with anger as if their argument were feeding something.

A few quick steps, and she wrenched open the dresser, grabbing one of the few jerseys she had thought to bring with her. Though she couldn't look at him, not directly, from the corner of her eye she didn't think he had moved. She pulled the sweater over her head, grabbed her handbag off the bed, and before she knew it, her hand was on the doorknob. She couldn't even bring herself to pause.

When the door closed behind her, all she heard was a throaty "Fuck" from Mike and the sound of flesh hitting out at something. The counter? The wall? It didn't matter. Her tears were really rolling now, blinding her to almost everything. Her body was in autopilot. It knew where to go, even if she didn't. Her legs carried her down the stairs. A small part of her so glad she met no one in the hallway.

Outside, though the rain had stopped, the air was chillier than normal, and the wind still blew with a fury. A few lights glowed from behind pulled curtains; everything else was dark, but for the aesthetically placed garden lights, which threw shadows around her like spectres in the night. Hannah slowed her run to a walk. Where the hell was she going to go? Did she really plan on leaving? And do what?

Options raced through her head as she continued down the path. She could head to reception and ask for another room, wait until the morning to decide what to do. But God, the thought of having to explain anything to the poor girl at the office desk. She had her phone with her but no one's number, so calling the likes of Rua was out of the question.

Each option came with an equally good reason she shouldn't. Her legs carried her of their own accord down to the beachfront, anyway. Overhead, the palm fronds thrashed at each other, and Hannah pulled her sweater closer to her body, almost hugging herself as she came to a stop. Even the lagoon was choppy; she could make out the small waves from the ambient lighting of the resort. Dark grey-blue clouds still hung heavy in the sky. One was a little brighter than the others, suggesting it hid the light of the moon.

Wooden beach chairs were the only invitation. She just needed a moment, she thought, to process the night; then she would make her way back to her room. Mike would have calmed down by then, surely.

What the hell had happened? She wondered again. They had never argued before. Not like this, anyway. He had never used her parents' death against her. How had things got so out of control?

A fresh wave of tears built up, ready to overwhelm her, and for a moment she bent over in two. Emotion sucker punched her. This was not how a honeymoon was supposed to be.

A new roaring filled her head against the white noise of the trees and wind and waves—almost like a drumbeat coming closer and closer. She glanced around, half expecting that Mike had followed her out, but no one lurked there, just shadows distorted from tears and darkness.

She was alone. *Alone.* She eyed the hammock where she had lain the first day. The tree where she had traced her fingers over the taunting nursery rhyme "Row, row, row your boat." The resort was laughing at her, and her husband wanted her gone. Grief threatened to overwhelm her.

What to do? She couldn't stay on the edge of the beach all night. The wind calmed a little, but she was still cold. Under her jersey, her dress was still damp from the earlier downpour. She shivered, teeth chattering.

She couldn't stay here. She had to go back to Mike. Back to the room that seemed to thrive off their anger and hurt. She hadn't *imagined* it. She had *felt* it. Like something was enjoying their pain. Thriving on the hurt behind their words.

Oh God.

Wiping her eyes with the sleeve of her shirt, she took a deep breath, willing herself to turn around.

A drumming sound thrummed. A little like the performance

from earlier. The night had grown darker, the shadows dense by the trees. She could barely make out the hammocks now. The shadows seemed to be moving, growing, reaching for her. Her heart gave a little leap in her chest. What the hell?

She swung around, ready to face the resort, the light, her room. Mike.

Shit. Nausea rose in her chest. The garden lights, the resort lights – they weren't there. The chairs, the gardens, it had all disappeared. Just more shadows. More darkness. The moon poked its head out from behind a cloud, giving Hannah a small glimpse of what stood in the resort's stead. Ruins. The same ruins she had seen on her first day. On the day she nearly drowned. The abandoned resort. No, that resort didn't exist, remember? The distant sound of drums continued, building into a crescendo of sorts.

This wasn't right. Where the hell *was* she right now? And how did she get there? She twirled around again, just able to make out the sea behind her. The shadows from the trees thickened, taking human form, reaching out for her. She spun again to face the resort. Ruins. Where the hell was everything? Panic burnt through her veins like a fire. Her heart beat so hard it felt like it was going to erupt.

What's going on? She was going crazy. Losing her mind. *That* was what was happening. The drums were almost inside her skull, reverberating against bone. Hannah put her hands to her face, wanting so desperately to shut out the drums, the shadows, the encroaching darkness. Make it go away.

His name fell from her lips without a conscious thought.

Amiri? She spun around again. This time firm hands grabbed her by the arms, holding her in place. Electricity tore through her limbs and silenced the drums. Her heart leapt into her throat. For a second, she stood there, too scared to open her eyes. Her entire body throbbed with fear, panic, surprise. It was him. She knew it.

CHAPTER 31

Time stood still. The world stood still. Even the elements had gone quiet.

"Hannah," a breathy male voice whispered.

Her legs threatened to buckle underneath her. The grip on her arms tightened, and she willed herself to pull her hands away from her face, slowly lowering them to her sides. She opened her eyes.

He was there. Dark molten amber eyes staring straight back at her. Liquifying her insides.

"It's okay," he said, releasing his grip on her arms. "It's okay."

"It's you…" Hannah whispered. "You're here." She tried to make sense of it. This enigmatic stranger who seemed to be everywhere and nowhere all at once. She had begun to think he was purely a figment of her over-stressed imagination.

"You're real!" Heat flared in her cheeks as she realised what she had said. "Of course you're real. I'm sorry, I'm just—" She looked around herself disconcertingly. She was just what? Lost? Surprised? The reality of the moment hit back at her. She was outside in the middle of the night after a horrible argument with her husband, standing before this man she didn't even know but for the fact he had saved her life.

Something broke inside her. A tsunami of emotion swept

through her body and nothing could contain the resulting sobs. Fat tears drowned her cheeks, and she trembled with more feeling than she had ever endured before.

"It's okay. It's okay," Amiri said. Tentatively, he drew her close to his chest, wrapping his arms around her while her body shook.

Her head lay against his shoulder, a never-ending deluge of tears on a stranger's chest, her entire body wracked with pain. He held her tight, and she gave in to it. His chin rested on the top of her head. His arms tight around her back. She let all the pain, all the mental and emotional exhaustion of the past few days out. And the whole time, he held her, saying nothing.

You don't let go of them, no matter what. Understand? Familiar words echoed through her mind. Who had said them? She couldn't remember. She only knew he was the one holding her together. If it weren't for Amiri, she was sure her legs would have buckled, and she would have sunk to the ground never to get up again.

The emotions kept coming. Wave after wave.

The rush of the wedding, her silent fears about their honeymoon location, all the memories of her family, her near drowning, Bethany's brush with death, the protestors, the talk of curses, feeling like she was losing her mind, and the horrible fight with Mike. And all her stupid comparisons to her parents' relationship. Her relationship with Mike was nothing like what she remembered of her parents. Her dad had given his life to try to save his wife. Mike had told her to leave.

After a while, her sobs slowed. Pure exhaustion crept in, replacing her tears with a pounding headache and full-body numbness.

"Where are we?" she asked in a small voice. She pulled away slightly from the solid chest she was pinned against. Embarrassment stopped her from meeting his eyes.

The wind had stopped, the only drumming was now that of her head. There were still no resort lights, no Rest Easy Resort, just the eerie suggestion that she had somehow got herself turned around, finding herself back at the ruins.

"You're with me," Amiri answered, his voice barely a whisper, but the warmth of his breath tickling the side of her neck. "I don't know how … but you're here with me."

Hannah shivered again, unsure whether it was from the cold or his words.

"You shouldn't be here," Amiri continued, his tone soft.

Hannah bit her lip. Where should she be exactly? Back with Mike?

"Maybe," came his reply.

Her jaw dropped. She was sure she had only thought the question.

"You need to leave this place." His hands had moved to her shoulders, and he held her at arm's length, looking at her.

She still couldn't meet his eyes. He gently cupped her chin in his hand and tilted it up to him. Her legs felt weak, but she knew she wouldn't fall. He had her.

"It's not safe here. You need to go back to your husband and leave right away." He slid his hands down her arms until he held her hands in his own. His touch sent waves of electricity through her body, putting every nerve ending on notice.

"It's not so easy," she said. "I want to, I do …" Her voice trailed off as she remembered the resort was gone, replaced with these ruins. The very ruins her own husband had dismissed as not existing.

She let go of Amiri's hands, as much as it hurt her to do so. She took a step backwards, doing a full circle to take in her surroundings again. The shadows had retreated to the safety of the trees. The lagoon was as it had always been, but the ruins remained before her, where only a short while ago a fully functional resort had stood.

"Where is the resort?" she asked, willing her eyes to meet his.

He grimaced. Pain crossed his face, and he took a step towards her. Instinctively, she took another step backwards. There was something between them, she could feel it, like a tightly wound cord. It almost hurt to pull away, but it wasn't right. She had a husband. This was her honeymoon.

And you don't let go of them, no matter what, understand? Not even for a resort.

"The resort is here," he said. "You just can't see it right now."

"That makes no sense," she said with a shake of her head. Nothing, *nothing* made sense.

Row, row, row your boat, gently down the stream. Merrily, merrily, merrily, merrily, life is but a dream...

"I ... I need to be getting back." She wrapped her arms tighter around her chest.

"I know." He kept his hands loose at his sides as if at a loss with what to do with them, unsure what to say.

A crack of the heavens overhead pre-empted another deluge. The rain bucketed down as if the sky had completely split open, drowning them where they stood.

"We need to get out of the rain," Amiri said, raising his voice to be heard. "Follow me." He grabbed her by the hand and dragged her with him as he started a jog towards one of the ruined resort buildings.

Not knowing what else to do, she followed, the rain pelting down, like needles being driven into her skin.

He pulled her around the side of a building, into a lobby area, then a staircase. It was slippery with God knows what, so she slowed her pace but did not let go of his hand. Her clothes heavy and wet, she followed him as best as she could up the stairs that teased her with a melancholic familiarity.

"It's the same place, isn't it?" she said between breaths. "This … this is the resort?"

He didn't answer but pulled her into one room, with the sound of rain hammering heavily outside. Two steps into the room and she planted her feet, refusing to budge despite so desperately wanting to be near to him. He was warm, she told herself. Her body just craved warmth.

He turned around to face her.

"This is the Rest Easy?" She thought for a moment he was going to pull his hand out of hers. She gripped it harder, demanding an answer. The room was much like the one she had seen the first time she had gone exploring. Unfinished. Smelly, dank, decayed. She could make out the shadow of the hot tub in the room's corner. Part of her wanted to run. To rush back out into the deluge outside, to take her chances at finding her way back to civilisation. Another part of her wanted answers, and this elusive man might be her only chance at getting them. After the week she'd had, she deserved answers.

"Tell me," she said with a force of voice that surprised her.

A range of emotions blew across his face as he wrestled with a response. Hannah took the moment to look at him, as much as she could in the dusky light. He stood at least a head taller than her. He was in jeans, ripped at one knee. A non-descript logo T-shirt stuck to his body, thanks to the rain. He was mostly a shadow amongst shadows, but for the faint aura separating him from the dark.

"Yes," he said. "It's the same."

Hannah released her hand from his in shock.

"How is this even possible?" she asked

"I'd like to know that too," he whispered.

Hannah was sure he wasn't talking about the resort.

"How are you here?" he said almost to himself.

The questions made her head swim. The rain beat its own percussion on the roof and pelted in through the open wall to the outside.

"Come. We'll sit down and talk."

She followed him towards the jacuzzi, away from the rain fighting its way into the room. Hannah hesitated as he perched himself on the edge of the tub, waiting for her to sit beside him. Heat flooded her cheeks again as she remembered her dream from the night before. Her wedding ring had loosened with the rain and had twisted the diamond, cutting into her finger. She adjusted it so it sat upright on her finger again, and a wave of guilt made her grimace. She shook her head at his invitation and stood on weary legs before him.

"Tell me," she said. "All of it. Who are you? Where are we, and what the hell is happening?"

Amiri sighed, dragging his hand over his mouth, shoulders slumping. She felt bad for talking so harshly, but shook it off. She needed answers, and she needed them now.

"I don't honestly know what's happening here," he said, his body slouching forward a little. "You're not supposed to be here."

Something tugged in Hannah's chest. She wrapped her arms around her middle, shaking again from the cold. Wherever home was, she wanted to be there with a hot shower and a warm bed.

"Where am I?" her voice, so small, so scared, knowing the answer but wanting to hear it anyway, to know she wasn't crazy.

"This is the Cook Island Resort, or what was the Cook Island Resort, anyway."

Rua had said something similar.

"So they didn't complete the renovations," she said half to herself, trying to make sense of it all. "But I don't understand. How did I get here? I was right outside the Rest Easy, and then … then…"

"Then you were here," he finished for her. "I don't know how you got here. I always thought of this place as a memory. A twisted, messed up echo of what was."

"And who were they, those people?" It was clear now, those shadows, the drumming – they were people approaching her, surrounding her. She shivered, this time not from the cold.

"You saw them?" he asked, surprise flashing across his face. He gave his face a scrub with his palm. "Please, sit down."

She wanted to. She really did, before her legs completely gave out under her, but something made her stay where she was. Fear, but a separate fear from all the other fears she was feeling, just that she knew, for as long as she could, she needed to keep a distance between the two of them.

So she stood where she was and answered. "Yes, I saw them. "Well, I kind of saw them, their shadows at least, and I heard them. Why were they drumming?"

"Shit," he muttered under his breath. "Another thing you

shouldn't have seen."

"Why not?" She was getting frustrated. He made as much sense as Rua. Why couldn't anyone just give her straight answers?

"Because you don't belong here," he said. "This isn't a place for the living." He left it hanging in the air between them.

Rubbing the goosebumps rising on her arms, she said, "But you're here?" she whispered.

Amiri stood up and paced, wiping his brow with one hand. "We'll wait out the rain, then we'll get you back," he said. "But you have to promise me something, okay?"

"What?" Hannah replied. She knew she should be more scared than she was, but exhaustion was creeping back with a vengeance. She reached out for the side of the jacuzzi with her hand, and on feeling it, sat down.

"You're safe here with me now, but when I get you back, leave okay? The guy you're with…"

"My husband," Hannah said reflexively.

"Your husband," Amiri said, correcting himself with a slight grimace. "You both need to leave. Go back home, go somewhere else, but don't stay here. Do you understand?"

"No," Hannah said, finding her voice, a flare of anger and frustration battling against exhaustion. "I don't. I don't understand any of this!" Her hands clenched into fists. She wanted to run again. To get away, but she had nowhere to go. She looked around herself, trying to think of an escape. But it wasn't Amiri or this room she wanted to escape. It was her life. Nothing made sense, and the need to get away was near overwhelming.

"Hannah!" he said, crossing the distance between them. He plonked himself down on the side of the tub and grabbed her hand again. She tried to pull away, but he held tighter. "You're safe with me, but you can't go out there right now."

The intensity of his gaze burned her. She knew he was right. Outside, the wind howled, and the rain was white noise.

"Wait," he pleaded, "until the rain stops. We can't go back out there. It's too dark. We need to wait until it's safe."

Until the shadows disappeared, Hannah thought. What could she do? Amiri was right. If she went outside now, she had no idea what she'd face. And finding her way back could be impossible.

If she stayed here, it would be just her and Amiri. Alone. Her stomach somersaulted at the thought. The lump was back in her throat. He was so close she could smell him. An intoxicating blend of male, musk, and something else. Something so familiar. Warm. Safe.

His fingers unwound from hers, and for a second, she mourned their loss.

What could she do? She could leave and try to find her own way back, but back to *what*? A resort that had somehow disappeared into thin air? A husband who had told her to leave? Hannah flinched.

And who were those people? Shadows? Well, what about them? Or she could risk spending time with a stranger in some abandoned ruins, which by her husband's account didn't exist.

Colour burning high on her cheeks, she hoped to God he couldn't read her mind. As much as she hated to admit it, here with Amiri was the safest she had felt in a long time. And that alone terrified her.

CHAPTER 32

The rain continued to beat down, pooling on the tiled floor. Concrete-coloured clouds and the onslaught of rain hid the moon. Shadows darkened the corners of the room as the last bit of light disappeared for the night.

She peered outside. What if she couldn't find her way back in daylight either?

"You need to move away from the window," Amiri said.

Hannah paced. It seemed the two of them had been taking turns. He was right, though. The wind was blowing a gale again, the rain coming in sideways through the open hole where ranch sliders would have separated them from a balcony, had the resort been completed.

She was cold. Her clothes clung to her body, wet and heavy. She bit down hard to stop her teeth from chattering.

"Come," he said. "I'm not going to hurt you. We can buckle down here until the storm passes. She could just make out his hand reaching for her, encouraging her to come closer. She wanted to. But something made her hold back. Loyalty to Mike? Maybe.

"My phone!" she said, remembering suddenly that her cell phone was in her handbag. She had completely forgotten about it. She rummaged through, going by touch. Her fingers found the smooth rectangular face of her phone, still somewhat dry. Her purse was saturated, but its contents seemed to have survived the assault of the elements.

By habit she found the power button and pressed, expecting the screen to come to life and illuminate some of her surroundings. She tried again. Again. Nothing. It was dead. She had taken an extensive number of photos at the dinner and performance, but not enough to have drained her battery, surely. Another few futile clicks and she dropped it back into the bottom of her bag with a growl of exasperation. Tears battled for escape from her eyelids again.

Amiri moved to her, drawn by her frustration, she guessed. Saying nothing, he took her hand in his. It seemed like his go-to move, but instantly some of her frustration and fear ebbed. His hand was warm, and a powerful part of her welcomed the simple human touch. He led her to the jacuzzi. Or it's incomplete, neglected husk, at least. She was too overwhelmed by so many extremes of emotions to argue.

When he stepped over the edge of the jacuzzi and slid down to a sitting position, she followed suit, curling up beside him, giving up on keeping distance. Too cold and weary to worry about the dirt and moss that no doubt covered every inch of surface too. The jacuzzi seemed to provide more shelter from the elements threatening the rest of the room. She had no choice but to press herself up against his body in such a small space. His warmth was welcoming and seemed to spread through her own body. Amiri hadn't let go of her hand. He gently pulled it across his body. She didn't fight it. Instead, she tucked her head gently under his chin on his chest, her arm resting on his torso.

"We're safe," he said again softly, as the wind roared outside, howling through the open orifices of the resort's corpse. "It's okay," he said.

Her eyelids flickered, so heavy now. Inexplicably so, as if it would be impossible for her to stay awake even had she wanted to. And she didn't think she wanted to. She was melting into the warmth beside and half under her. The day, the ugly horrid emotions, disappeared as did everything else, and she gave in to sleep. A drug-like escape.

The dream started the same way it always did.

She was small. Lying sprawled on the overturned hull of the aluminium dinghy. Her small fingers gripped the slippery ridged surface of the boat's bottom as it rocked precariously side to side, threatening to tip her into the granite coloured depths of the ocean. She heard screams but still couldn't discern if they were hers or someone else's. Her bloated lifejacket made it hard to hold on.

She lifted her head up to see where the yelling was coming from. That's when she saw the top of her mother's head, her eyes wide with fear, her mouth open, gasping for breath while another wave sent her under. Her mother's long white fingers – artist's fingers, Hannah thought – broke the surface again, grasping for something that wasn't there. This was the part of the dream where she would see her father, pure panic on his face, reaching for her mother as she went under. He'd be terrified as he lost sight of her, separated again by the fury of the ocean. Only this time that didn't happen. This time her father never showed.

A hand broke the surface of the water a short distance from where Hannah lay on the hull of the boat. She wasn't a toddler anymore. And the bulky orange life jacket was no longer strapped across her chest. The rocking of the boat had almost ceased and the size of the waves had mostly diminished. Hannah pushed herself onto her knees, waiting for fingers to break the surface of the water. She was bigger now; she could save her. But where was her father? Why wasn't he there?

The top of a head broke the surface, a hand clasping at thin air.

It was Mike. He reached out to her as his head bobbed up and down in the water. His fingers, thicker than her mother's, stretched towards the boat just out of reach.

"Mike!" Hannah yelled, surprised. The waves had almost ceased, but he struggled to keep his head above water, as if invisible hands were pulling him down.

"Mike!" She shuffled her body closer to the edge of the boat, stretching her arm over the side, trying desperately to reach him. For a moment, her eyes focussed on her wedding and engagement ring, on a hand stretched towards the very man who had given them to her.

Pure terror filled his face. Water washed over him again. Warm tears rolled down her cheeks. For all she was trying, she couldn't reach him. He was centimetres out of reach.

Mike's struggling grew weaker. Hannah scanned wildly for something, anything to save him. She couldn't lose him this way.

A firm, heavy hand planted itself on her shoulder, startling her for a moment. Then came warm breath by her ear as a voice whispered, "It's okay, you can let him go. He wasn't meant for you anyway." Liquid calm spread through her limbs. The tickle of the voice remained in her ear, and she sat straighter, withdrawing her outstretched hand and watching calmly as the face of her shocked husband slipped for a final time beneath the waves. Fat, soundless tears wet her cheeks as she turned her head to see who had broken the spell. Her eyes met those of melted amber pools, which she instantly fell into as they peered into her soul. They were eyes full of love and empathy and knowing.

"No," she whispered aloud, turning to focus back on the place she had last seen Mike. The water was deadly calm now. He had gone.

CHAPTER 33

She woke with a start, heart beating hard against her ribcage. Her dream, still a living entity of the world she woke to, took a moment for it to fade, for those two worlds to become one.

A rooster crowed somewhere in the distance, and she knew the sun was out even before opening her eyes. She blinked a few times to make sure she wasn't still dreaming. No more filthy jacuzzi, no abandoned resort room, and no Amiri. The last realisation hit the hardest.

She had fallen asleep. Beside him.

God, she thought.

And now here she was, sitting against a wall between potted hibiscus plants, on a cold tile floor. Clean tile. Tile she recognised. Tile very near to her and Mike's Garden Suite.

Her bag lay beside her within arm's reach. Putting it over her shoulder, she stood up to make sure her bearings were correct. She was right. The stairs were behind her. If she continued down the terrace, her room would be just around the corner.

How the hell did I get here? she wondered.

Looking down, she saw she still wore the same clothes as the night before. So that had happened; she and Mike had gone out for dinner. Had there really been all that drama with the protestors? And her fight with Mike; was that real too?

She reached up for her locket, rolling it between her fingers. "Oh, God," she whispered again. What the hell was going on?

Hannah turned around, leaning on the balustrade to peer out across the resort. It was exactly as she remembered from this direction. But something felt different.

A moment passed before she realised what it was. The garden was there, and the rooftops of other distant resorts. But everything looked so calm, so untouched by the savagery of the previous night's weather. Surely with the way the wind had blown and the rain had pelted down, there would be debris, palm tree fronds or even overturned beach loungers. But there was nothing.

The sky was clear and calm, the sun in the distance just beginning to rise. Early morning, then. She could only guess how she looked, even if she had imagined the extremes of the weather, the raw flood of emotions she had gone through the night before wasn't imagined. No way to keep the stress off her face. She cringed at the thought of anyone seeing her like this. Her cheeks flamed as her stomach dropped in remembering that Amiri had. He had seen her at her absolute worse.

If she hadn't dreamt it all, of course.

There was nothing else for it but to seek sanctuary in her room. To hell with Mike.

A lump bubbled up in her throat at the thought. Was she still angry with him? No. She hurt. She had never felt so unwanted. So second best to his job. Worse, this was supposed to be their honeymoon. This trip was meant to be about them, wasn't it?

Swallowing down her emotion, she pulled her fingers

through her hair and used the cleanest corner of her shirt to wipe any mascara smudges from under her eyes. Putting her handbag over her shoulder, she pushed back her shoulders as resolutely as possible. She would not cower. She would march in, clean herself up, have a shower, pack her bags and organise a shuttle to the airport. From there she would wait it out until she could get a flight out, and from there … she had no idea.

One step at a time, she told herself.

She headed down the corridor, turned around the corner and paused for a moment outside of their room. The key. God, she hoped she hadn't lost it. Taking a moment to fumble in her purse, she located it. As quietly as she could, hoping beyond hope the room was empty, she slipped it into the card slot and pulled down on the handle, pushing it open with a deep inhale.

He was waiting for her, jumping up from the sofa as soon as she entered the room. His hair was tousled, eyes red and puffy. A pained expression of remorse covered his face. Seeing him like this emotionally winded her.

"Hannah," he breathed, taking a step towards her, arms outstretched then quickly dropped them to his side. His lips moved, trying to form words, struggling to know what to say next.

Hannah said nothing. Her legs felt cemented to the ground. Part of her wanted to rush to him, throw her arms around him and forget everything that had happened. Another part of her wanted to turn around and walk out, repelled by the man before her.

"I am so, so sorry," he said. "I never should have said any of those things. I was so worried about you." The words tumbled out in a flood of repentance.

Hannah didn't move.

"Are you okay?" he tried again, softer this time, shaking her from her reverie.

"Hannah?" Genuine concern showed on his face. He, too, seemed almost anchored to the spot, as if he was too scared to move any closer.

"I need a shower," she said, meeting his eyes before heading straight for the bathroom, closing and locking the door behind her. She turned on the shower tap and let the tears fall, choking back her sobs so he wouldn't hear her. Unable to bring herself to look in the mirror, she let the room steam up before dropping her clothes in a pile on the ground and stepping into the warm waterfall. With her eyes closed, she imagined the water washing away everything. Their whole honeymoon. Their argument. The whole night and its uncertainty. Dirty water spiralled down the plug hole at her feet.

She stayed there a long time. How long she didn't know, but like a zombie she stood still, letting the water run down her head, her face, her body before she even had the energy to wash her hair. When she did eventually turn off the shower, she had to admit she felt marginally better.

Though she still wanted to leave, she would pull herself together and listen to what he had to say. Hannah looked down at the rings on her finger. He would get it, surely. It would be okay. Just like Amiri said.

Wrapping a towel around her, she finished drying her hair and putting on the bare minimum of makeup before stepping into her robe and opening the bathroom door into the bedroom. Mike was waiting for her there.

"Hi," he said nervously. "Can we talk now?" Dark circles underlined his eyes. He patted the end of the bed beside him.

She sat down and licked her lips. Her mouth felt dry.

"I really am sorry," he started. "I don't know why I got so angry, and I never should have said the things I did." He paused, but she really didn't know what to say.

He continued in her silence. "You mean the world to me. I was so scared when you didn't come home last night. Where were you?"

She thought for a moment. What could she tell him? That she slept in a non-existent room, with a man she had only met a couple of times, in a dirty old jacuzzi? Or that she slept on the terrace outside their room?

"I went for a walk," she said instead, hoping to drop the subject. She had never been in the habit of lying, and didn't want to start now, not to her husband.

Her *husband*.

Her eyes teared up again. Stay strong, she thought.

"I want us to leave," she said with a firmness she hoped belied the storm of emotions beneath the surface.

"You know it's not that easy, Han." Mike sighed heavily, running a hand through his hair. "This resort means a lot to us, to our family. The money…"

Hannah's shoulders drooped at his response.

"I know this hasn't been the honeymoon we planned—"

"Not the one *I* planned," Hannah said.

Confusion etched Mike's brow.

"You knew this wasn't the honeymoon I wanted, but I did it for you. For your family's business."

"Our business," he interjected.

Hannah ignored him. "I went along with it because that's

what spouses do. It was important to you so … we're here. But something is wrong with this place, Mike. Surely you see now?"

"Look, Hannah. Yes, there have been some birthing pains, but it's only a few days until the opening. We can get through this. Make it work."

"Make what work, Mike? The resort or us?" She twisted her wedding ring on her finger. She hadn't meant it to sound as harsh as it did. It wasn't meant to be an ultimatum.

Mike held still, and goosebumps crept beneath Hannah's skin as something flashed in his eyes. But as quickly as it burned, it disappeared again.

Mike sighed. "I get it," he said. "It's our honeymoon, and I keep getting pulled away to deal with resort stuff. It's not fair on you. So why don't we just take today, enjoy each other's company, and we'll see how you feel tomorrow morning. If you still have your heart on leaving, we'll make the arrangements and … we'll make it happen, I guess."

Hannah wasn't convinced. She wanted so much for them to go back to how things were. Back to enjoying each other's company. She could give him that, couldn't she? One more day? And if she still felt like leaving in the morning, she would. She pushed away the niggling fact he hadn't explicitly said whether he'd be coming with her.

He must have seen the cracks form in her armour because he took her hand in his, gently bringing it up to his mouth and kissing it.

"I really am sorry," he said again. "I never want to hurt you."

"I know," she said. "Okay. Let's try to enjoy today. Then we can decide in the morning." The small sense of relief surprised her. Amiri's image flashed through her mind – being wrapped in his arms, crying while she felt herself break. Who was she staying for?

She bit her lip.

CHAPTER 34

Few other people were in the Moonlight Bistro when they finally made it down for breakfast. Mike had returned to his usual playful self, determined, Hannah thought, to get her to change her mind about leaving.

They ate breakfast with Mike carrying most of the conversation. Hannah did her best to be present, but thoughts of the night before kept invading her mind. She tried pushing them away, but so many things troubled her, and it went beyond her argument with Mike. She saw those shadows closing in. Heard the drums amongst a building wind. Felt Amiri's hands gripping her arms, pulling her to him as she felt she would crumble into the earth. Surely, she hadn't imagined the resort ruins. Or the rain. Or falling asleep in a dilapidated jacuzzi against this other man's chest, only to wake in the foyer outside her room. But no signs remained of the storm Hannah had experienced the night before. *Had* she imagined it?

"So …" Mike began, making a face. "I have to check in with Mariana about last night?"

"Last night?" Hannah asked, surprised. How was it Mariana's business?

"About the protest?" Mike finished, a line appearing

between his eyebrows.

"Oh, yeah. Of course," Hannah said with relief. She had forgotten about the protest. It felt like another lifetime ago. The torches, the police, Mike hitting a protester. How the hell had she forgotten that?

Mike's shoulders relaxed.

"I can just go back to the room or something?" she said.

"I won't be long. Just want to fill her in on it all. Then we can head off into town. Walk around the markets or something, if you like." He was trying.

Hannah gave him a weak smile back. "Sounds great," she said, not feeling it.

"And I have to make a statement at the police station. It won't take long," he said hurriedly. He kept his eyes on hers.

"I understand," she said, hoping her face conveyed as much. She still felt numb, but she'd give him today, like she'd promised.

He searched her face, and she squirmed in her chair, uncomfortable under the scrutiny. It was hard to know what he was thinking exactly. But whatever it was, he quickly covered it up with one of his wide grins.

"God, I love you," he whispered, reaching across to hold her hand, tracing her wedding and engagement ring with his thumb.

They got up to leave, and Mike gently pulled her towards him, lightly brushing her lips with his own. Something defrosted inside her. He was good, she reminded herself.

Mike headed towards the reception area while Hannah made her way out the front of the bistro, ready to head back to their room. Instead, she kept walking. Past the staircase, down the path, almost to the beach but angling off through

Rua's gardens towards the rock.

She assumed she'd find Rua where she always found him; kneeling in front of the cracked commemorative stone in the gardens. She was taken aback when she rounded the corner to find the path before her bare. Rua wasn't there.

It was ridiculous; she chided herself. It wasn't like he didn't have other parts of the resort to tend to. Disappointment hit her anyway.

She had so many questions, and if she was going to leave tomorrow, she wanted as many of them answered as possible. Rua had seemed like the best bet to do so. He might even know Amiri; might know how she could contact him, thank him for looking after her for the second time in a row.

A sigh escaped her lips. What the hell was wrong with her? She moved closer to the commemorative stone. The ugly jagged scar still cut through the stone, slicing it in two. The metal plate seemed to be the only thing holding the rock together. The etched words were still visible on its smooth surface.

Hannah bent down for a closer inspection. Something about it both tugged at her and repelled her at the same time. Rua had called it a cancer.

The gravel crunched under her feet as she crouched. Eyeing the surrounding vegetation, she saw this was the only spot the plants weren't flourishing. Hannah knew next to nothing about horticulture, but even she could see something was very wrong with the plants near the rock. No flowers bloomed, only long, twisted stems and blackened leaves. Previously they had all grown towards the rock as if by magnetic force, now they all arched away as if it were poisonous to touch.

Though the rock itself was a nondescript dark grey, raw

and unpolished, something about it made her stomach twist with nausea. Was it possible this had been the noise waking the resort two nights ago? Hannah shivered, goosebumps prickling her skin. Cautiously, she reached forward with her hand, wanting to touch the commemorative plaque as if doing so would reveal the answers she wanted. Her fingers lightly brushed across the etched writing. It was ice cold despite the hot Kulani sun. The nausea strengthened, making its way up her chest.

"Hey, I've been looking for you." Mike's voice cut through her trance, forcing her back to reality.

She withdrew her hand sharply as if stung, and the nausea receded. He'd given her a fright, and she rocked on her feet a little in her crouching position. She had to put a hand on the gravel to steady herself before pulling herself upright. A nervous giggle escaped in surprise.

"Hi," she said back. "I got side-tracked on the way to the room." Her heart clamoured a little in her chest, feeling guilty for being caught at the stone.

"I went back to the room to get you and you weren't there." His eyes narrowed on the rock. "Why are you here?"

Hannah tried to steady her racing heart. She didn't need to feel guilty. She had done nothing wrong. "I thought I'd stop off to say hi to Rua. He's normally here tending the plants," she said, stepping aside.

"Rua's away today. He's sick," Mike answered almost automatically, not taking his eyes off the area Hannah was trying to shield with her body. Mike walked closer, looking at the spot she had been hiding.

"The plants…" he said, his voice trailing off. It was true. They stood out in solemn contrast to the lush green foliage and bright pink blossoms of the rest of the garden.

"I know," she said, standing close beside him. "The last few times I've seen Rua, he's been tending to these plants. Something about them … they just … it's like they're dying…"

"Rotting from the inside," Mike finished for her.

"Yeah."

They stood in silence for a moment. She could tell Mike was a little unsettled. Whatever his thoughts about the stone and its superstitions, the state of the plants had caught him off guard.

CHAPTER 35

"Do you think it could have something to do with the commemorative stone?" Hannah whispered, frowning at the plants.

Mike's forehead crinkled again. "It's not possible," he said. "It's just a rock." He gave a little shudder and took a step back. "Look, no more talk about curses, okay. Just for today, let's just leave the curse thing alone and try to enjoy the day together."

She could tell he had tried to tone down the sharpness of his tone, but it still bit through, regardless. Feeling chastised, Hannah took a small step away from him.

Mike flashed his teeth, the corners of his eyes not quite crinkling. "Still up for exploring the markets?" he asked. Subject change.

"Sure," she said, struggling to push away her unease. "Is Rua okay?" Hannah couldn't shift gears as fast as Mike. There was more to this stone – this resort – than Mike might admit, and Hannah's need to find out more was growing.

"I guess so. Mariana said he had called in sick. It's the first time he ever has. Which she found odd. But he's a hard worker, that man, so you can hardly begrudge him a day off, sick or not." Mike chuckled, his moods changing so fast it made Hannah dizzy.

He moved closer to her, placing his arm around her waist as he led her back down the path towards the resort.

"If you're worried, we can always stop in and check on him on the way back from town. I've been to his house before. But let's head into town first, okay?"

Hannah nodded. Part of her looked forward to exploring the markets. It would be a welcome distraction. Hannah relaxed a little.

The market was easy to spot. Utes, motorcycles and scooters all lined the left side of the road as they neared the centre of the town. Locals and tourists amassed in a buzzing throng of activity, weaving their way in and out of small tented areas. Hannah and Mike found a spot further down the road where they could pull their vehicles up on the grassy curb. After climbing off his scooter and hiding his helmet in the under-seat compartment, Mike turned to Hannah.

"Why don't you have a look around while I head over to the police station?" He pointed further down the road to the large concrete building where they had earlier received their scooter licenses. "I'll meet you back here in an hour. It'll save you getting bored at the station."

Hannah battled a quick succession of emotions. Annoyance that they had just arrived and Mike was already off, and relief she wouldn't have to sit around in the police station while Mike rehashed the events of the night before.

"That's fine," she said. "See you in an hour."

Mike placed his hands on her shoulders and gave her a quick kiss on the top of her head. "Love you," he said.

"Love you too," she said as he turned around and crossed the road. She stood there for a moment, watching him.

Mike was fifteen minutes late in getting back. Hannah

barely noticed. She was enjoying herself. She liked being a faceless tourist lost within the bustle of visitors and locals, all sampling the local wares: clothes, fruit and vegetables, sarongs in brightly coloured fabric, artwork, hand carved nick-knacks, jewellery and other bits and pieces. The place buzzed with conversation and laughter. Everyone, to Hannah's mind, looked like they were there because they wanted to be. She had walked around all the stalls at least six times, only purchasing two pairs of shell earrings, one set for herself and one set for her aunt.

"How was it?" Mike asked on arriving back at the scooters.

"Great," Hannah said. "I wish you'd been able to see it all." And she meant it. She had enjoyed herself, but part of her mourned not having Mike by her side.

Mike's lips curved. "I'm glad. I've seen it all before, but it's nice you checked it all out."

Hannah had forgotten. None of this was new to him, like it was to her. This was her first time at Kulani, not his. "How did it go at the station?" she asked, wanting to push the thought aside.

"Fine. They let the last of the protestors go this morning. They've all had some stern talking to's and have a thirty day no-trespass notice against them for coming onto the property."

"Thirty days? That doesn't seem like a lot. Were there charges laid against them? They could have burnt the place down last night. They put people's lives at risk." Hannah couldn't believe they'd be let off so easily.

"No charges. They didn't hurt anyone." Mike shrugged. "Well, not badly anyway. These things spiral sometimes, but they weren't really going to burn anything down. The police around here, they know them. All bark, no bite. In thirty days, the resort will be open to the public and they'll see there's no curse, and then they'll be off to find some other crusade to champion for."

It surprised Hannah Mike was being so relaxed about it. He still had a slight red bruise on the side of his jaw, and she suspected his hand still hurt underneath the layer of bandages.

It felt nice to be back on the scooters. The breeze tamed the sun's warmth, and Hannah's confidence on the scooter was increasing with every trip, allowing her more time to enjoy her surroundings while they rode.

Rua's house was nestled amongst trees off a back road circling the interior of the island. Like many other houses on the island, it was a modest rectangular building that looked arbitrarily plonked on a piece of land with little thought to aesthetics. Its once white cladding had turned a grey green from the elements. Over grown jungle-like brush and tall grass grew around the house, a stark contrast to the particularness of the gardens Rua cared for at the resort. A coconut shell wind chime hung from the roof's slight overhang above the entrance, swaying in the breeze with a hollow wooden melody. The blinds were drawn in the window facing the road. On closer inspection, they appeared more like sheets of patterned fabric than curtains.

Hannah and Mike rode their scooters up the small driveway, parking beside Rua's white ute. A shovel and an array of shoes of various sizes littered the ground around the front door.

The door was slightly ajar.

"Hello," Mike called, simultaneously knocking on the door frame. "Rua? It's Mike and Hannah. We wanted to make sure you were okay?"

The two of them waited for a moment before a shuffling

sound came from inside. To Hannah's surprise, the formidable form of a rather large woman blocking the doorway greeted them. Furrowed deep brow. Sky-blue dress with white printed flowers. Her thick fingers grasped the doorframe before a wave of recognition washed over her face.

"Mr Mike!" she said, throwing the door back in enthusiasm and engulfing Hannah's husband in a giant bear hug, almost lifting him clear from the ground.

"Liana!" Mike responded with equal exuberance; his arms pinned to his sides. He gasped for breath when Liana returned him to the ground and loosened her embrace.

"This is my wife, Hannah," Mike said, gesturing in her direction.

Hannah managed an awkward smile and a wave of her fingers. "Hi," she said, unsure what the response would be. Within seconds she was also trapped against the ample bosom of their hostess, her own arms pinned to her side by Liana's giant arms. She murmured something in welcome that Hannah couldn't quite catch, as her ears were smothered against her chest, wrapped in a bear hug. After what felt a considerable time, she released Hannah, but only to arm's length. The larger woman eyed her up and down as if she were a doll brought to her as a gift.

"Ahh, Mrs Mike. So beautiful." She beamed in Mike's direction, showing a clear gap between her two front teeth. Hannah felt the colour rise to the surface of her face, unaccustomed to such flamboyant attention.

"Hannah," Mike said. "This is Liana. She's a friend of Rua's."

Hannah murmured an uncomfortable greeting as Liana let her go to stand beside Mike, who protectively placed an arm around her shoulders. He brushed his lips against Hannah's hair. Liana grasped her hands to her heart in response.

"Ah, blessed love birds, come in, come in. Mr Rua! We have company!" She yelled behind her into the depths of the house.

"We don't want to intrude," Mike quickly interrupted, "We just wanted to make sure Rua was okay, Mariana said he had called in sick."

"Ah, Mr Mike." Liana shook her head. "Aye, he's sick but no excuse not to receive guests. Come, come." She turned, holding her hand out, waving for them to follow her as she moved deeper into the bowels of the house.

The hallway opened into a small living room with an attached kitchen. Brightly coloured handwoven rugs crisscrossed the floor. Hand-painted artwork of various plants and the typical sea-and-sunset scenes adorned the walls. A seventies-style steel-and-laminate yellow kitchen table sat to one side of the room. Two dark-green lounge chairs with wooden arms sat against the other wall. Rua reclined in one. He wore knee-length shorts and a dirty white T-shirt with a faded palm tree and sea scene on it. Rua looked older than the day before, his face unshaven and stubbly. His eyes more aged than Hannah remembered.

"Mr Rua, sit up, man! You have guests!" Liana went about fussing around him, propping an extra cushion behind his back, and moving the footstool away to the side so Rua was no longer reclined. Rua ignored the fussing and welcomed them with his usual enthusiasm.

"Mrs O," he said to Hannah first, his eyes dully twinkling. The edge of his mouth turned upward. "Mr O, sit, sit," he said, gesturing to the other armchair and the kitchen chairs. "That's enough, Liana," he said, warmly. Liana had continued to flutter around him. "Maybe you could get our guests some drinks?" he said, sending Liana off to the nearby kitchen.

"There's really no need," Hannah protested. Mike stayed a hand on her arm, a quiet sign it would be rude to protest.

"Sit, sit," Rua gestured again.

"How are you feeling, Rua?" Mike asked, easing himself onto a chair.

The banging of cupboard doors and the knocking of glasses together came from the direction of the kitchen. Hannah was torn between offering to help Liana or to stay where she was and talk with Rua. She had so many questions she wanted to ask him, although it wasn't necessarily the right time. Any question she asked would pique Mike's interest, and she had promised him no talk about curses.

"I'm fine, I'm fine." Rua tut tutted. "I'll be back to work tomorrow, Mr O. Don't you worry." He and Hannah shared a grin.

"No need, Rua. You know that. I'd rather you take your time and get healthy. The grounds will survive a few days without you."

"Huh!" came the reply from the kitchen. "There's no use telling 'em that; he won't believe it for a second."

"Ah, hush, woman," Rua replied with a good-natured chuckle. Whoever Liana was to Rua, they were close. Best friends? Siblings maybe? Hannah wondered if they always ribbed each other like this, even without guests to entertain.

Liana came back with a tray holding glasses of what appeared to be orange juice. Hannah gratefully accepted the glass. Despite the windows being open, the heat was stifling in the small room.

Liana plonked herself down in a spare chair, and the four of them made small talk about the island and the cultural performance, carefully avoiding all talk of the resort. As the conversation turned to Mike's business back home, Hannah's mind wandered.

Liana must have noticed as she interrupted. "Let's leave these two to shop talk, huh?" she said to Hannah. "I have something I think will be perfect for you. We'll make an islander out of you yet." She gave a wink.

CHAPTER 36

Hannah placed her empty glass in the kitchen sink as she followed Liana to a room at the very end of the narrow hallway. It was set up with a single bed pushed up against the window, where a colourful pink-and-orange sarong acted as a curtain to block out the full bite of the sun.

A wooden dresser stood beside what Hannah suspected was a small closet. A square mirror sat atop of the dresser, its back leaning against the wall. On the other corner of the room, under the window, directly in front of the door, was a cane chair with a pile of linens. On the wall above it were three framed photos. One drew Hannah's attention right away, but she held back from studying it as Liana swung back the wardrobe door and started rummaging loudly amongst the items hanging there.

"I know it's in 'ere somewhere. As soon as I saw ya I knew it would be perfect." She was bending over now, the girth of her bottom blocking any chance of Hannah seeing what she was doing exactly.

"Ah-ha!" she said, swinging around with a beautiful piece of azure and purple fabric in her hand. She held it out in front of her, letting Hannah see the full extent of the fabric littered with a beautiful purple-and-white flower design. A sarong, Hannah assumed at first glance.

"This will look beautiful on you. Make you a real islander," she said, passing it to Hannah. Not knowing what to do with it, she held up the rectangular piece of fabric in front of her body. The colours were so vibrant, and Hannah couldn't help but love it. Still, it took her by surprise that Liana was gifting it to her.

"It's beautiful!" she said, "But it's too much, it's—"

"Nonsense," Liana said, hands on her hips. "As soon as you walked through the door with Mr Mike, I knew this pareu was meant for you. Come on, let me show you how to use it," she said.

It was weird having someone fuss over her. Weirder still to have a complete stranger order her down to her underwear and bra. Hannah was thankful she had given up both for a bikini top and bottoms that morning for no other reason than if she wanted to strip off to sunbathe, she'd be already dressed for it. Still, it made her feel weird to be standing there so exposed.

Liana talked the entire time. "You're too skinny," she said, poking her in the ribs as she held the fabric length ways in front of Hannah. She chatted about her nieces – of which it sounded like she had a few – and how many of them were dancers, and all the different ways you could wear a pareu, and how once one of her nieces hadn't tied hers properly and it came undone right there on stage during a performance. Her niece continued on in her underwear as if nothing had happened, and the applause had been deafening. Liana's hands quickly tied two corners of the fabric into a double knot and placed it over Hannah's head so it hung almost like an apron.

Pulling the fabric where it hung at Hannah's waist, Liana tugged it around Hannah's back and tied another knot, letting the fabric fall to cover Hannah's butt.

"All done," she said proudly, twirling Hannah in a circle so she could admire her handy work from all directions.

Hannah couldn't help but smile at the women's warmth and exuberance.

"Let me get ya mirror so you can see yourself," Liana said, making to leave.

"Oh, it's okay, I can just use this one here," Hannah said, moving towards the one sitting atop of the dresser.

"Pfft!" Liana replied. "You'll see nothing but ya face in that one. You wait 'ere, I'll be back in a moment." Liana left the room, leaving Hannah alone. She ran the palms of her hands down her sides, the fabric thin and soft. Her eyes caught the photos hanging above the chair and she drew closer to get a better look.

There were three, two smaller photos flanking a larger one, which was the one she was drawn to. It was a black-and-white photo in a simple black frame. A posed photo, a family portrait. There was a friendliness, a feeling of deep love from the people in it, obvious from the arms slipped around waists and the big smiles. Hannah scanned the faces. Taken a great deal of time ago, it included at least four generations, by Hannah's estimation. The patriarch sat front centre. An old man, one of the few not smiling, solemn and somehow both frail and powerful. Hannah's heart skipped a beat when she saw what he held in his hand. A stick. Like the one she had seen in her dream, her nightmare where an old man had used a stick to curse the commemorative stone at the resort. She swallowed hard. Could it be the same person? She peered closer, trying to see past the graininess of the photo. It could be him. He appeared older, weaker. No. That had been a dream, she reminded herself. It was a coincidence, nothing more.

In front of the man were several children. A few babies and toddlers, and a young boy who might have been about nine years old. Damn it, she thought. One toddler also looked familiar, like the girl from the same dream, and yes, there was her mother, further back. Hannah's heart thudded heavily in her chest. How was that possible? It was a dream. She continued scanning the photo. Behind the man to his right was another face she recognised. This one she could make sense of. Rua. She was sure of it. Younger, but she could still tell by his broad smile, and even in the photo the twinkle in his eye was clear. She grinned affectionately towards the old man. He hadn't changed at all. His very presence allowed her a moment of calm. The rest had been pure coincidence; she was sure of it. Her mind playing tricks on her.

Until she saw him.

Way over on the left, nearer to the back, with two other young men. She would have recognised him anywhere. His eyes. The quirking upwards of the corner of his mouth. His lips. He was wearing the shirt he had worn the first time they met when he pulled her out of the pool, saving her from drowning. It was Amiri, no doubt about it. Appearing exactly as he had only the night before. Untouched by time. The blood drained from her face, her heart racing faster now, beating against her rib cage like it was trying to escape. Cold sweat broke out along the back of her neck. It wasn't possible.

None of it was possible.

CHAPTER 37

"'Ere we are," a loud voice broke into the room. "Let's have a look at ya then."

Hannah turned around slowly, as if in a dream. Liana stood there. Her full form taking up most of the doorway. A narrow, full-length mirror held against her chest. Hannah's reflection bounced back to her. All she saw was the fear on a drawn white face. For a moment, she thought she was going to faint as black spots danced in front of her eyes. It was so warm in here, her mind panicked. She needed to get out.

Liana must have noticed something was wrong at the same time.

"Aue!" she said, quickly leaning the mirror up against the wall, grabbing Hannah by the hand and leading her to the bed. Sitting her down, she pushed Hannah's head between her knees. Hannah gulped in a big lungful of air, willing the feeling of faintness to disappear. She could feel Liana's warm body beside her, her hand holding back her hair, like one would if they were going to throw up.

As the black dots disappeared, Hannah pulled herself up to a sitting position, embarrassed she had caused such a scene.

"Oh, my dear," Liana started. "I was sure you'd seen a ghost." She let out a little chuckle.

"I think I might of," Hannah whispered, shaking her head at the thought. Liana went quiet.

"You'd better tell me all about it," she said with a motherly sternness.

Hannah took a deep breath. She had a million questions and now was as good a time as any to have some of them answered.

"That photo," Hannah said, pointing to where it hung on the wall. "The large one." She paused, struggling for the words. "I… I've seen some of those people."

Liana let out a loud guffaw of laughter. "Of course, you have," she said, getting up and taking the photo off the wall. She plonked herself back down beside Hannah, holding the photo on her lap for Hannah to see.

"See right 'ere, well that's Rua." She poked a thick finger at Rua's face and let out another chuckle. "I don't think you will 'ave seen any of the others, but there'll be no mistakin' Rua. I swear he hasn't aged in thirty years."

Hannah had to agree. Although he looked younger than the man she had left chatting with her husband in the other room, there was no disputing the fact he held his age well. Hannah shook her head, though, and sucked in a deep breath. Now or never, she thought.

"Who's this?" she said, pointing to the face of Amiri. She was sure it was him. Her blood chilled a little at seeing him so clearly in a photo taken such a long time before.

"Aue." Liana said. "Well, that one's a story, he is."

Hannah waited with bated breath, trying to talk her heartbeat down to a respectable pace within her chest. She wrung her fingers and played with her wedding ring.

"He was Rua's nephew. Such a good boy, that one," she said

with a slight shake of her head.

"Was?" Hannah asked, suppressing a shiver.

"Aye, it's a sad story." Liana chewed on her lip. "You would've heard about the curse, eh?"

"On the Rest Easy?"

"Yes, yes, on the land. Aue. That name, though. Whose idea was it?" Liana said. "Who names a resort after a platitude you pay someone who's grieving? It's not right, but then … there's not much right about that place." Liana's voice had dropped. All hint of humour bubbling beneath the surface had left.

"Well, ya might have heard of the curse, but I wonder how much you've heard is true, and how much is malarky. So, let me tell you it right. We don't like talking about it 'round here, but something has you spooked, so I'm a gonna take a chance on you." She gave Hannah a cursory glance, as if checking she was doing the right thing.

"Well, it goes back some time, it does. Back to the eighteen hundreds, in fact. The land used to belong to the Tangaroa family. The land neighboured the Wallaces' place. They were a white family, came over with the missionaries, they did. And More Tangaroa and Robert Wallace, well, over time they became best buddies, always fishing together, planting their crops. Their families were close. So close in fact that More's daughter Moana and Robert's son William they fell in love. The tried their best to hide it from their families. More already had plans for who his only daughter would marry, and friendship or no, it was not a white man."

Hannah listened, intrigued, not knowing how this had anything to do with Amiri's face appearing in a photo taken a few decades ago.

"Well, one day a quarrel broke out, eh? Some say it was

over land boundaries, others say it was over a gambling debt. Whatever it was, those two men dug at each other from that point on. One night, words were had. Maybe it was that they'd learnt Moana was pregnant."

Hannah cringed, suspecting the story didn't end well.

"It was said Moana and her mama watched as the two men fought it out, and then one of the guns let fire. And there on the ground lay Moana with her mama's arms wrapped around her, bleeding out from a hole in her belly. The gun shot drew enough attention to bring William, young Billy, running from the Wallace house. Can ya imagine? There he was, a young boy all of nineteen watching the love of his life bleeding out on the ground and his father and her father standing there looking like the idiots they were, in shock."

"How awful," Hannah said. "Could they save her?"

"Such a tragedy." Liana shook her head. "Nah, Moana and her baby passed where they were. Billy was heartbroken. Aye, they all were, but both men – they blamed the other. Over her dying body, they continued to brawl. Billy tried to break it up, but it was Mama Tangaroa who ended it. Aye. You don't mess with Mama. She was known as a medicine woman on the island. A woman of great power, she could talk to spirits and the like, and she was *mad*." Liana shook her head again, a tear escaping her eye.

"So she cursed the spot where her daughter and grandchild were killed. Cursed their land and the Wallaces'. Nothing could flourish there. These men and their ego's, for whatever reason, their falling out cost the life of her most loved. In the moment, she cared nothing for the effect the curse would have on her or any future generations. Oh, yes, she was angry. So nothing, *nothing*, not money, nor business, nor relationship can flourish on that land. It is dead, eh? Barren. It's where things go to die."

Hannah shuddered. "And that's where the resort is?" she asked in a whisper. "But I thought the curse took place much later."

"Aye, well, that's the second curse. The land has been twice cursed. The first curse, was put in place by Rua's grandmother. It was his father who revived it. See, both that land and the Wallaces' fell into ruin within ten years. Uninhabitable. It hadn't been lived on for long. Over time, the government, they claimed it for their own and sold it out under Rua's family to some overseas investors. And they went about breaking ground for a fancy resort. This part you probably know, eh?"

She eyed Hannah, who gave a small nod. "Some, I guess. It was the Cooks Hotel Resort, right?" she said.

"Yeah." Liana nodded. "So they made a big thing of it, see. Promised lots of jobs, promised the island economy would flourish. Promises, promises." She waved her hand dismissively. "So, they did this big thing, eh? The mayor was there, got some locals to dress up and perform, and these business guys, they did their little spiels and what not. Showed off this stone with a plaque and all to celebrate their breaking ground."

Hannah swallowed hard. This was all sounding too familiar.

"Then Moana's younger brother, Rawiri, all grown up—" She poked a finger at the older man centre-front. "He was Rua's father, he was. Well, he took the tokutoku stick, and he brought it down on that stone in front of everyone. He reset the curse, eh, and cracked the stone while doing so."

"I've seen this," Hannah whispered, her hands noticeably white with how hard she was wringing them.

Liana looked at her quizzically. "No, dear, that was a long time ago, only a little while before this photo was taken."

"I dreamt it," Hannah said. She needed to tell someone. It made no sense that something she had dreamt was true.

"Aue," Liana said, her face drawn.

Recognising a few more faces, Hannah pointed to them, a beautiful woman standing to the side of Rua, and a little girl sitting in the front with a big grin on her face.

"They were there too," she said, pointing to both of them.

"Aye, I suspect they were. This here's Meilani, Rua's niece, and you've met this one." She chuckled. "Oh, she's a fiery one, this one." She pointed at the little girl. "This one's Awhina."

The shocks kept coming. This little girl was Awhina, the woman who's protesting had caused so much trouble for the resort.

"But you," Liana said, pausing before shifting her finger towards the figure Hannah had first questioned her about. "You want to know about Amiri."

Amiri. Just the sound of his name sent shivers through her. There's no way it could be him. His father, maybe?

"This curse, aye. It's real. And it's a bugger. It hurts everyone. It doesn't care if you're family or not. These things, when you unleash them, they take on a life of their own, and there's not much you can do but get outta the way. Well, Amiri, he wasn't like that. Stubborn like his uncle, he was. See, Amiri was Rua's nephew, Meilani's brother. He musta been almost thirty here. Well, his sister, she was dead set against the resort being built, eh? Most of the family was. You don't go building nothing on land where blood's spilt, let alone cursed. And those white investors, they shoulda had no claim to it, but the government saw an opportunity and took it I guess." She shook her head again.

"Amiri, he didn't believe in curses or the like. So he got himself a job, working on the construction site, eh? With a group of his mates, he helped build the thing. Most of the labour came from overseas and whatnot, but for a moment the government did right, created jobs for its people, and Amiri took 'em up on it." Liana paused, lost momentarily in the past, Hannah thought.

"But things started happening, aye. Bad things. It started small. Quarrels and such. Then came sightings. Strange animals. White pigs. A white cow."

"A white cow?" Hannah asked, with a sharp intake of breath, remembering the first time she'd stumbled on the resort. The old resort. The one that couldn't actually be there.

"Aye. There was no one to account for them. Some locals thought they were spirits or ancestors giving warnings, but commerce don't stop for any spirit. And the white guys, they just saw dollar signs, and they were in a rush too, aye. So it wasn't safe. Amiri and his crew used to tell stories of mounting injuries on the site.

"One of Amiri's friends near lost his whole hand. He was lucky it was only half a finger in the end. The site manager, he done himself in. Found 'im hanging in one of the rooms. Then one of the local children went missing – he had drowned in one of the pools there. It wasn't even full, just a bit of rain water, but the poor boy must've fallen, knocked his head and drowned anyway.

"Meilani begged her brother to quit. They'd lost their mum only a few years before, and she didn't want to lose Amiri. But he laughed it off. That's what he did, silly boy. He should've listened."

The air felt thick and humid. Sweat had broken out along Hannah's hairline, and she was beating back rising nausea. She wanted so badly to hear what happened to Amiri, another part of her wanted to race from the room, and leave.

It wasn't possible, she thought. No way could this be the same Amiri. Surely not. He would have aged more, and the ice in her veins told her there was no happy ending to Liana's story.

"He died, didn't he?" Hannah felt the words slip from her tongue. She needed to know.

"Aue," Liana said, wiping another tear. "He fell. That boy could climb coconut trees like no one. Been climbing since he could walk. But he was helping on the roof and just … fell. It was flat as anything, yet he got too close to the edge, lost his balance or something, and broke his neck. He was a special one too, eh? All he wanted was to make enough money to help his family. Meilani's man had left her, see, so he liked to help provide for her and his niece. Time's had been tough. He'd seen this job as a blessing. He had no wife or tamariki of his own. Silly boy, he was always waiting. Wanted his ducks in a row, eh? He coulda had anyone too, a boy like that. But he was a romantic, he was. Believed love was for life and all, but he waited too long." She lifted her shoulders and wiped another tear from her eye.

"Aww, no," she turned to Hannah. "I didn't mean to make you cry. It was a long time ago now. He'll be in a better place, eh?" Liana put a thick warm arm around Hannah's shoulder and pulled her in for a hug but kept talking. "And you know the rest of it, I suppose. Not long after, work on the resort stopped, the investors pulled their money. Rumours of it being dirty money and the likes made the rounds. I don't really know, but it stirred up mixed feelings around here, for sure. You can see why this new resort has been met with some ambivalence, eh?" She gave a gentle chuckle.

"I don't know that he is," Hannah mumbled.

Liana furrowed her eyebrows.

"You said he'd be in a better place. I don't know that he is," she said.

Liana frowned.

"Amiri," she added to clarify. "I've seen him."

CHAPTER 38

Liana pulled away. Her eyes narrowed and bore into Hannah's.

"Whatcha mean?" she said after some time.

"I've seen him … at the resort. Only it wasn't the resort, but its ruins, and … he said his name was Amiri." The words slipped out almost with a sigh of relief. "He's still there, or—" Hannah didn't know what to say. He couldn't be dead. Someone so alive could not be dead.

The colour slipped from Liana's face. "No," she said. "No."

"They look so similar…" Hannah's voice was thick with emotion.

"Oh, hell!" Liana said, interrupting her. "Not good. Not good at all! The stubborn fool. Aue!" Liana's bottom lip was trembling and her eyes wide with fear. Hannah felt her own heart race. She shouldn't have said anything. Now this woman was going to have a panic attack or tell Mike or worse, and it was her fault. As if reading her mind Liana asked, "How much does Mr Mike know?"

"About Amiri? Nothing," Hannah said. Or at least she thought he knew nothing.

"Okay, well, we'll keep it that way, huh? You say nothing to him, you hear. I know enough to know he don't think he suffers the supernatural. Ignorance is dangerous, eh? But you keep it to yourself, and you get him to leave. Blow the resort. It's just money, eh?

"If Amiri's shown himself to you, there's a reason, but you stay away. He's a good boy, and nothing will change that. But if he is there … it's done him no good; it won't do you none either. I do need to tell Rua, though. He should know, but I'll wait until you're gone, 'kay?"

"What does he need to know exactly?" Hannah asked. The story was overwhelming, but she wasn't willing to let it go so easily without knowing more. Especially about Amiri.

"You've seen Rua, eh? He's told me. You've seen him near the stone. You ever wonder what he's doing?"

"Looking after the plants?" she said.

"Aye, he cares for the plants, but there's more to it. He's part of the curse, eh? Through his bloodline. He's got some of Mama and Rawiri Tangaroa in him. So he looks after the place. He does what he can to temper the curse, keep the evil in its place. As best he can. But it takes it out of him. Takes a piece of him each time. Makes him sick.

"If you really 'ave seen Amiri, I bet he's doing the same thing, the silly boy – only from the other side. It's his bloodline as well. Too much like Rua, he was. It cost him his life. It shouldn't 'ave cost him his afterlife too."

Liana was right. She couldn't tell Mike. Not yet, anyway. Not any of it.

She'd seen a different side to him, and it wasn't a side she wanted to see again. They needed to leave, turn their back on the resort and walk away. She knew it within every fibre of her being. Just as she knew from the hollowness in her chest, she needed to see Amiri, one more time.

With deep breaths, Hannah reset her face. Smile. Fake it. She walked into the living room where Mike and Rua were talking. Mike stood up from his chair, eyes wide with appreciation. "Wow, you look amazing!"

"It is beautiful, isn't it?" she said, patting the fabric on her hips. She gave a small twirl to show off the pareu. It was show time. She could think about everything else later.

"Mr O is a lucky man," Rua said.

Liana stood with a hand held to her heart. She smiled, but her lower lip quivered.

"Liana, thank you so much," Hannah said, turning to the woman. "You really didn't have to."

"Nonsense," Liana said in response. "I know these things. It was waiting for you."

Hannah shivered. The pareu, the resort, or Amiri?

"Sorry we took so long." Hannah turned to Mike and Rua, hoping her face wasn't giving anything away. She wasn't sure how long she and Liana had been talking. It had felt like a lifetime ago that she had first entered their home.

"Mr O was telling me about some things I've been missing at the resort," Rua said, eyeing Hannah as if he had been privy to the entire conversation she had had with Liana. "I will have a talk with Awhina about it. I can't promise she'll listen to me, but she should know she's gone too far."

"Rua's told me that Awhina is his great niece," Mike said, turning to Hannah.

"Oh," Hannah replied, not letting on she already knew.

"Anyway, I think we've probably taken up enough of your time, Rua. You need some rest. Get yourself better. Thanks for the drink, Liana," Mike said to them both.

Rua pulled himself up from the armchair. His eyes still

sparkled with warmth despite the dire tiredness scarring his features. She could see now the family resemblance, particularly around the eyes, between him and Amiri.

As they said their goodbyes, Liana embraced Hannah in another big bear hug. "Look after yourself, Mrs Mike. It might be time to head home, eh?" she whispered, holding Hannah close. "Remember, if you can see them, they can see you." She released Hannah a little, holding her by the arms to inspect her. "Be safe," she said before stepping back to say her goodbyes to Mike.

Rua came forward to clasp Hannah's hands in his own. "Aww, it is always a pleasure to see you, Mrs O."

Hannah blushed. "I hope you feel better soon," she said.

"Oh yes," Rua said. "You take care, okay, and we'll talk soon."

He knew, Hannah thought. He knew, as if he had heard the whole conversation. Hannah leaned in and kissed the old man on the cheek before releasing his hands and heading with Mike towards their scooters.

From the scooter's seat, she pulled out her helmet and replaced it with her discarded clothes.

Turning around, she saw Liana and Rua were already heading back inside.

"Everything okay?" Mike said. "You were chatting with Liana a while."

"Yeah," Hannah said, unable to meet his eye. "She was showing me some family photos and things." It wasn't a complete lie. But everything was not fine. Not by a long shot. Something significant had changed. With her. With Mike. With their relationship. And she doubted there was any going back.

CHAPTER 39

The first few drops of rain hit Hannah's face as she followed close behind Mike on the way back to the resort. Heavy grey clouds had come from nowhere, hiding the sun from view. The weather forecast had hinted nothing but a beautiful tropical sunny day, but Hannah could feel something coming. Her skin goose-bumped with a chill that had risen unbidden in the air. She caught Mike's eye in his side mirror and indicated she was pulling over. Mike did the same a little further up from her. She walked up to meet him.

"I'm going to stop off at the supermarket. I want to get a few things before heading back. Is there anything you need?" she asked.

"Let me guess," he said. "Chocolate?" He grinned.

"Don't judge," she said playfully. Chocolate was her comfort food, and he did not understand how much comfort she needed right now.

"Nah, I'm good," he said. "Just be careful on the ride back. It feels like a change in the weather." Another few fat drops of water splattered on the ground in front of them as if to stress the fact.

"I'll be fine," she said, waving away his words.

Mike took her arm and pulled her towards him. "You are beautiful," he said.

Hannah could only imagine. Sure, the pareu might look good, but the big bulky white scooter helmet would not do her any favours in the fashion department.

He pulled her closer and gave her an awkward kiss on the lips, trying not to knock their helmets together, but failing. He grinned. "Be careful," he said again.

She felt like she had been hearing that a lot lately.

"Love you," he said.

"Love you too," she replied, giving him a smile.

She watched as he pulled out and continued back to the resort. Sitting for a moment, she fingered the filigree patterns of her locket while trying to calm her racing heart.

She did love him, didn't she? A few bad days couldn't change that, surely? Hannah pressed down on the little latch, opening the locket. A small picture of her mum and dad stared back at her. Even as a child, she had known something was special about their relationship. The way they looked at each other, laughed together. They were soulmates. She knew it. Not everyone knew love like theirs.

Was *that* the problem, then? Hannah's expectations were so high no one could meet them?

No one?

Or just Mike? The question drifted through her mind.

What about Amiri?

She slammed the door on that duplicitous thought as soon as it rose. It was as if her own mind was attacking her.

Another fat rain drop fell, this time perfectly covering the face of her mother. Hannah brushed it away with her fingertips. She needed to get going before the weather really let loose.

Pulling out, she followed the road for a while until the supermarket appeared on the right. She pulled into one of the scooter parking spaces. She didn't really need anything. Space maybe. A moment to herself to process everything she had been told.

She and Mike needed to leave. Leave the island and, most importantly, leave the resort. Their marriage depended on it; she needed to get Mike to see that.

Too much had happened, and it was only day four of their honeymoon. The resort hadn't even officially opened yet. What would happen when it did? When it was booked out with tourists? Who would get hurt?

Both she and Bethany had nearly drowned. Mariana's husband, and now Rua, were sick. Mike's hand got sliced. The commemorative stone split, the plants around it dying. And other little things, if Mike's own accounts were to go by: plumbing problems, freezers and dishwashers breaking down, towels and robes going missing. The protests were definitely not supernatural, but they also weren't a good look for a new resort.

Then came all the things she couldn't explain: the ruins, the shadows, the drums, the strange weather. Amiri.

It was more than an overactive imagination. And it was bloody scary. At the minimum, she needed chocolate. Then she needed a plan.

With an enormous sigh, she hauled herself off the scooter, squished the helmet into the seat compartment on top of her clothes and ran a hand through her hair. Her rings were biting into her again. She needed to get them resized.

When she walked into the market, only a few customers

were around: a tourist pulling at the arm of a young child to follow her down the aisles, an older man with grey hair and moustache at the checkout waving to a woman filling up a SUV at the petrol stand, and Hannah. She took her time surveying the stalls. She didn't really know what she wanted. Besides a distraction.

It all looked much the same as last time. The small fold-out table in the entranceway still held an assortment of home-baked goods: biscuits, muffins, slices of fudge. Behind that, the wall was lined with refrigerators, the first one full of shelves of chocolate bars to stop them melting in the heat. Hannah heard a distant growl of thunder and eyed out the entrance to see the rain was gaining momentum. She opened the first fridge and grabbed two Cadbury milk chocolate bars. Closing the door, she turned around in time to be shoulder checked hard by the person next to her. It took her a moment to register whose eyes were staring her down with such hatred. It was Awhina. Again. The second time she'd met her outside of the protests, and it was in the supermarket.

"Sorry," Hannah muttered. She tried to step around her but was closed in by the folding table. In return, she got a feral growl from Awhina. Hannah made to turn around and backtrack out the way she came.

"Get out of my way," the voice from behind her said, menacingly close.

Something snapped inside Hannah's head. No more. She was tired of being told what to do. No. More. She swung around to face the hostile woman. They were about the same height, maybe the same age.

"What is your problem?" she attacked back. She had done nothing knowingly to this woman; she didn't even know her.

"You are. You and your money and your disrespect for my people!" Awhina spat back.

"I'm sorry, what?" Hannah retaliated, her voice rising.

"You come here. You take land that's not yours. You mess with matters that are best left alone. And then what? You go home, back to your comfy lives, and we … we have to clean up the mess." Awhina's eyes blazed.

Hannah wanted to look away but also didn't want to give her the satisfaction. Heat rose from her chest up her neck to her cheeks. "You know nothing about me," she said, coldly. Calmly.

"Yes, I do," Awhina interjected. "You're all the same."

"Is this about the curse, Awhina, or is there something else?" Hannah had no idea where her confidence had come from in saying that, but for the shock slamming across Awhina's face, it was worth it.

"How do you know my name?" she snarled, trying to claw back her dip in composure.

"I know lots about you. And your family," she added, for a moment enjoying the upper hand. "Liana told me." Surely she knew Liana, Hannah thought. "You're Rua's great niece. I know all about the curse too. I get it."

Awhina's jaw dropped, and she swore under her breath, but the fire in her eyes barely dimmed.

"You know nothing," Awhina threw back at her.

"Oh, I do," Hannah said, sharpening her voice to that of a knife blade. "Not only do I know about it, I *believe* it." She took a small step forward, closing the gap between them. "And if I could, I would pull our money from the resort and be done with it!" Is that really how she felt? she wondered. Yes. It was.

Awhina stood there, speechless.

"But it's not my decision to make, so get the hell out of my way." She stepped forward and pushed past Awhina, slammed the chocolate bars down on the table and walked out the door. Adrenalin sped through her veins, making her breaths sharp and short. From the corner of her eye she saw the stunned faces of a couple of cashiers and a customer.

The rain was falling much heavier now, soaking through her flimsy pareu and making greasy rivers from the sunscreen down her arms. She didn't care; she had had enough. She grabbed her helmet from under her seat, brushed wet tendrils of hair from her face and placed it on her head. Turning the key in the ignition, she heard a voice behind her yell out, but she didn't bother turning around. She had had enough of being told what to do. Of being pushed around. Of being made to feel crazy. Or feeling crazy. *Enough.* And at the same moment, it had never been clearer to her what she needed to do.

CHAPTER 40

The rain fell harder now. The weather had turned. Hannah slowed the scooter to a crawl as powerful gusts of winds threatened to send her and the bike either off the road or onto its side. Her pareu was soaked through, providing a second goose-bumped skin. Palm fronds blew across the road, and a few of the long-stemmed trees bent harshly in the wind as she neared the entrance to the Rest Easy. The weather, a sombre reflection of her mood.

She pulled her scooter up beside Mike's, then swapped out her helmet for the clothes and purse under the bike seat. As she headed towards the reception, streams of water puddled under her feet on the terracotta coloured tiles.

Mariana stood behind the reception desk, glasses slipping slightly down her nose. Beside her was the young office girl Hannah remembered seeing the night before.

"Kia Orana," the girl said in spotting Hannah first.

"Hi," Hannah replied, attracting Mariana's attention.

"Oh my gosh. Look at you!" Mariana said, eyeing her bedraggled state.

Hannah gave her a wry smile "I wasn't expecting this weather," Hannah said with a half shrug of the shoulders.

"None of us were, dear," Mariana said, stepping out from

behind the reception desk. "Julie, go get Mrs O'Connor a towel or two, will you."

Julie hurried off to the store room beside the office.

"I'm fine," Hannah said. "I'm going to head up to the room for a hot shower."

"Of course. You know, this weather … it was supposed to be a beautiful day, a hint of sun showers later this afternoon, but nothing like this. I guess the weather gods make their own rules." She gave a shake of her head.

They sure did last night, Hannah thought. Only no one else seemed to have experienced the weather as she had. At least this time she knew it wasn't all in her mind.

The young office girl came back with a couple of towels and handed them to Hannah.

"Thanks," Hannah said, hugging them to her chest, "I have to go." She was eager to get up to her room and strip out of her drenched clothes. She gritted her teeth to quell them from chattering.

"Of course," Mariana said, wringing her hands. The expression of concern in her eyes was clear.

Hannah hurried through reception and down the path to her hotel block. The stairs up to the second floor were a little slippery from the rain, so Hannah took them slowly, touching the wall of the balustrade with one hand to balance herself. She paused outside of the room. First things first, she needed a shower, but then she was going to have to have a talk with Mike. If they were ever going to get their relationship back on track, he needed to listen to her. She knew she'd be asking him to make a huge sacrifice, but that's what married couples did. That's what soulmates did. And if they were soulmates, like her parents, they'd get through it. In the end, it *was* simply about money. No one had to die.

The TV was on, an action movie playing while Mike lay fully dressed, asleep on top of the bed. An afternoon siesta. As usual, the air conditioner was set to a chilly temperature that set Hannah's teeth chattering despite her determination not to do so. The sound on the television was up high enough that he didn't wake when Hannah entered the room. It surprised her to find she'd been holding her breath, wondering how to say what she needed to. For the moment, she needn't have worried.

After slipping into the bathroom, she undressed and enjoyed the moment of peace. The cleansing water cleared Hannah's mind, washing all her fears and anxieties down the drain.

There was so much to process, but it came down to one thing: would Mike choose her or the resort?

Liana's revelations threatened to unravel her. Her mind wanted so badly to scrutinise to death everything she had been told, everything that had happened but shouldn't have. Her mind wanted so badly to think of Amiri. But she couldn't take the chance. The possibilities of what could happen scared her.

She felt somewhat better when she eventually left the bathroom, dressed again in her robe. The TV was off in the bedroom, and Mike was gone. She found him instead in the main living area, sitting, staring at his phone with stern consternation.

"Is everything okay?" Hannah asked on entering the room.

"Did you get what you needed from the supermarket?" Mike asked right away, deflecting the question.

A small tingle of heat flashed across her clavicle. "Not exactly," she said, embarrassed. "Awhina was there."

The smile on Mike's face tightened. "She didn't give you any trouble, did she?"

"No. I handled it," Hannah said without thinking,

"Handled it?"

Hannah shrugged her shoulders. "I still think we should leave," she said. Though her voice was barely a whisper, she kept her eyes trained on his. Her husband's. The man she loved. Till death do us part. "You told me to think about it, and I have. I want us to go home. I want us to pull the plug on this resort. Your dad can find someone else to oversee it, or sell it. Just not us." To her annoyance, her eyes filled with tears. She tried to beat them away with her eyelashes, hoping none would betray her and fall.

Mike remained silent. Still. The forced smile on his face slowly faded into a thin, stretched line.

"It's not going to happen," Mike said, his voice flatlining.

Hannah's mind: *Don't cry, don't cry.*

"Not anytime soon, anyway," Mike continued. "Trees are down and the road is closed. We're not going anywhere."

CHAPTER 41

ost of the resort patrons must have opted for room service. Hannah and Mike were some of the few left to eat dinner in the bistro. The storm outside screamed like a banshee. Hannah had little appetite. Her stomach sat lodged in her throat. Storms had never bothered her in the past, but she had never been stuck on a small island, surrounded by sea, cut off from all the rest of civilisation at a cursed resort.

She had twisted her rings so often on her wedding finger, a raw pink mark had formed where her skin had chafed.

Their dinner was almost silent, with no disguising the tension between them. Hannah knew Mike was not open to leaving the island, even if it had been a remote possibility. Which it wasn't. There was no way he'd disappoint his father and back out of overseeing the resort.

The lights on the bistro's ceiling flickered in and out, and Hannah wondered how long it would be before they lost power completely. The weather was much worse than what she'd experienced the night before. As if the island itself were trying to lock her down so she couldn't run away.

A few palm trees had fallen across the road, cutting off the main entrance to the resort from both directions. Although,

Hannah guessed, they weren't cut off. If anyone wanted to get to them, nothing was stopping them from making their way down the beach. They would have to avoid high tides, fierce winds and flying debris, but she assumed it could still be done.

The lights flickered again when Mike took another bite out of his food. Shadows danced in the corners, making her scalp prickle as she remembered the human shaped shadows from the night before. The tea light candle in the centre of their table quivered before sputtering out.

"Maybe we should get back to our room before the lights go out completely," Hannah said, thinking their room would somehow feel a little safer than the large but nearly empty restaurant.

"What's going on with us?" Mike said, ignoring her question and taking Hannah by surprise. Hannah put the glass of water in her hand down on the table. The air hung heavy between them. Hannah searched her brain for something to say.

"I – I don't know," Hannah said, casting her eyes down to the plate before her. She'd barely eaten anything, just pushed the food around with her fork.

"This is supposed to be our honeymoon," Mike said. "I know it's not the location you would have chosen for us, but ... surely it's not so bad either."

A mixture of emotions swept through Hannah. Her mouth twitched as she struggled for the words to reply. He didn't give her a chance to.

"You haven't been yourself since the moment we got here."

Hannah's eyes widened with shock. *She* hadn't been herself? "That's not true," Hannah said, feeling on the defensive but wondering if maybe he was right. "You know why I'm not a fan of places by the sea…"

"I honestly thought you'd get over that."

His words stung. Get over what? The death of her parents?

"You know how important this resort is to our family."

Your family, Hannah thought, surprising herself with the severity of the words.

"We've invested so much into the Rest Easy. Its success will set us up for life." They were going in circles again. It was the same conversation they'd had the night before.

"What life? This is our honeymoon, and you've been more preoccupied with the resort than … than your wife."

Her words struck a nerve, and Mike gritted his teeth. So strange, she thought. It hadn't been too long ago she had wondered if Mike was ever unhappy; nothing ever seemed to get to him, but now…

"That's not fair," he said, letting his simple statement lie naked on the table between them.

Hannah checked in with herself. It really wasn't fair. If she was honest, she hadn't been particularly present either. She'd been second-guessing their relationship the whole time and getting caught up in the resort's drama herself.

The lights above them flickered again, before going out completely.

"Shit," Mike said.

For a moment everything went silent, as if even the storm was holding its breath. A crashing sound came from the kitchen, metal on tile or the like, followed by nervous laughter and a few murmurs Hannah assumed were from some kitchen staff. Someone found a flashlight and waved it around the restaurant. A server made their way to their table.

"I'm so sorry for the inconvenience. Someone is checking

on the generator, and I'm sure we'll have the power back on in a moment. In the meantime, is there anything else I can bring you? A drink refill?"

Hannah shook her head. "No, we're fine. I think we're ready to head back to our room now, anyway." She flashed a smile at the server.

"Actually, another drink would be great," Mike interrupted her, holding his glass up for the server. "Rum and Coke."

"Anything for you?" The server turned to Hannah. Hannah shook her head again, and the server took Mike's glass from his hand, swept the torch over the table once more, and headed to the bar.

"I'm sorry," Hannah whispered. "You're right. I've not been all that present, and it's not fair to you."

Mike reached his hand across the table and curled his fingers around Hannah's. "I'm sorry too," he said. "You know how much you mean to me. This resort – I meant it to be for us. Not for my parents, but for *our* family. The family we might have one day." He paused.

Something in her chest squeezed again. "There's something not right with this place, Mike." She held eye contact with him, hoping that even in the dull light he would see she was pleading with him. "We need to leave."

"No more curses, Hannah. We've talked about this." His words had an edge. "You're better than that."

She felt like a scolded child. The need to tell him everything was fighting so strongly with her own self-doubt. Maybe he was right. Maybe the whole curse thing was superstitious hocus pocus, and she was imagining things. Losing her mind. Having a temporary slip of sanity, what with the pressure of the big wedding, the honeymoon and all the memories it brought up about her parents. Maybe it was childhood trauma finding an adult outlet. Or maybe … it wasn't. The pit in the bottom of her stomach told her it wasn't.

Before she could say anything, a figure approached their table. "Mike. Hannah," Mariana addressed them. "I'm so sorry to interrupt your dinner, it's just …" She cleared her throat.

The pit in Hannah's stomach grew some more.

"Um … the generators, they're not working. There's no reason for it; Sam was out here last week checking them over again. They were working fine. But now … I don't know what's going on, and I don't want to panic the rest of the patrons. There's been no reports of a storm, but the weather is definitely getting worse." She tipped her head at Mike. "I know it's a big ask, but I thought maybe you'd have an idea?"

Mike was more than just an investor, a developer and the man with the money. Somehow, he'd also become the resort's go-to person.

He must have sensed some of Hannah's thoughts. "You know I'm always here to help Mariana, but who would usually look after this kind of thing?" He remained focussed on Hannah when he said this, as if to say, See, I'm trying – you come first.

Mariana let out a small high-pitched sob and quickly covered her mouth with the back of her hand, letting the flashlight beam drop to the floor.

"Mariana?" Mike said, his tone concerned.

"Sam. Sam usually takes care of the generators. He showed me and two other staff before he left what to do in times like this, but nothing we try is working, and now Sam's not answering his phone." The words came out fast. She punctuated it with another small sob.

"Are you okay?" Hannah asked.

"It's his cancer. It's getting worse. It hasn't been a pleasant week and I'm … I'm … worried. He's not picking up his phone and—" Mariana's voice cracked and she covered her mouth harder. Real sobs wracked her body now.

Mike jumped up and pulled her into a hug. "It's okay, it's going to be okay," he soothed. Those words shot arrows into Hannah's heart. She heard them not long before, only it hadn't been Mike who'd said them to her.

"Is there someone we can call who can check in on him? He's probably sleeping, is all."

"This weather came from nowhere. It's supposed to be months before cyclone season, I guess we weren't prepared," Mariana said as a way of apology.

"It's fine. It's a minor storm. If the weather reports haven't even picked it up, I'm sure it'll be over before we know. I can look at the generator and see what I can do. Could be worse; we're not open to the public yet." Even without seeing his face fully in the dark, Hannah knew by his tone he was trying to lighten the mood. No doubt he was sending Mariana a broad, dimpled smile.

"And everyone's calling reception asking when the power's coming on, and I don't know what to tell them …" The tears were coming strong.

Hannah ached for this woman. She wasn't the only one who'd had a tough couple of days. She didn't know Mariana's financial status, but possibly with her husband as sick as he was, she needed this resort to be a success more than most.

"Why don't you show Mike the generators, and I can see if I can help at the reception." As only twenty or so people were staying at the resort at the moment, Hannah couldn't see it as a big thing to offer a little reassurance to the few people on site. Mariana sniffled and nodded her head.

"Thank you," her voice quavered.

"Of course," Hannah said automatically, standing to leave. She felt around for her phone on the table and then remembered she hadn't brought it with her. It was still in the room. As if reading her mind, Mike offered her his, as Mariana held a flashlight already. Thankful, Hannah accepted. Turning on the flashlight app, she was glad for once that Mike had brought his phone to dinner with them. She let Mike give her a kiss on the cheek and then headed towards the reception desk.

The rain was coming down at a hard angle. Putting the phone temporarily in her pocket, Hannah braced herself for the small run to the covered walkway from the bistro. Solar garden lights still lit the path enough so she wouldn't need the flashlight. She was grateful they had stored enough energy from earlier in the day.

Heavy clouds blacked out any chance of moonlight or stars. Hannah wrapped her cardigan tightly around her body, crossing her arms to keep it in place, counted to three and – head down – made a run for it, being careful not to slip on the concrete path.

The covered walkway gave little reprise from the elements. The wind drove the rain at such an angle she might as well have been fully exposed. She continued at pace, being momentarily relieved the power was out and she wouldn't have to be seen for the second time that day in such a bedraggled state.

The glass doors to the reception area, normally left open, had been closed, and it took Hannah a moment to work out whether she was expected to push or pull. Finally, pushing the door open, she stepped through and took a moment to regroup, catching her breath.

Julie was still manning the desk, which now glittered with about five candles in different sizes. She was talking on the phone in the calm professional manner most receptionists did when they were on the cusp of losing their shit. On seeing Hannah, she put a hand up as if to say, Stop, I'll get to you soon.

Another phone rang from the back room. She looked so flustered turning in its direction as she told the speaker on the other end of her ear piece that, yes, they were checking into the generator now, and they should have it up and running shortly.

Without pausing, and seeing she was ready to protest, Hannah shot behind the desk and into the back office, using her ears to pinpoint where the ringing was coming from.

Grabbing the receiver, she answered almost automatically, "Kia orana, Rest Easy Resort, Hannah speaking."

"Hello, is Mariana Willcox there, please?" the voice on the other end of the line said. A crackle of static garbled the voice.

"No, I'm sorry, but I can pass on a message if you like," Hannah replied.

White noise kept breaking up the clarity of the call. "... neighbour ... been an accident ... husband."

"I'm sorry, I can't hear you properly. Can you repeat that?"

The caller persevered, sounding more and more urgent as she did so. "Mariana ... husband ... I'm so sorry." The last couple of words poured out before the line went dead. Hannah's heart thumped in her chest. Surely not. Surely something hadn't happened to Mariana's husband. Not now.

CHAPTER 42

Hannah vigorously pressed buttons, hoping she'd get a phone connection again. Nothing.

She needed to call emergency services. The island was small enough they could locate where Mariana and her husband lived. They needed to send someone out there to check on him. If they hadn't already.

Oh, God, she thought. This couldn't be happening.

Giving up on the landline, she remembered Mike's cell phone. Pulling it out of her pocket, she pressed the on button. Nothing. Frantic, she tried again and again. She could swear it had a good battery life only minutes before.

She almost collided with Julie as she went to join her in the reception area.

"Do you have a cell phone?" Hannah asked.

"Yeah. Here it is," she said without hesitating. Hannah tried to find the on button.

"How do you turn it on?" she said, panic making her hands shake.

"Here," Julie said, taking it from her and fiddling with it. "It's dead!" she said, surprised. "I don't understand, it had lots of juice when I was using it before."

"Shit!" Hannah said under her breath. Until they could

find a working phone, they'd just have to pray that Mariana's husband was okay, cared for.

Maybe sensing Hannah's panic, or else battling with her own, Julie sniffled beside her. Hannah pitied her. For all she knew, this could be her first job, and with all the pressure of the official opening coming up and then the curveball of this freak storm ... well, it was a lot for anyone.

"It's okay," Hannah said, trying to console her. "Mariana and my husband, Mike, are checking on the generators now. Hopefully, they'll be able to spur them into action. In the meantime, there's not much to be done. If you're okay to continue manning the desk in case anyone comes in, I'll go check on them now."

Julie gave a nod and thanked Hannah again.

"Do you know where the generators are?" It was not something she ever thought she would have needed to know.

Julie gave her brief directions to a room on the bottom floor of one of the hotel blocks. She did her best to hold the instructions in her mind. Following directions had never been a strength.

The wind continued to howl, and the rain came down like a frenzy of needles. No wonder Julie was scared. She was about to be stuck alone in the reception of a resort that was supposedly cursed, having only the night before been privy to protestors and fighting. It was a wonder she hadn't already broken down.

In the meantime, Hannah needed to find Mariana. She didn't want to add to the poor woman's stress, but surely the right thing to do was to let her know about the phone call. Hopefully, Mariana would have a cell on her and be able to check in on whoever had called, or call an ambulance or ... or something. Too many doubts raced through Hannah's mind. Why hadn't the mystery caller contacted Mariana's cell first instead of the resort?

Cold and wet from the trek over to reception, Hannah took a deep breath, pulled her cardigan tightly around her again as she prepared to head back out into the fierce weather. She jumped as the glass doors to the front entrance swung open of their own accord, and two wet figures with a rain coat held above their heads lurched into the room.

Julie gave a sharp intake of breath. It took Hannah a moment to realise who was standing there, adding to the wet puddles on the tiled floor.

The taller figure shook the raincoat out, caring nothing about the water splattering over the desk and the nearby wall of brochures. Her hair was tied back in a thick plait down the middle of her back. Hannah's jaw dropped.

"Awhina?" she spluttered, even more shocked when she realised she had been shielding the hunched figure of Rua under her jacket. Rua coughed, a raspy, phlegmy bark that made Awhina glare at Julie.

"Get him some towels, will you," she snapped, sending an already anxious Julie racing for the backroom to do as ordered.

"Rua. Are you okay? What are you doing here?" Hannah moved to him, took his arm and led him towards one of the corner chairs. Awhina helped, refusing to make eye contact with Hannah. They eased him into the chair and waited for his coughing to abate.

"Mrs O," he finally said between coughs, as a way of greeting.

"What are you doing here, Rua? You should be at home resting." She couldn't help the double-edged scold for him and Awhina that she knew had slipped through in her tone. But he appeared worse than when she had visited with him earlier. Even in the candlelight, his skin was pallid. Hannah brought her gaze up to meet Awhina's while Rua wiped the edge of his mouth with a handkerchief he'd pulled from inside his jacket.

"He insisted. Nothing I could do," Awhina said, her steely stare daring Hannah to argue. "From the looks of it, it's a good thing too. If anyone can put an end to this thing, it's Papa."

Julie came back into the room with several towels in her arms, interrupting them. Hannah bit down on the brewing questions. Julie was visibly shaking on recognising Awhina. Hannah took the towels from her arms and passed some of them to Awhina, then went about trying to wrap one around Rua's shoulders. She had never seen this man as frail before, and it worried her.

Julie went and stood behind the desk as if it would somehow keep her safe. She twiddled with a pen behind the desk.

Taking in the situation, Hannah rubbed the side of her face. "Julie, can you go get Mariana? I need to stay here. Will you be okay to do that?"

Julie looked relieved she didn't have to stick around.

"No, no, Mrs O, it's fine. I'm fine," Rua said, pulling himself more upright in the chair.

"We're not here for her, we've come for you," Awhina interrupted with her usual abruptness.

Hannah's pulse rushed. "There is an emergency," she half whispered to Awhina and Rua, "and Mariana needs to be here. Now." Hannah looked back at Julie, who was hovering at the door.

"Go." Hannah said. Julie dove out into the rain, and Hannah

lost sight of her as the darkness and rain swallowed her.

Hannah turned back to her new guests.

"What do you mean, put an end to things?" Hannah asked, not wanting to waste time.

"Liana told me," Rua said between raspy breaths. "She told you about the curse. The real story." He paused while Awhina let out a low growl in the back of her throat. "And it seems it knows about you too," he said.

"I don't know what you're…"

"Just stop it!" Awhina said, stepping into Hannah's space, eyes like daggers. "You said you believed in the curse and you want to put an end to this resort."

"That's not what I said," Hannah argued. "Yes, I believe in the curse. How could I not? But the resort opens its doors in a few days. There's nothing I can do about it."

Awhina balled her fists and opened her mouth to say something, but Rua beat her to it.

"Liana said you've seen Amiri."

For a moment, Hannah's heart stopped.

From the way Awhina's jaw dropped and colour drained from her face, this was news to her.

"I – I…" Hannah didn't know what to say.

"What are you talking about, Papa?" Awhina turned to Rua, her voice quiet, edged with fear.

"You've seen him, haven't you?" It was more a statement than a question. Rua's eyes eagled in on Hannah's.

Face flushing, she twisted the rings on her fingers.

Awhina could judge her all she liked, and maybe she was crazy, but she couldn't lie to Rua. Maybe she'd hallucinated it all; it didn't matter.

"Yes," she said solemnly, bracing for whatever backlash she

would get from Awhina.

"More than once?" Awhina asked in a small voice.

Hannah nodded her head, her eyes filling with tears. Glancing in Awhina's direction, she saw the candle light catch the welling in her eyes too.

"I told you she was special," Rua said, turning to his niece. "Only, in this place, I don't know if that's a good thing."

CHAPTER 43

"Mike doesn't know," Hannah said, glimpsing movement outside the resort doors, and pleading with her eyes for them not to say anything. Rua nodded his head in understanding. Awhina gave no indication of grasping what she'd hinted at.

The doors swung open, the burst of wind making the candle flames dance wildly. Mariana led the party, fear and worry washing her features. Julie was right behind her, followed by Mike. Hannah couldn't meet his eyes.

Mike was the first to speak, pushing himself to the front of the others. "What's going on?" he asked before glimpsing the two additional guests.

"Rua? Are you— What the hell is she doing here?" he said on noticing Awhina. "Julie, call the police. This woman's trespassing." He shot daggers at Awhina, who snarled in his direction.

"Wait!" Hannah stepped in front of Rua and Awhina. "She's here for Rua."

"Rua. What the hell are you doing here, man? You should be at home resting, not out in this weather." His fondness for the old man winning out over his fury towards Awhina. "How did you even get here? I thought the roads were closed."

255

Worry was drawn on his face.

"They are," Awhina said. "We took the bikes."

Hannah guessed maybe it made it easier to manoeuvre around fallen trees and whatnot, but surely the rain and wind would have made even their quick trip, near impossible. From the expression on Mike's face, Hannah suspected he thought the same thing.

"The worst of the storm is *here*," Awhina said, as if it answered everything. Maybe it did, Hannah thought.

"Hannah?" A small voice finally pulled itself to the front of the group as if she was expecting the worst. "Julie said you needed me?" Mariana looked older to Hannah now. Her hair plastered to her head and most of her makeup washed off. It stressed dark circles in the candlelight.

"I do," Hannah said as gently as she could. She wasn't even sure what she was telling her. "There was a phone call." She closed the gap between her and Mariana, who, at almost a head shorter than her, seemed to have shrunk in size. Hannah reached out for Mariana's hand. It was all the comfort she knew to give.

"What's happened?" Mariana asked in a whisper.

"I don't really know," Hannah answered truthfully. "The line kept breaking up, but I think it was about your husband. The person on the other end said something about an accident." Hannah almost choked on the last word. How could anyone infer anything but something bad having happened from that?

Mariana's legs wobbled under her. Hannah put her arm around her to steady her and led her over to another chair in the waiting area.

"Did you call an ambulance?" Mike asked.

"I tried; the cell phones and landlines are dead."

"What are you talking about? I always have reception." He gestured for Hannah to give him his phone.

She pulled it out of her pocket and passed it back to him. He tried turning it on. Nothing. He shook his head and let out a grunt. Hannah stared at him a second longer than intended. This was not the man she had married. Even amid chaos, he had always maintained an air of optimism. Now a frown seemed permanently affixed on his features.

"There's someone with him, now. A neighbour maybe? Hopefully, they got help," Hannah said. She really did hope they had.

"Shit," Mike said, dragging his hand through his wet hair.

"I need to get home," Mariana said, hauling herself up from the chair. "If the two of you could get here" – she pointed at Rua and Awhina – "I should be able to get home."

"It would be madness to go out in this weather," Mike said.

"He's right," Awhina added. "Trees are down on the main road. We could get around them on our bikes, but the wind almost threw us off them several times, and it's only going to get worse." She paused, eyes pinned on Hannah. "I can feel it."

"Hannah said there's someone with him. He'll be in good hands, I'm sure. In the meantime, we need to sort the resort. Make sure everyone's safe and looked after," Mike said.

"We should prepare as if for a cyclone," Rua said, joining the conversation.

"A cyclone? We would have heard on the news if there was any risk," Mariana said, her eyes sparking with fresh worry. As if to shake them from their musings, a large palm frond slammed into one of the reception windows, startling them all.

"We need to make sure everyone knows to stay indoors, in

their room. Away from the windows if possible," Mike said taking, charge. "Julie, can you get some other resort staff to help you? If the phones are down, you might need to knock on everyone's door, give everyone on site the heads up they need to stay indoors."

"Okay," Julie said, looking uncomfortable with going outdoors again.

"A few people are staying in the beachside rooms. We should get them moved inland to one of the garden suites and make sure no one's staying on the ground floor. On the off chance there's a sea surge," Mariana said, taking Mike's lead.

"What the hell is a sea surge?" Hannah asked, panic rising like bile in her chest.

"You're *fine*, Hannah. You can stay here, man the office and keep your eye on the reception desk if anyone we miss comes in. Just until I get back," Mike said, dismissing her question.

"Julie, if you can put together a list of everyone on site and where they are staying, we can touch base with everyone and get guests moved," Mariana said.

Julie disappeared into the back office right away.

Graham and his family were staying in one of the beachside rooms. Hannah didn't envy whoever tried to get them moving without argument. They could all be thankful, however, that so few people were on site.

"I'll help," Mike said. "We'll be able to move some guests faster that way. "Rua. Awhina. We can set you up with a room to weather the storm, although I still don't understand what you're doing here," he said, shaking his head.

"Of course you don't," Awhina said, the fire back in her voice. "You didn't listen and now look. This storm is no accident. There's a reason its focus is here and not over the rest of the island. We tried to warn you."

"Awhina!" Rua scolded.

"God! What is wrong with you people? There is no bloody curse!" Mike raised his voice louder than Hannah had ever witnessed. He waved his arms as if he were near to strangling someone.

"We'll stay and help Hannah," Rua said, just as Awhina was ready to start a new tirade. "I know this resort inside and out. If anyone comes into reception, I'll know what to do."

Awhina stayed strangely quiet.

Everyone hustled together. Hannah helped Mariana and Julie pull out as many flashlights and towels as they could find from the storage room behind reception. They left a pile of towels on the desk for their return. It looked like the rain had temporarily stalled, but the wind seemed to pick up even more. Plant debris continued to smack into the glass windows at different intervals.

Mariana snuffed out the candles in the reception area and handed out flashlights to everyone. Hannah helped stuff some towels into a rubbish bag to give out as needed when the others were moving guests from rooms. Julie made a list of all the staff and visitors on site and their room numbers. Giving a copy to Hannah, Mike and Mariana, and keeping one for herself. They set a plan for Julie to touch base with everyone on the reception side of the resort. She wouldn't have to be outside much, and it wasn't too close to the water, so relatively safer.

Hannah was torn between going with her and staying at reception. She didn't want to leave the young girl running around on her own, and Mike had made it clear he didn't trust Awhina. As she was here with Rua, he wanted them together.

Mike and Mariana were going to get those in the beachside bungalows moved. Hannah had instructions to wait. Mike would come back for her or send a messenger when everyone on site had been accounted for. Then he'd meet her in their room, and they'd buckle down and see out the storm together.

There was a speed and efficiency that worked well between Mariana and Mike. Julie, now having a purpose, seemed to have bounced back. She was the first to set out, holding a radio so she could stay in touch with Mariana and Mike. Mariana and Mike followed suit seconds later.

"Please stay safe," Hannah said to the pair of them. It scared her. The weather was nasty and whatever a sea surge was, it filled her with more dread than she wanted to admit.

"I will," was all Mike said, not even humouring her with a peck on the cheek. The darkness outside swallowed them almost immediately but for the bars of their torches and the faint glow of the garden lights.

Then just the three of them remained. Alone. Hannah, Rua and Awhina.

"Why are you really here?" Hannah quietly asked as the wind howled around the building, making the glass windows bend with the pressure.

"To put an end to this," Awhina said matter-of-factly.

"You believe in the curse, Mrs O?" Rua asked

Hannah nodded her head slowly.

"Then you should know, everyone who is here, who is connected to this place, is in danger."

"If something's happened to that woman's husband," Awhina said, referring to Mariana, "then it'll be because of this place."

"That's not possible," Hannah said, just as the thought popped into her head that Mariana had told her Sam hadn't got sick until he started working here. Rua must have noticed the realisation dawn on her.

"And how is Mr O," Rua asked gently.

Hannah turned away.

"He's different, eh?"

Hannah said nothing. There was no point lying. Plus, she was tired of all the lies and half-truths.

"I do not know what you've experienced here, but I suspect the spirits have been playing with you," Rua said, not pressuring her for confirmation. "And if Amiri is here … well, then … he'd only show to protect a person, so you must be in trouble."

"But why me?" Hannah asked, realising too late how whiney it sounded. "Why can I see them but others can't?"

"Some people have the gift," Rua said. "Some people invite them in," he said with an air of solemnity.

"But I never …" She thought for a moment. "I've seen nothing before and I didn't ask for this."

"You need not ask; you just need to send an invitation. In a place like this, fear is an invitation." Rua paused as a tsunami of memories flooded through Hannah's mind. "What is it you fear, Mrs O?" he asked.

The water. Her parents drowning. Her relationship with Mike, and it not living up to that of her parents. There was so much she feared. So much. She bit her lip.

CHAPTER 44

"Have you really seen Amiri?" Awhina asked quietly, as if everything depended on her saying yes again. Hannah nodded her head.

"Tell us," Rua said.

So she did. She told them everything. The resort ruins, her near drowning, first meeting Amiri, the dreams, the rock, Bethany's near drowning, and then the events of the night before. The storm that apparently never happened. The drumming and shadows and Amiri showing up again, as if he were protecting her. Falling asleep in the ruins to wake in the hall of her hotel block. She told them everything, except how he made her feel. Saying it out loud would break her.

Other than a few hmms and haas they both remained silent and listened until the end when Hannah heard a sniffle coming from Awhina's direction. Relief that she'd finally told someone was quickly shadowed by remorse for dredging up painful events of the past. Liana had said Awhina had almost worshipped her uncle and here Hannah was saying she had not only seen but also spent time with him, a man who had supposedly been resting in peace for the last thirty years or so.

"I'm sorry," Hannah said. "I know it sounds crazy."

Awhina sniffed again, then pulled her shoulders back, resuming her hardened posture again.

"No. If Uncle is here, it means he will help us. You get now why this resort must close."

Hannah shook her head. "No. I—" she tried to protest. This was Mike's dream, their investment. She might not care, but her husband would. For better or worse, those were their vows. She owed it to him to stand by them … didn't she?

As if reading her mind, Rua said, "You owe it to Mr O. For his safety and your own and everyone else here. There is no price on human life."

"What did you have planned?" Hannah asked.

She would never have believed it if anyone had told her this would be her honeymoon. With a torch in one hand, Hannah followed Awhina out into the storm, towards where Rua and Awhina had dumped their bikes. The rain had lessened, while the wind whipped around them screaming, shrieking, throwing plant debris and dirt their way. Hannah had tied her hair back, but the wind took mere seconds to unleash most of it, making it a struggle to see where she was going. They had left Rua behind to man the fort, hoping he could make an excuse for them if anyone came back to the reception early.

"They're here," Awhina said, stopping halfway down the drive. Partially hidden amongst the plants on the verge were two red jerry cans. Awhina had hidden them there, on the night of their last protest.

It had shocked Hannah to hear Awhina and her supporters had meant to do actual damage that night. Awhina told her they had tried talking to Mariana. She had lived on the island long enough that Awhina had believed she might get through to her. But it hadn't worked. Their next step would have been to burn down the reception area, or at least damage it enough to stall the official opening. Those tiki torches had not been there for theatrical effect.

They needed more time, Awhina had said. More time to work out how to contain the curse. Surprising even Hannah, containing the curse was even more important to Awhina than the historical land claims.

The handles of the jerry cans were slippery from the rain, but each carrying one, they fought their way against the wind back to the reception area. Hannah couldn't believe she was doing this. The "plan" was not much of a plan at all. But time was running out, and they had to do something. It was getting dangerous. Hannah could feel it. As if the curse were ramping up to something bigger.

They didn't need a big fire. Even damaging part of the reception area would be enough to win them another couple of weeks to come up with a better idea. Maybe by then, she could get Mike on board to walk away from the resort.

She needed him to see straight. And she didn't like its effect on their relationship, although this … course of action … would not do their relationship any favours. Not at first, anyway.

She didn't even want to think about how illegal it was. So much could go wrong. With everyone moving rooms or hunkering down from the storm, away from reception, she hoped no one would get hurt.

If they were caught, she was at risk of jail time. Gasoline was not inconspicuous as an accidental burning. She was going to have to stall the others, play dumb and allow Awhina and Rua to take the hit if it came to that. She had argued against it to no avail. Rua and Awhina knew people in the police force here.

They were better protected than her. Hannah was puffing by the time they made it back into the reception area. The glass door slammed behind them, and she momentarily grimaced, waiting for the sound of shattering glass to follow. It didn't.

Rua came out of the back room. A frown upon his face. "This is not what I would have planned," he said with a shake of his head. "But I have tried. I have prayed and tended to the curse spot, but its energy has been growing as we've got closer to the resort's opening. I am the son of Rawiri and the grandson of Mama. It is in my bloodline. If I cannot remove it, we must protect those in its path, as I believe my nephew is doing."

At the thought of Amiri, a jolt of pain flared in her chest. She needed to see him again. Before it was all over.

Awhina hid the jerry cans behind the chair Rua had been sitting on. A faint smell of gasoline hung in the air.

Rua wanted to try one more thing first. Their first point of call was going to be the commemorative stone. The centre for all the activity – or the curse spot, as Rua called it. One more attempt to cleanse the stone and subdue the curse. This time they'd try with fire. Obviously, it would do no harm to the rock itself, but fire was said to purify. The rainfall would make it hard for the fire to get traction, hence the gasoline. The hope was they would need only a small amount. The wind would be the game changer. They would have to be careful to not let it get out of hand.

CHAPTER 45

Hannah taped a note to each door facing outside from reception, telling people to return to their room and stay put through the storm. The group of three headed outside. Awhina had poured a little petrol into an emptied water bottle. A small amount spilled on the tiles, making the room smell even stronger of gasoline.

They wouldn't need much. They hoped to pour a small circle around the commemorative rock. Rua had some special herbs for the occasion in a small backpack. He planned on adding them to the fire, to help cleanse the stone and dispel any negativity. The curse itself, despite his direct bloodline, was not something he could kill, he told Hannah.

He had tried. With the prayers he'd come armed with, the best he could do was try to mollify it somewhat, buy them some time. The curse, Rua said, had been amplified by all the emotions of fear, hate, heartbreak and racism. It had seeped into the soil and poisoned the grounds; it had morphed into forms of fear and attracted negative entities to it.

They would use the commemorative rock as a focal point, as his uncle had done to reset the curse. It was a stab in the dark, but worth trying before they stepped it up to arson.

The rain was minimal now, but the atmosphere felt heavy

and waterlogged. In the sky, a twirl of inky black and sooty grey clouds blocked the stars and moon. The wind still thrashed at the gardens. Debris and dirt flew across their path. Hannah hated to imagine what the state of the resort would be like tomorrow.

They hurried the best they could. Awhina's and Hannah's hair whipped across their faces, making it impossible to talk. Each holding of one of Rua's arms, they helped steady him as they walked. Their bodies bent into the wind, forcing themselves forward as if through a wall of phantom hands trying to block their path. A few times, a gust of wind would send Hannah teetering on one foot as she struggled to regain balance again.

They followed the path past the front of one hotel room block. To her right, Hannah could make out the sound of sloshing water as the wind no doubt wound the pool water into a frenzy. Taking a left turn down the side of the building block and then taking a slight fork to their right, they moved away from the buildings and the small amount of light from the garden lights to where the stone lay half hidden along the path.

Their flashlights distorted the shadows as they moved to single file with Awhina leading the way. Rua yelled directions as they went. Likely, Awhina had not travelled this path as often, if at all. Hannah now knew it well, but still felt disoriented as everything looked so different in the dark.

They drew closer. No lights, but their flashlights shone now. Still fighting the wind at every step, as if it had changed directions to stop them, Rua flew backwards a metre or so, landing hard on the ground at Hannah's feet. She regained her balance and kept from falling on him in time, yelling out for Awhina to stop, her voice barely carrying on the wind. Turning around, Awhina saw Rua and rushed to his side as Hannah bent down to check he was alright.

He let out a groan and started coughing. Hannah put a hand on his shoulder and one around the backpack on his back.

"Are you okay? Can you stand up?" she said.

"Yes, yes," he said, gasping for breath and making no sign of moving. He held his hand against his chest as he tried to stifle his coughing and draw in a deeper breath. "It knows we're here," he said.

"It?" Hannah said, perspiration sliding between her shoulder blades.

"It knows we've come to subdue it, and it's fighting us. This is no normal storm," Rua wheezed.

"Grab his arm," Awhina said, looping her own arm under one of Rua's. "We'll get him up. A few more metres and we're there."

The two of them, again on either side of Rua, forced their way forward through what felt like a heavy suffocating wall, until Rua's legs buckled under him, pulling them down with him. The sharp gravel cut into Hannah's knees with the impact, but she hardly noticed the pain as she saw in the beam of her flashlight the shiny wet surface of the commemorative plaque on the rock.

Rua struggled to get the backpack off his back, so Awhina took charge, helping him and then pulling out supplies. Hannah moved her flashlight around the stone. The greater circumference of plants had blackened and died. It even smelt rotten to her, and nausea rose in her throat as she imagined it to be the smell of something dead. She leaned forward, planting her hands into the gravel as she gulped big mouthfuls of air and tried to quell the queasiness.

"Are you okay, Mrs O?" Rua asked.

She shook her head no, quickly placing a hand over her mouth. The smell was so strong; it had crawled into her nostrils, and she could almost taste the death and decay on her tongue. Pivoting on her knees, she threw herself forward into an untainted patch of garden and threw up, sweat cooling quickly on her forehead.

After heaving a few more times, she turned, embarrassed and teary-eyed, back to her companions. "I'm sorry," she said.

"You should have stayed behind if you have a weak stomach" Awhina said, her sharp no nonsense manner apparent in her voice.

"The smell, it's just—" Hannah couldn't find the words to describe it.

Awhina stared at her for a moment, and Hannah blinked as the flashlight burnt her eyes. "What smell?"

Hannah's jaw dropped. How could she not smell it? It had a viciousness to it, like it was poisoning her skin.

"They're playing with you, Mrs O, ignore it the best you can, don't give in to the fear," Rua said.

Another gust of wind roared up. The howling sounded supernatural.

"We do it now." Rua gave a nod.

Awhina held the water bottle of gasoline. Uncapping it, she poured a circle around the rock.

"You need to move back," Rua said to Awhina and Hannah. "And you must not interrupt until it's done." They both nodded, stood up and took a step away from the stone. The ground and plants were still wet from the rain, so it would not be much of a fire even if it ignited, Hannah thought, but she also wasn't confident they were playing by the normal rules of science right now either.

They stood slightly apart, behind and to either side of Rua. He pulled something from a leather pouch and sprinkled it around the rock where the gasoline had been poured, while reciting words in a native tongue Hannah could not discern. The wind died down to an eerie stillness, and for a second, Hannah thought she could hear the thudding of her own heart in her chest, waiting for the moment Rua would light a match and set the gasoline ablaze.

It wasn't her heart that was thudding. The drumming was back again. Quiet. Methodical. Haunting. On the periphery of her hearing.

CHAPTER 46

Rua pulled a pack of matches from his pocket and stood up, not taking his eyes off the stone, and still chanting. Awhina kept her flashlight in his direction so he could see what he was doing. It took two strikes for the match to light. Rua took a step back and threw the lit match at the circle of gasoline. It went out. He went to strike it again.

The drumming continued. She wanted to ask Awhina if she heard it, but Awhina's gaze had locked on Rua's back and what he was doing. She too was reciting something under her breath. The drumming grew louder. She was sure that was what it was. It was coming from further down the path where she had walked the first few time's she'd stumbled on the ruins. It was a trick; she told herself. She was an easy target.

Quietly taking a few steps further down the path, she left Rua and Awhina to their prayers and chanting. She didn't want to disturb either of them, but another noise came from that direction now, and it had her worried.

Beyond the faint rhythm of drums in the background, footsteps had sounded too. Gravel crunching under shoes. And it wasn't her own. This was moving faster, darting here and there. Hannah continued another couple of paces.

Whatever Rua and Awhina were doing must have worked because the wind had died down to nothing more than a gentle breeze.

A spiel of laughter made Hannah take pause. She recognised it, though it echoed as if from far away. Turning, she checked whether the others had heard it. Both remained focussed on what they were doing, with neither showing any sign of acknowledgement. A small glimpse of light on the ground had Hannah guessing the fire had taken. Swinging her flashlight back and forth, she took a few more steps down the path, holding her breath. Listening. She was sure she hadn't imagined it.

There it was again. A girl's laughter. Closer now. Louder.

"Jake," a high-pitched voice whined, then squealed with laughter again.

Surely not. Surely Graham and Edith hadn't been daft enough to let their kids out in this weather? In the dark. Sure, the wind and rain had died down considerably, but the heaviness in the air made it feel like they were in the eye of a storm not on the other side.

Hannah stole one more glance in Rua's and Awhina's direction. They were completely immersed in what they were doing, and if it might work without them having to resort to more drastic measures, she would not disturb them.

Hannah picked up her pace, almost jogging. She needed to get the kids inside where it was safe – or safer, at least. The sound of running footsteps came from ahead. Crunching gravel, brush moving. In the distance behind her, she thought Awhina called her name, but she didn't turn around.

"Bethany," she called, hoping she would hear. "You need to go back to your room."

The wind built again. Sand whipped up from the beach, stinging her face and making her eyes gritty. She squinted into the poor light of her flashlight, which did so little to define the inky shadows.

"Hello? Bethany?" she called again. Another squeal of laughter. Hannah paused, orienting herself. It must have come from further ahead. As if to confirm, a flash of white whip across the path ahead. She jogged again until another sharp peal of laughter sounded right behind her ear. She turned on her feet in fright, swinging her flashlight wildly. No longer was she able to see Rua and Awhina, who had disappeared around the corner. Nothing but the tropical grasses and few plants rustled either side of her. No longer those of Rua's garden, but of a different familiarity. Had she really wandered so far? Done it again? And not just her this time, but Bethany too. The ruins couldn't be too far ahead, which sent a new chill through her bones.

"Bethany," she yelled again, louder this time, twirling on her feet, checking all directions. Another flash of movement on the periphery of her vision. It had to be Bethany. It sounded so much like her. She didn't want to think what it could be otherwise.

"Wait," she called in equal amounts concern and fear. The laughter rolled again. "Wait!" She took a few fast steps forward before a hand gripped her firmly by the arm, bringing her to a halt.

She screamed in fear as she rounded on her toes to face her assailant. Still with a firm grasp on her arm, another hand grabbed her by the shoulder, holding her in place in front of him.

"Amiri!" Hannah gasped, relief flooding her and threatening

her legs to give out. His expression was barely visible in the dark, but she saw enough to make out the fear etched into the shadows of his features. "What—" Words failed.

Warmth spread through her chest. She hadn't realised how much she had wanted to see him until he was suddenly before her. A million questions raced through her mind, but nothing came out. Here she was again, face to face with this man – this man, whom now she knew couldn't possibly be real. Yet he held her. The pressure of his fingers burned through her clothes, and for a moment, she didn't want him to let go.

She shook the tangled web of questions from her mind; time for that would come later. The wind continued to howl and Hannah felt her teeth chatter again with the cold. "There's a girl, Bethany, maybe even her brother too. I need to—" She turned and tried to dislodge herself from his grip.

"No," he said, his voice low. He held her tighter.

"Yes, there is," she repeated. He had to believe her. He dropped his hand from her shoulder but kept a forceful hold on her arm. She wasn't going to fight him off. For the moment, it was the only warm part of her. "I'll show you," she said, attempting to pull him with her.

"No," he said again. "That's not a child, Hannah. It's a trickster spirit."

Hannah's mouth fell open.

He shook his head. "You need to leave."

"But I heard her. She's staying at the resort."

He said nothing and refused to budge.

"I don't understand," she said. A trickster spirit? How did she know *he* wasn't one too?

He must have noticed the twist to her lips. He dropped her arm, and she took a tentative step backwards. Shining the torch in his face. He instantly shielded his eyes with one hand and looked down at the ground. Hannah moved it out of eyes but so she could still see his face.

"What do you mean, a trickster spirit?" Hannah's voice rose to be sure he heard her. The wind began its banshee howl again. The sound of grass rustling and plants thrashing was like background white noise. He didn't respond, so she took another step backwards. Her heart leapt into her throat again. She didn't want to believe he might be a trickster. How could someone so warm, so safe, be evil?

"You're supposed to be dead," she whispered when he still made no move to say anything. Tears welled in her eyes. She so badly wanted him to laugh at her right now; tell her how ridiculous she was being.

He gave a weak smile and nodded his head. Her heart continued to thrash in her chest. How was it possible?

"I am," he said.

"Then how can I see you?" she asked, panic rising.

"I don't know. It makes no sense. You're the first," he said, hunching his shoulders and tucking his hands into his pockets. "You're different. I knew as soon as I pulled you from the water."

Hannah choked at the memory. The thick water filling her lungs. The feel of fingers around her ankle. If it hadn't been for him, she would have drowned.

"Is it the curse?" she asked quietly.

"Maybe," he said. "I don't know. But, I think, because you can see me, it puts you more at risk. You're not safe here, no one is, but you especially."

"Rua and Awhina are here," she blurted out. "They're trying to do something. Over by the stone, contain the curse, or something." She shook her head.

"It won't work," he said, defeated. "Rua's tried before. I've seen him." He paused. "Awhina's here?" he asked in a small voice.

At Hannah's nod, his eyes filled with tears. "Little Awhi," he said with a faint smile.

"She was special to you," Hannah said.

"Yeah. She was only four when I died. I tried to do what I could to support her and her mum, my sister. I thought working here would help them out. My sister, she was so against it. She believed in the curse, eh? But I didn't. Even if I did, I assumed I'd be immune, being in the family and all," he said, shrugging his shoulders. "I guess that will teach me, eh?"

Hannah looked away. How was it possible this man before her was dead? She had spent a night with him, sheltering from a storm. Yeah, but the storm hadn't been real, nor the shelter and neither the man. A voice of reason corrected her. Shit, she thought.

Another giggle sounded from behind her, making her jump on the spot. Hannah turned around as Amiri lunged in front of her and pushed her behind him. Hannah swung the flashlight beam down the path. A rustling sound came from the brush up ahead on their right.

"Move," Amiri whispered out the side of his mouth, taking a step backwards and forcing her to do the same.

A few more paces, then a figure emerged onto the path. The white horned cow stood in front of them, blocking the path to where the ruins would be. It paused and slowly turned its head towards them. Its eyes glowed red in the flashlight beam. When it released a mournful bellow, pins and needles jabbed through her bones.

Hannah stumbled backwards in fright, letting out a small shriek as she lost her footing and fell backwards on to her bottom. She dropped the torch which rolled away from her grasp before promptly going out, leaving them in near complete darkness.

Amiri turned to her and reached for her hand. "Get up," he said. "You need to get back to the others." His hand grasped her own.

How could he be anything but real? she thought, as a spark of warmth flooded through her, replacing the chill. He pulled her to her feet.

"The torch" she said, bending back down to feel for it with her hand.

"Leave it," he said. "You hear that?"

She did. The drums were getting louder; the beat increasing in tempo; the wind picked up again as if to add to the percussion.

"We need to get you out of here."

"Hannah?" A voice called against the wind. Awhina again.

Hannah gripped Amiri's hand tighter. "Come with me," she said.

"I don't think they'll see me," he said.

"It doesn't matter. Come on." They moved as fast as they could, tracking the sound of the gravel under their feet. The drumming followed them, but that was it. No sound of footsteps other than their own reached her ears.

Voices called her name again. Awhina's and … Mikes? What was Mike doing there? Her heart stalled mid-beat. A small prick of guilt made her take pause, surprising Amiri and making him slam into her back, his hand still in hers.

She turned around to face him. Unable to make out his

features in the dark, but able to feel his warm breath on her face.

"Thank you," she said. One of her hands rose to rest on his chest. She didn't know why. It was as if she wanted him to feel her words, not just hear them.

"Hannah?" he said, confusion lacing his voice.

"You sacrificed yourself for all of us. There must be some place better you can be—but you're here." She paused, feeling the warmth of his chest and his solid torso through his thin T-shirt.

He brought both of his hands up to her shoulders.

"It is my family's curse. It's what I have to do. But, God, I wish things were different…" His voice trailed off, edged with raw pain.

There was a magnetism between them. A fire. She had felt nothing like it before.

She heard her name again. They were getting closer, but she didn't want to let go, didn't want to say goodbye. She pressed her fingers harder against his chest, savouring the feel of him. He was real; she knew he was. Oh, God, what was happening?

"Hannah," Amiri whispered, pulling her to him so her head rested on his chest. He wrapped his arms around her, the warmth of his hands sending heat waves through her skin where they rested. His heart beat beneath her ear. "You need to leave. Promise me you will. And you can't come back." His breath tickled the top of her head. "As long as you and the others are here, people are going to get hurt, and I can't do much to stop it."

She knew it now. The last thing she wanted was to leave. Though she didn't want others to get hurt – despite all the horrible things that had happened – here, within his arms, she was safe. Safer than she had ever felt.

"Please," he said.

She tilted her chin towards his face, his breath warm across her lips. She was drawn to him, an otherworldly tug that put a pause on all the drama going on around them, leaving just the two of them alone. Her eyes closed in anticipation of his touch. She wouldn't fight it, no matter how much she should. Without explanation, she needed him.

His lips met hers with an electrical charge, a soft buzz. Gentle at first. She wasn't sure if it was with her urgency or his as she pressed harder against him. Her tongue searched for his. And then, she was drowning, but this time in liquid light. An inexplicable sense of rightness filled her. Like she'd come home. Finally. Home after having just gone to war.

CHAPTER 47

"Hannah!" A voice yelled from behind her. Reluctantly, she pulled away, her cheeks wet with tears. The man before her dissolved under her touch as if he had never really been there. An emptiness fell heavily over her and she reached for her locket, pulling it out from where it rested on her chest under her shirt. It was warm beneath her fingers.

She knew now. She understood.

Hannah bit her lip and used her sleeve to wipe her eyes before slowly turning on her feet once more. Two flashlight beams were aimed at the ground in front of her. She could just make out the figures holding them. Mike and Awhina. Enough light bounced off their faces for her to see Awhina, wide eyed with her hand covering her mouth, and Mike... Anger and heartbreak disfigured his face.

She couldn't be sure what they had seen, but by their expressions, they had seen something. The honeymoon was over.

Mike was the first to move towards her. Awhina stood paralysed. Shock turning her to stone.

"Hannah?" Mike's voice was raspy, dangerous even. "What the—" His voice broke off, and he shook his head.

She had no answers for him. A fresh surge of tears overwhelmed her. Streams of grief and guilt ran down both cheeks. She couldn't even look at him.

"Come on!" Awhina had somehow recovered enough to cut through her reverie. She pushed past Mike and grabbed Hannah by the arm. "We need to get back," she said, a lump in her voice belying the undercurrent of emotion she too was struggling with. "Rua and Mariana are waiting for us."

She let Awhina lead her down the path, past Mike, whose head hung low, eyes downcast. She diverted her eyes but listened to his footsteps following behind her amidst the wail of the wind.

As they neared the rock, she whispered to Awhina. "Did it work?"

"I don't know. Maybe a little. But not enough."

Hannah's heart sank further. That didn't leave any other choice. She had to convince Mike. Pull their money if they could. Walk away. Now. Save themselves and give everyone else a chance to do the same. And if she couldn't convince him. Then what? Arson? Potential jail time? She'd caused him enough pain, but this resort, this land, this curse, it could do worse.

As if to mock her, a powerful gust of wind roused up, almost pushing her and Awhina over on to the rock itself. The drumming had disappeared, Hannah noticed, replaced now with the howling of the wind through the nearby trees and vegetation, and the assault of flying sand. They paused against the sudden onslaught of the elements. Hannah held her arm up to protect her eyes. Someone roughly grabbed her, pulling her around. It was Mike. He too was struggling, trying to shield himself from the rain and sand.

"Who was he?" he yelled into the squall at her. His voice breaking with the wind. His fingers dug into her arm, bruising them, and she tried to shake him off.

"Who was he?" he demanded again, his voice breaking with emotion.

"We have to leave," Awhina interrupted. "Rua and Mariana are waiting for us." She tugged at Hannah's other arm. A tug of war with her in the middle.

The wind was blowing a gale. They had to lean into it just to stand upright now. A large palm frond came flying past their heads. All three of them ducked, shielding their faces. One of its sharp leaves slashed at an unprotected part of her cheek.

"Now!" Awhina yelled. "You two can fight later."

"You go," Hannah yelled back, trying to shrug her off. The pain in Mike's eyes held her back. His blond curls were darker, looser, dripping rivers of water down his face. She owed him a moment.

"I'm ending this," Awhina threatened. The jerry can. Nothing was going to stop her now. Awhina was going back to the reception, and with or without them that place would be ablaze. She had seen Amiri, Hannah knew she had. For him, she would burn the place down.

Hannah had to do something.

But what? Liana had said the curse was bred of heartache. A man's love for a woman. A parent's love for a child. She couldn't undo that.

Rua had said the best weapon against evil was love, but she'd broken her vows to Mike; she knew that. All she could do was try to keep him safe.

"Go," Hannah said to Awhina.

Awhina's jaw dropped slightly. Then she left, her flashlight bouncing around the path ahead of her as she fought against the wind.

Hannah faced Mike. He still gripped her arm.

"Mike…" she started, having to yell against the wind to be heard.

"You were with someone. I saw him, then he … he just disappeared. What the hell, Hannah?" He stifled a sob. For a moment, all Hannah wanted to do was draw him to her. Wrap him in her arms like a child. Tell him everything was going to be alright. But it wasn't. She knew that now.

"I love you," she said, laying her free hand against his cheek. She did. She loved him.

He leant down and rested his forehead against hers as the world toppled around them. Three years they'd been together. He had always done right by her. He wasn't perfect, but neither was she. She had to do right by him. Even if it broke his heart.

Her heart hammered fast in her chest, as if an echo of the island drumming she'd heard before. The air thickened around them. Heavy, as if others were close by, watching. Waiting. Closing in.

"Do you love me?" she asked him. She held his eyes with her own, needing to know he did.

"Of course," Mike said.

"Then we leave this island. As soon as we can, we leave. We pull our money and we never come back. Do you understand?" She needed to know he understood, needed to hear him say it.

"Hannah…" he protested.

The wind whipped her hair around both of their faces. She

shoved it away. "Promise me, no matter what, you won't come back here. It's cursed, Mike, this place *is* cursed." Promise me, she thought; willed him with her mind. The wind whirled around them.

"Come on. We'll talk about it back at the resort," Mike said.

"No! Please, Mike," she pleaded. But his expression told her everything she needed to know. He loved her, yes. But it wasn't enough.

Hannah didn't see it coming until it was too late. The thrashing of the wind hid the roar of the water. The waves hit them at the knees, bulldozing where there had once been gardens. It knocked them both off their feet. Hannah's arm hit something hard. The rock.

A crippling pain seared her shoulder joint as her limbs tangled with Mike's. Someone yelled before she went under. She sucked in a mouthful of water, fighting for the surface. Everything was murky, black.

Mike. Mike was screaming her name. She hit something else solid. The rough trunk of a tree, maybe. Struggling to right herself against the current, she used her fingernails to grip onto anything. She tried to stand, her ankles giving out under her. Mike's flashlight had been knocked away, a flicker of brightness reflecting off in the distance before disappearing.

"Hannah," Mike yelled again. She felt him near. Hands trying to pull her to him. The water kept coming. Hannah swallowed a mouthful and choked, coughing and spluttering as memories of being pulled down in the pool and drowning, played out in her mind. His body pressed against hers, pinning her to the tree and protecting her from the onslaught of debris swept up in the sea surge.

"Annie!" She heard her father yell for her mother. She saw him then, her father, she was sure it was him, coming up for breath in the distance. The two scenes inter-played. No, it was Mike. He wasn't with her. He'd somehow found his flashlight again. It still worked – a dim glow in inky darkness, but she could see him, see his silhouette; it was him.

"Mike," she cried. The water kept coming, buckling her at the knees again. If it wasn't for the body pressing up against hers, she would have lost her grip.

"I have you," a voice in her ear. Amiri. Her saviour. He was here.

"Hannah." She heard the echo of Mike calling for her.

He was so far away.

She was losing her grip. Her shoulder ached. "I have you," the voice said again.

The current was so strong, rising so fast, it was almost at her chest. Hannah closed her eyes. Make it end. Make it end. She repeated the words in her head, but all she saw was her mother disappearing under waves and her father doing the same. He sacrificed himself, sacrificed a lifetime with his daughter for his soulmate.

With a sudden flash of insight, she knew what she had to do. Love demanded sacrifice.

"Let me go," she whispered.

"No," the voice said in her ear.

"Please," she pleaded. She remembered now what Edith had said: Soulmates transcend death.

"I'm not letting you go," he said again, his cheek pressed up against hers.

"No. You're not letting me go. Not really." She spluttered on another mouthful of water as the deluge crashed against the tree. "Please."

She felt rather than heard his pain in doing so. His body slipped away from hers. The full force of the water took his place. Her shoulder ached; she didn't think she could hold on much longer, even if she wanted to.

But it was the only way.

She let go.

She let the water take her. Like it had her parents. Like it should have done for her twenty-odd years ago. She let it all in. The inky blackness of death.

CHAPTER 48

"Are you ready?"

A jolt of nervousness surged through her chest. Was she?

The hand in hers gave a squeeze. Yes. Yes, she was. With him by her side, she could face anything. She gazed up at him. His amber eyes almost glowed, warming her in a way not even the sun could. A gentle smile played on his lips, enough to light up the dimple on his cheek, and her knees went weak.

This is what it feels like, she thought, to have your heart truly belong to someone else. She returned the smile. He gently brushed her cheek with his free hand before tilting her chin up so he could brush her lips with his own. He smelled of the island. The good smells. Mango and mahogany trees after a gentle rain, coconut and frangipani, sweat and sea.

"Okay. Let's do this," she said.

The storm had done some serious damage. A few of the palms on the beach had toppled, and Rua's gardens were destroyed. The pools were murky from dirt and rubble, the path only visible in places. Broken glass, coral, plant debris and sand, so much sand, covered everything. Most of the resort buildings still stood. The buildings closest to the road or on the second story surviving the best. But not the reception area. Awhina had kept her word. Its charred corpse would need a complete rebuild.

The sea had gutted most of the beachfront properties. Smashed glass and broken furniture. The whole resort was battered and bruised.

Strangely enough, it gave Hannah a sense of hope. There would be no grand opening. Not soon, anyway. The worst of the storm had hit the Rest Easy, which had fuelled even more talk about curses.

They made their way down to the beach. It too was looking worse for wear. The beautiful, smooth, golden sands now a rubbish tip of sea-surge debris.

The lagoon was quiet now. Small waves rippled along the coastline. Further out, small breakers crashed against the reef. The sky was postcard-perfect azure. The water was murkier than normal, but was still picturesque in its own way. How much prettier everything appeared when the fear was gone.

They had already gathered; a small party of familiar forms, standing awkwardly on the beach, gazing out to the sea. Hannah recognised Rua between the two contrasting shapes of Liana and Awhina. One on either side, each one resting a hand on his arm, as if they were holding him up. He looked older than Hannah remembered, but he was still Rua. Awhina wiped a tear from her eye with a tissue, while Liana pressed her free hand to her heart, letting tears flow unstemmed down both cheeks.

Graham and Sheryl were there, positioned off to the side. Graham wore another bold Hawaiian floral dress shirt while his wife dressed more subduedly in black. Even Bethany and Jake were there. Hannah felt a small rush of relief at seeing them alive and well, even as they snuck punches to each other's arm behind their parents' back.

Mariana was there too, standing beside a balding man leaning on a walking stick. The way she clung to him suggested he must be her husband. Hannah sent up another prayer of thanks. He was alive too. Two figures walked arm-in-arm towards the semicircle. How strange, Hannah thought. Henry and Edith had come.

Hannah moved closer. She needed to see one more person. Ached to see, in fact.

Mike was kneeling in the sand where the water touched the shore. His broad back and curly hair sent a ripple of affection through her. And guilt. There would always be a bit of guilt.

He held something in his fingers. Playing with it, winding it around his hands and whispering. He tried to stifle his sobs, but the movements of his body gave him away.

Amiri's hand squeezed hers; then he let it go. She needed to see this on her own, but he would wait for her. Always. He wasn't going anywhere.

She hadn't wanted to hurt Mike. But he would love again. She knew it. She hoped his heartache might be what saved him; took him away from this resort and kept him safe. If he did love her, had loved her, he would honour her wish. He would leave. Pull his money from the project and be done with it. Maybe that would be enough to stall the fixing of the resort. Maybe it would return to ruin once again. Resting, if not in peace, at least resting easy, dormant, until the next fool tried to resurrect it. If the curse could rest, they would all be better off for it.

As if reading her thoughts, Amiri bent down and whispered in her ear. "He's safe now. They all are."

Mike stood up on shaky legs. The sun glinted off the gold

locket he held in his hands. She didn't need to hear him to know what he was saying – a bonus of being on this side. She just knew.

He was saying goodbye. Not only to her.

He would leave. And he wouldn't be back.

Hannah smiled and wiped tears from her eyes. On the periphery of her vision, she saw a ring of shadows surrounding those who were alive. They knew it too. These shadows. People who had lost their lives or been affected by the curse. They too could slumber for a while. This land was never meant to be built on.

Mike took one more step forward towards the water. The surrounding people held each other. A small sob escaped from someone.

Mike drew back his arm, the locket held loosely in his palm. With a deep breath, he threw it out into the lagoon, to be taken by the sea. As her parents had. As she had.

Mike stood there for a moment, watching the ripples on the surface of the water where it sunk.

She had learnt something. She *was* like her parents. She could sacrifice herself for love. When you loved someone, you sought to protect them. And that's what she would do. She loved these people. Between her and Amiri, they would do everything they could to protect them from the curse.

Mike turned his back on the lagoon and walked, head down, shoulders slumped, back towards the resort, towards where she and Amiri now stood. He wouldn't see them, Hannah knew. She had tried to get his attention when she had first woken up, if that was what it was. Amiri and Hannah stepped to the side so he could pass without walking through them. For a moment, he looked up, an expression filled with puzzlement beyond the dark circles and cuts and bruises along the side of his face, and it was as if he saw her. Finally *saw* her. His eyes were bloodshot, but his tears had made his irises even bluer than before.

"I'm sorry," Hannah whispered. He wouldn't have heard her, couldn't have, but all the same, his body seemed to convulse and his hand went up to shield his eyes as he sobbed again.

How cruel that to save someone she loved, she would have to hurt him so badly.

He continued past them and disappeared. The crowd on the beach slowly scattered and disappeared back to their own lives.

"Are you okay?" Amiri asked.

She nodded before turning to face him.

"How is it that a person can be both heartbroken and so heart-full at the same time? My heart has never felt so full, and yet never felt so raw."

Amiri wrapped his arms around her and pulled her to him in a hug. "I don't know," he said. "It kills me to see what you've sacrificed, but I feel like the luckiest man on earth. You had your entire life…" He shook his head.

"But now *we* have our whole afterlife." She would never have thought death would be what brought her to her soulmate.

She leaned her head on his chest, feeling the warmth of his body on her cheek. Here in his arms, she was safe. And here, with Amiri, she could keep others safe as well.

Edith's words from when they landed in Kulani echoed back to her: *Every moment, every second with your soulmate is a thing to treasure. And you don't let go of them, no matter what … not even for a resort.*

She was both right and wrong, Hannah thought. Every

moment with your soulmate *was* a thing to treasure. But sometimes, you had to let go – for your soulmate, for those you loved, and especially for a resort.

The End.

Acknowledgements

A novel, particularly a first novel, is never the work of one alone. Without a wonderful bunch of cheerleaders in my life this book would still be a "some-day" dream.

Thank you to my wonderful hubby, Martin, who cooked dinner and bought takeout more than his fair share to allow me more time to write, and for putting up with my meltdowns when I fell behind schedule.

Thank you to my mother, Nicky, for always being the first to volunteer to read my stories. On the bad days I can always depend on her to tell me what an awesome writer I am. Sometimes all a writer needs to keep going is the bias of a mother's love.

Thank you to my father, Ian, for teaching me to be big and brave with my dreams and as ridiculous as I want with my story-telling.

Much appreciation to my friend, Rebecca, for showing interest in this writers' journey: checking in, cheering me on and understanding when I disappear to meet deadlines.

So much gratitude to my amazing editor, Hannah, who morphed the ramblings of a first-time novelist into this manuscript and taught me so much along the way.

And finally, a big shout out to my readers, social media followers and newsletter subscribers. You keep me accountable
in ways you can't imagine.

Get Between the Shadows For FREE!

I love building relationships with my readers. It's my readers that keep me writing.

I regularly send newsletters with details on new releases, special offers and other bits of news relating to my books and writing life.

And if you sign up to the mailing list, I'll send you a copy of my short story collection, *Between the Shadows*, for **free.**

Sign up at https://www.jobuer.com/

Enjoy this book? You can make a big difference and keep this writer writing!

Reviews are an authors' secret weapon.

Honest reviews of my books help bring them to the attention of other readers.

If you've enjoyed this book, I would be super grateful if you could share the love and spend a couple of minutes leaving a review. (It can be as short as you like on whatever platform you prefer.)

You can jump right to the page by clicking below.

Thank you so much!

About the Author

Jo Buer is a gothic suspense and ghost fiction writer living in New Zealand. She is a sucker for the supernatural, time travel and all things woo-woo. From an early age she came to realise that sometimes truth *is* stranger than fiction, and what we think we know isn't always true.

Jo lives in an ordinary house in an ordinary town with her muggle hubby, feline familiars, Atlas, Gaia and Zeus, and ghost-kitties, Loki, Rhea and Odin. When not doting on her cats, devouring self-help books or gorging on chocolate, she writes slightly dark, sometimes scary, often ghostly stories with a smattering of romance.

Jo makes her online home at https://www.jobuer.com/ . Alternatively, you can connect with her on Facebook at https://www.facebook.com/jobuerauthor, or Instagram at https://www.instagram.com/jobuerauthor/, or send her an email at jo@jobuer.com.

* 9 7 8 0 4 7 3 5 5 8 8 5 7 *